125

a novel
# ELLING
by ingvar
ambjørnsen

a novel

# ELLING

by ingvar
ambjørnsen

MACADAM CAGE

MacAdam/Cage
155 Sansome Street, Suite 550
San Francisco, CA 94104
www.MacAdamCage.com

Published in Great Britain as *Beyond the Great Indoors* by Transworld
Publishers, 2005.

Library of Congress Cataloging-in-Publication Data

Ambjørnsen, Ingvar, 1956-
  [Elling English]
  Elling / by Ingvar Ambjørnsen; translated from the Norwegian by Don
Bartlett and Kari Dickson.
     p. cm.
  ISBN 978-1-59692-255-6
  I. Bartlett, Don.  II. Dickson, Kari.  III. Title.
PT8951.1.M35E4413 2007
839.82'374–dc22

                                        2007037190


Paperback edition: November 2007
ISBN: 978-1-59692-256-3
Cover design by Dorothy Carico Smith
Manufactured in the United States of America
10 9 8 7 6 5 4 3 2 1

# 1

'I loved redcurrants when I was a kid,' Kjell Bjarne said. 'Can't stand them now.'

The way he said it led me to believe that something had happened in the meantime. That was not really very surprising, since he had lived half of his life already. And somewhere along the way he had lost his taste for the tart red berries.

Personally, I have nothing against redcurrants. I like redcurrants. What I had lost over the years was the ability to enjoy myself. Life was not as much fun as when I was a boy. But I didn't say anything. That would only have confused him. Besides, it's strange – when you say something out loud it somehow becomes twice as true. And in this case, half as palatable.

Anyway, I didn't have much to complain about. I really did not. Quite the contrary – the truth was that I was a spoilt young man. As are so many other young men in this country. You didn't have to go to Africa to find people who were worse off than us. You just had to cast a glance at the black people in Oslo to know immediately how things stood. As far as I was aware, they were treated like criminals. Even by the police, or rather, particularly by the police. 'Come here, Sambo,' the police said. 'Let's have a wee look at your false papers.' Well, that's certainly what you read in the newspapers.

Kjell Bjarne was standing by the window, staring down at the street below. I wondered what it was he had seen that had suddenly reminded him that he didn't like redcurrants any more. But I knew better than to ask. It was quite possible that he had seen nothing whatsoever that could logically be associated with redcurrants. Not even a red Volkswagen Beetle. He was just saying whatever came into his mind. That's just the way he was. The first time I met him he asked if I knew anything about cows. Which of course I didn't. And when I asked him later why he had asked precisely that question, he replied that he had no idea, he didn't have a clue. It had taken a long time to get close to him. And even longer before I dared to let him get close to me.

But now we were blood brothers. Involuntarily, mind you, but our blood had mingled.

'Sit down,' I said. 'Don't just stand around like a spare part!'

I knew only too well how easy it was to find yourself sidetracked once you started to study reality through the window of a small flat. Before you knew it you'd lost touch with the real world. Now that we shared a common purpose, we had to use every means possible to get back on track. Take part in everyday life, as it were. There were pitfalls everywhere; it was like trying to pick your way through the minefields of Verdun.

'Sit down,' I repeated.

He did as I said and sat down on the edge of the sofa, gazing at his two gigantic hands. I suspected that he knew what was coming.

'Do you know what day it is today?' I said, without remorse.

'It's Thursday.'

'Thursday the fifteenth,' I persisted, 'which means that Frank is coming.'

He began to rub his temples with his fists. A sure sign of nervousness and guilt.

'I'm sorry,' I said, 'but I'll have to take the matter up with him. If you cannot stop this moronic sex-lines stuff, we'll lose the telephone. That is, we won't be able to afford to keep it. It's as simple as that.'

His fists sank and he sat staring at them. 'Haven't phoned anyone.'

'No,' I said. 'You've phoned a recording. You've

3

phoned a recording of a woman telling you that she's desperate for your body. That she's fantasizing about all the things you're going to do to her. I heard you last night! I heard you get up and fumble around with the telephone.'

He took a deep breath. 'Aw, don't tell Frank.'

His hangdog look was too much to bear. He reminded me of a cocker spaniel that had just had a steak whisked away from under his nose after fourteen days without food. All the same, this was not the time to go soft and give way. It was only after intensive telephone training that I had finally come to terms with this practical device and now I intended to keep it, whatever the cost. I had quite simply become a telephone man, and I was not prepared to let Kjell Bjarne ruin it all. The last telephone bill had been astronomical. We had to live on dry bread and instant soup for weeks. Frank said that it served us right, that it was the perfect way to learn. 'The choice is yours,' said Frank. 'Dirty talk or a decent meal. With the benefits you get, you could actually live quite well. It just depends on how you want to spend the money.'

And he was right. It was our responsibility. I had learnt that at Brøynes Rehabilitation Centre, where Kjell Bjarne and I first met.

That is, it was my responsibility. I held the purse strings in this two-man enterprise. Kjell Bjarne lost all control whenever he had money in his pocket. But, on the other hand, he was a good cook. He reigned supreme in the kitchen. I kept the accounts and Kjell Bjarne cooked and fried. It was as simple as that. When he was in a jocular mood, Frank used to call us 'the two thrifty bachelors'.

Kjell Bjarne pleaded with me again not to tell Frank.

But I could promise him nothing. The role of tell-tale is absolutely alien to my nature, but as I saw it, this was not actually telling tales. It was about sticking to an agreement, and the agreement was that we would discuss any problems or grumbles with Frank, to clear the air so that we could get on with our normal lives and day-to-day reality. The telephone is a part of normal life. That's just the way it is.

It had taken a superhuman effort to crack this telephone thing. In all the years that Mother and I had lived in a kind of nerve-tingling twosomeness, she had played the role of spokeswoman whenever the outside world penetrated our reality or had to be contacted via old Mr Bell's invention. Personally I found it impossible to hold an intelligent conversation with someone I could not see. I was easily distracted as I stood there, trying hard to imagine what the other person looked like and what was happening in the room around them. If it was someone I knew, I ransacked my memory in order to reconstruct every detail of the person's face as closely as I could. And if it was someone I didn't know, everything went to pieces as my imagination ran completely amok. I simply could not relate to a disembodied voice. In order to understand what was being said, I had to be able to invoke a being of flesh and blood.

Once when I was alone at home, a woman from the social services called. In the end I just had to give up and put the receiver down. This was a shameful defeat that did not go unremarked. I just could not decide what she was wearing or what kind of hairstyle she had. Part of my brain conjured up an attractive young woman with dark hair cut in a page-boy style, a little delight fresh from college with a straight nose and full, red lips. Hungry and submissive at the same time. But then, another part of my brain superimposed a different image, one of a sweaty, leathery face. Open pores and unhealthy, pasty skin. Gimlet eyes peering at something that I could not see, but that I knew was indecent, even a bit threatening. A lewd sculpture from Ancient Greece that she kept on her desk, perhaps. As I said, I had to put the phone down, and then, to protect myself, I pulled out the telephone connection. I got a fearful telling-off when Mother came home and from that time on, I generally put my fingers in my ears whenever the phone rang.

However, with Frank's guidance, things improved considerably. He helped me to relax. He got me to play games with the telephone. The first thing we did was buy a ten-metre-long lead so that I could move around more freely with the phone, even take it with me from room to room. In all the years I lived at home, the telephone always had its fixed position – on a low table beside the television. The flex was just long enough to reach the socket in the wall. Mother and I would never have dreamt of imitating the telephone habits we were exposed to in American films, where people roamed restlessly from room to room, happily chatting away. Or they lay seductively draped over a pink quilt, sipping a Martini and talking to their loved one in Illinois.

Mother, who remembered when the telephone was first invented, maintained a deep respect for it for as long as she lived. Whenever the phone rang, she dropped everything and ran to pick it up, as if she were frightened to the very core of missing something vital. And when she spoke on the phone, she stood bolt upright until the conversation was finished. I never saw her sitting and talking on the telephone; in fact, I am sure she would have thought it disrespectful to Mr Bell, or maybe to the person at the other end of the line. Kjell Bjarne had not yet moved in when the telephone was installed in our new flat; so without giving it a second thought, I had copied the old set-up with the phone beside the television and a short flex. Kjell Bjarne took it for granted, as he did most things. I don't remember even discussing it.

To begin with, Frank made me do solo dry runs, made me pretend that I was talking to someone, pulling the long lead behind me from room to room.

From the living room to the kitchen. From the kitchen to the bedroom. Naturally enough, I felt like an idiot, but I took care to wait until Kjell Bjarne was out of the house before starting to practise. Of course, he was aware of the problem I had – he knew what I was like. But I still thought it would be inappropriate for him to overhear the imaginary conversations I had with my deceased mother, or the father I had lost before I was even born. Not to mention my tirades against various politicians, or the tender words whispered to non-existent women. I wandered about shouting or cooing, depending on how the mood took me. And after a while, I began to like it.

Then phase two was introduced. Frank would ring me at an agreed time. To begin with I was stiff and tense and refused to utter a word, but gradually my jaws relaxed and the words started to slip out. Visiting Frank and seeing where the phone was in his study was a great help. The next time he rang, my mind was less cluttered. I could picture him clearly now as he spoke to me, sitting on his blue office chair by the desk, looking out over his garden with row upon row of apple trees. But Frank still thought that I put too much emphasis on details and said I would be better off trying to curb my imagination and train myself to concentrate on the conversation at hand. To listen to what was being said. So, after a while, he started to phone me arbitrarily from different phone boxes all over town.

Slowly my phobia began to recede and now I was at the stage where my voice was remarkably firm whenever I spoke on the phone. I gave my full name, stated the purpose of my call, and listened attentively to what the person on the other end was saying. The very idea of breaking off the conversation midway and hanging up didn't cross my mind now, in fact, it seemed absolutely absurd.

I will admit that, to begin with, we both got excited about sex phone lines. While Kjell Bjarne and I were at the Brøynes Centre, this particular personal service had undergone terrific improvements and now that we had our own phone and no-one could catch us red-handed we simply succumbed to the temptation. As a matter of fact, there were two types of service. One where you could chat to a real live woman, and a slightly cheaper alternative where the woman's voice was recorded on a tape. Obviously, the first option was out of the question. We tried a couple of times with Kjell Bjarne doing the talking, but all he did was splutter and stammer. Not even he knew how to handle situations like this. But the recordings, well, we had a lot of fun with them for a while. With my somewhat overactive imagination, I had no problem whatsoever picturing Patricia lying on the sofa, groaning with pleasure as she plied bananas or any other object she had to hand. And the language those girls used! We blushed furiously as we sat there, heads close together, the receiver between us.

One of them even used the telephone and we could hear the crackling sound of plastic against curly pubic hair and her crying out for more in a strangulated voice in the background. Kjell Bjarne and I were transfixed by lust.

But, as I said: one day the bill came. That was when it first dawned on me, and therefore also on Kjell Bjarne, precisely how disgusting it was and how degrading to women. Three thousand Norwegian kroner is a lot of money for two men living on social benefits, saving up for a video recorder. I worked out that we had set the video project back by half a year, and it was this that enabled Kjell Bjarne to see the seriousness of the situation. At least, that was what I thought. Until now.

'If you snitch on me to Frank, you can do your own cooking,' Kjell Bjarne threatened. ''Cause I'll move out.'

'If you don't stop that nonsense, neither you nor I will have anything to cook!' I countered. 'And where will you move to, when your bank account is overdrawn by a couple of thousand kroner? Not even the Salvation Army would have you. You're not an alcoholic. How long have you been doing this behind my back?'

'Haven't. Just couldn't sleep last night. It got me down. All the stupid things in my head.'

'So it was just this once? Tell the truth because you will be found out, anyway, when the bill comes.'

'Just this once . . . and then, once more.'

'Fine,' I said magnanimously. 'I won't say a thing. But you'll have to promise to talk to Frank about your stupid thoughts.'

'Why?' He glared at me, but I could tell that he was relieved.

'You have to find something else to do instead of listening to bloody expensive smut every time you get frightened,' I said.

'Wasn't frightened. Just mad at my mum.'

'Same thing. The unit cost is precisely the same whether you're frightened or angry. You could call the Christian helpline instead. It's free, I think.'

'Not really the same thing, though, is it.'

'Who knows,' I said. 'A lot has happened in the church since you and I were confirmed. If we are to believe what the papers say, there is a good chance you'll get a lesbian priest on the line and if you tell her about how mean your mother was, you may even get her to groan a little.'

We were blood brothers once more. We laughed the way blood brothers laugh. Loud, raucous laughter.

Kjell Bjarne went out into the kitchen to make the food. I could hear him rummaging about the tins in the cupboard, mumbling to himself about lesbian priests.

'Meatballs or fishballs?'

'Meatballs and fishballs,' I yelled. For some

11

reason I was in a daredevil mood and pranced around, swatting wildly with the newspaper.

Frank arrived at seven, as agreed. Seven o'clock sharp, as he says. When he drove through the gates into the back yard, Kjell Bjarne and I were already waiting by the kitchen window on the second floor. We raised our hands in greeting and Frank waved back. I felt a surge of warmth as we greeted each other, and I knew that Kjell Bjarne felt the same close companionship.

It wasn't always like that. At first we hated Frank. We would sit around in the evenings imagining how we would torture him to death. We imagined him handcuffed to the back of a train, being dragged along through the ice and snow. Or screaming in an acid bath. Abandoned to the company of tormented pit bull terriers. Of course, it was nothing more than fantasy and hot air. It is not in Kjell Bjarne's nature to harm anyone other than himself, and the same is true for me.

But Frank was forever interfering! He had something to say about everything we said and did. It was unbearable! Nothing was good enough and when I did muster up the courage to tell him exactly what I thought, he told me bluntly to shut up. It was a difficult time particularly at the beginning, when I was still on my own in the flat, and I often longed to be back in the Brøynes Rehabilitation Centre where nice Sister Gunn was in charge. I wrote to tell her that I had landed somewhere near hell, but she wrote back that I should not exaggerate so much and I should be more positive. And in any case, my good friend Kjell Bjarne would be joining me shortly. She passed on his best wishes.

Exaggerate? Be more positive? When Frank mocked my ideals and derided my aesthetic taste? Who was going to live in the flat, him or me? How he chose to paint the rooms in his own house was entirely up to him – but in all fairness it should then be up to me to decide how to decorate my home. I wanted orange walls throughout the flat and that was that. I spent the entire decorating budget on orange paint. But I had hardly even opened the first tin before Frank arrived unannounced and confiscated the lot. White, he said, and exchanged every single litre of paint in front of my very eyes. On top of that, I had to help him carry the tins. I stood beside him in the shop while Frank and the shop assistant, who was a despicable pea-brain by the way, made jokes about my choice of colour. When I embarked on an ever so tiny lecture on democratic thought, he laughed in my face and said that that sort of thing went out with the ark. He was the one who made the decisions now. And in any case, the flat was not mine, it belonged to Oslo City Council, so he could say what he liked about it.

That really hurt me. I liked to think of the flat as mine. Ours. Mine and Kjell Bjarne's. Kjell Bjarne wrote to me from Brøynes to ask how I was getting on with the decorating. I replied that it was not going too well. That a certain Frank was getting in the way the whole time. And the idea of having a hanging garden in the living room, well, we could just forget that. Frank wouldn't even discuss it.

Frank's footsteps sounded on the stairs. He is the only man I have ever met who always runs up the stairs; the more there were and the steeper, the better. Frank ran. And then the familiar code: three short and one long. The secret call of the Norwegian Resistance. I nodded to Kjell Bjarne, who rushed into the hall to open the door. I heard them talking to each other, slapping one another on the back, and I felt tears well up in my eyes. That I should be blessed with this! To be part of this good, solid, unsentimental friendship. I quickly wiped my eyes with the dishtowel and went into the living room.

Frank wasn't even out of breath. He had the fitness of a leopard. He threw himself down onto the sofa and started to scratch his greying moustache.

'Everything OK, Elling?'

I assured him that life was more or less in perfect balance. I didn't say anything about missing the joy and warmth of childhood. He couldn't possibly understand that. Some areas remain out of bounds, even to close friends from Oslo City Council.

'Great,' he said. 'And it looks a lot tidier here than it does in my house, as far as I can see.' He looked around the room.

And it was tidy. Spotless. I had picked up a trick

or two at Brøynes and knew how to keep things spick and span. In fact, I set great store by keeping things tidy. A quick zip around with a cloth and warm water and everyone's sense of well-being goes up a peg or two.

'How's Janne?' Kjell Bjarne asked, excavating his left nostril.

'Fine, I think,' Frank said. 'She's in Majorca. Just for a week – she'll be back on Friday.'

'On her own?' Kjell Bjarne asked.

'Yes, I can't get away. I have to run around making sure that boys like you don't get into trouble. Last week, a nutter up at Bjølsen tried to break through the wall into his neighbours' flat.'

'But we're not like that,' Kjell Bjarne exclaimed.

'What have you been up to since I saw you last?' Frank asked, as if he hadn't heard Kjell Bjarne. 'Have you been out to have a look at real life, or have you just sat indoors staring at the walls?'

'If I had a girlfriend, I wouldn't let her go on holiday alone,' Kjell Bjarne said. 'She'd have to deal with me first.'

'What are you talking about, you big old hippo? Who said she asked me? I asked whether you and Elling had been out for some air since I last saw you. That's what I want to know.'

He was all mouth, all mouth. But now I knew what he was like. It had not escaped my attention that he was trying to drop the subject of Janne as fast as he could. Kjell Bjarne was right; in a healthy relationship, no-one would go off to Majorca without even asking their partner. It just wasn't right. And here he was, playing the tough guy, while trying as hard as possible to disguise his own inner turmoil. I felt terribly sorry for him. Any idiot could imagine the temptations that Janne would face in Majorca. I had been to the Mediterranean myself and I knew. Cheap package holidays had not been invented to preserve monogamy, that's for sure. There were all sorts of goings-on from dawn until dusk. I forced myself to blank out an image of Janne with the local football team.

'D'you want a Coke?' Kjell Bjarne asked.

'My God, you two are completely hopeless! Yes, I do want a Coke! Have you done anything at all in the past fortnight?'

I really wanted to lie. You see, I knew exactly what he wanted to hear. He wanted us to tell him how active and extrovert we had been. He wanted us to create a life where Kjell Bjarne and Elling went out and painted the town red, made friends and contacts here, there and everywhere. New friends by the minute. Confidently chattering away in cafés, pubs and clubs. Two winning personalities bowling everyone over with their remorseless charm.

But we were not like that. Kjell Bjarne and I were simply not like that. We were more the anxious type. Loud, noisy places frightened us. And as we didn't know who our neighbours were, we would rather not meet them on the stairs. We felt

16

safest at home. Was there anything wrong with that?

'I go down to the supermarket all the time to buy food,' Kjell Bjarne said, putting a 1.5 litre bottle of Coke and a glass down in front of Frank. 'I'm sort of getting to know the bloke at the till down there. P. Jonnson, he's called. About twenty, I think.'

Frank made a vague show of applauding and opened the bottle of Coca-Cola. 'Can't you sit down, Elling? Don't just stand there staring at me. It makes me nervous.'

I sat down and tried hard not to look straight at him.

'And you?'

'Me?'

'Have you been down to the supermarket as well?'

I explained to him that supermarkets were Kjell Bjarne's department. And that it was the first I had heard about P. Jonnson.

Frank downed the Coke in one and burped. 'It's not good enough, guys. Where's your get up and go?'

'What do you want us to do then?' I asked. I could feel my righteous indignation making my voice tremble. 'Perhaps we should abduct people on the street and force them back to the flat?'

Frank pushed away his glass and stood up. 'Let's go to the flicks,' he said.

We went to see Storks and Stones, quite a ridiculous film, in my opinion. It was about a young couple who couldn't have children. There was something wrong with his sperm. But they desperately wanted a child and a child they were going to have, whatever the cost. After a while it became a kind of idée fixe and eventually they decided that she should go out on the town and mate with any old fool. By the time this fool appeared in the form of an awful poet, I for one had had enough. The rest of the film was all jealousy and intrigue, as you would imagine, and people sat there laughing! About what, I do not know. I like to think of myself as a modern urban man with liberal ideas and an open mind, but I refuse to applaud the disintegration of morality.

What annoyed me most about the film was that it finished where it should have begun. In the end, the couple sit there with not one, but a total of three babies. Triplets. An entire trilogy inscribed in the woman's womb by a mediocre poet she didn't even know. While her husband, the man she really loved, just sat there grinning inanely. He didn't seem to be bothered. Of course he was jealous when the love of his life was doing her utmost to squeeze as much sperm out of the poet as possible. But once she had conceived, all was well with the world. Poppycock! You didn't exactly have to be an expert in male psychology to know that this one event, this single-minded mating, would be used against the wife for the rest of her life. Whenever the husband felt that the world was against him, he would blame it on this poem-scribbling breeding hound. She, on the other hand, would insist that she did not enjoy the sex at all, that she didn't have an orgasm and that, in fact, the poet's Thomas was tiny. She barely noticed when he entered her and she spent the whole time staring at the ceiling, refusing to let him kiss her.

To no avail, of course. Not even the whitest lie nor the bitterest tears could alter the fact that the three children were not the product of the two protagonists' love for each other. What we saw at the end of the film was an artificial nuclear family. A false image. Nothing more, nothing less.

'Best film I've seen!' announced Kjell Bjarne as we came out.

It always was for Kjell Bjarne. Every time we went to the pictures with Frank, he saw the best film of his life. He was particularly enthused every time there was a glimpse of a naked woman. Then his voice went all husky, like now. We had seen Anneke von der Lippe's white backside in a clip that lasted all of two seconds. In my opinion, that was not enough to haul the film out of the morass where it belonged.

'Funny,' Frank said. 'Wasn't it, Elling?'

Not at all. I told both Frank and Kjell Bjarne exactly what I thought about the times in which we lived and the fact that Norwegian film producers seemed unable to take a moral lead in society. As far as I was concerned, people who worked in the cultural sector in this country had a social responsibility.

'Jesus,' Frank said. 'It was only a comedy!'

Kjell Bjarne laughed. 'Didn't you realize it was supposed to be funny?'

'I realized that it was very unfunny!' I snapped. 'And you have not understood a thing.'

'You know bugger all, you do,' Kjell Bjarne said. 'I understand what I want when it suits me.'

'Great,' Frank said. 'It's good when culture generates discussion.'

I didn't say anything. It was the same superficial claptrap every single time we went to the cinema. Kjell Bjarne had seen the best film ever and he and Frank refused to understand my objections.

'Nothing is ever good enough for you,' Kjell Bjarne said. 'It's always wrong.'

I didn't answer. There was no point in contradicting Kjell Bjarne when he was in that sort of mood.

'It's just turned nine,' Frank said. 'I could murder a pizza.'

All I wanted was to go home and read some general knowledge magazines I had, but I realized it would be impolite to say so. And anyway, what could be more natural than to wander down to a pizzeria together with a couple of old chums after a film? It felt right, somehow. A crispy slice of freshly made Italian pizza and easy, relaxed conversation.

'Wicked!' said Kjell Bjarne. He had quickly acquired a repertoire of teenage slang since coming to Oslo, which did not suit him at all. It was like Mother Teresa suddenly swearing.

We went to Peppe's Pizza and, after a show of hands, ordered a large pizza with ham and pepperoni. Two against one. As usual. I would rather have had tuna. Strange, isn't it, how quickly you become accustomed to being steamrollered when you first have friends. To begin with, I fought tooth and nail and stubbornly pursued the rights of the minority. Now I often felt the adrenaline being diluted by a mild sense of resignation. We had settled into a rhythm, we knew each other inside out, and when three grown men go out on the town, as we had started to do twice a month, things often got a bit boisterous. I had got used to it. And, in fact, I quite liked it.

When the piping hot pizza arrived on the table, Frank said, 'Oh by the way, before I forget . . . I've looked into what you asked about last time. And it's OK, you can get a cat.'

Kjell Bjarne and I looked at each other.

# 2

It was a perfectly normal two-up two-down terraced house, with brown-stained wood panelling, but my hands were sweating and my heart was racing. I had never approached a stranger of my own free will before. I glanced surreptitiously at Kjell Bjarne and realized that he didn't have much experience of this sort of thing either. He looked as if he wanted to rub his temples with his fists. But he couldn't. In his right hand he was holding a grey cat box and his left hand was stuffed as far into his jacket pocket as it would possibly go.

'Well,' he said. 'No going back now, chum!'

As usual, the word 'chum' gave me a boost. That word made me grow. And without even drawing a breath, I said, 'Come on, old boy', or something like that, and trotted up the steps. I was taking responsibility. I was being proactive. And as I pressed the bell, it hit me like an avalanche. What struck me in a blinding flash was that I had been reborn in midlife. That the man who was standing there with his finger firmly on the bell, who would not remove it until the door was opened, was not the same man as the one who had lived a sheltered existence with his mother for thirty-five years. This man on the doorstep had a far more proactive approach to life. For example, he had now decided that he wanted a cat. And a cat he was going to have! The first thing he did was to scrutinize the small ads in the paper. This had reminded him of the old days: reading the left-wing Arbeiderbladet line by line in his room, his eyes glued to the page so that he would not even miss a comma. Home wanted for eight-week-old kittens. Please phone. The final break with his old self. Yes, the name was Elling. His mouth was dry, his voice firm. Was he correct in understanding that there were some kittens looking for a home . . . ?

'My dear young man!' A tiny lady looked up at me from the doorway.

I took my finger off the bell.

'Afternoon,' Kjell Bjarne said. 'We've come for a cat. My friend here phoned you last night.'

I shook her hand and introduced myself.

She laughed. 'Oh, it was you who said all those silly things? Come in!'

Silly? Was it silly of me to give her a brief résumé

of my life when I was about to take responsibility for an innocent life that she currently had in her care? Surely she wanted to know who I was and what my intentions were? As far as I was concerned, there was a responsibility attached to taking on an animal. And likewise, the person who gave away the animal had a responsibility. You couldn't just hand over an animal to someone you didn't trust wholeheartedly. So I had gone to great lengths to make it quite clear that I was not some psychopath with a hungry boa constrictor hiding under my bed. I explained to her that one of my greatest dreams was about to be fulfilled. I had yearned for an animal's affection since I was a boy, but ridiculous regulations in a block of flats in the East End of Oslo had made it impossible. But now I was living with my good friend in a flat near Majorstuen, where all the neighbours were hale and hearty liberals. They had a completely different view of the bond between animals and people. In fact, several of them owned poodles or retrievers.

'Would you like a cup of coffee?' the woman asked. 'And a piece of cake?'

'Yes, please!' said Kjell Bjarne, still holding the cat box in his right hand.

Cakes. Coffee. I wanted to see my cat!

Then I saw them. They were everywhere. I had never seen so many cats in one place before. A large ginger tabby was lying on top of the fridge, staring at me. Four black cats were lolling around on the sideboard. There was a Siamese cat in the middle of the table that just looked straight through me, and everything else. And four half-grown miaowing felines were wrapping themselves around the legs of the woman who introduced herself as Dagny Rimstad, their pink posteriors flashing at me from under the dark fur.

'Please make yourself at home,' Dagny Rimstad said. 'Have either of you had a cat before?'

We could only answer 'no' to that question, but I quickly added that we were well prepared all the same. We had been to the library and borrowed all the books they had on cat care.

'Then forget everything you've read,' Dagny said. 'The most important thing is to keep the cat litter clean. The rest is common sense.' She put half an almond cake on a plate on the table and poured the coffee. Normally I don't drink coffee as it makes me terribly nervous, but now I felt obliged, out of politeness, to sip some of the warm liquid. The Siamese cat looked at me distrustfully, but sniffed my finger with curiosity when I held it out.

'Where's our cat?' Kjell Bjarne asked, with his mouth full of cake.

'Are you sure you only want one?' she said. 'It's far easier to have two. Then they can play with each other while you're at work.'

I was just about to reply, but Kjell Bjarne pipped me to the post.

'Don't work, neither of us.'

I sent him a warning look, and said that of course we would consider taking two. Job or no job, we had plenty to do. More than enough, in fact. We were always on the go, so yes, it would probably be better to have two. She needn't worry about the cat litter – we had a tray standing ready in the hallway at home. A lovely tray in cream-coloured plastic. With a top.

Dagny nodded happily and disappeared out of the room. Shortly afterwards, she returned with a large cardboard box. Mewing and scratching noises came from inside the box, and a black and white cat, presumably the mother, trotted behind.

The kittens were black and white, just like their mother. They were huddled together in a great ball so that it was almost impossible to see how many there were.

'Six,' she said, as if reading my thoughts. She lifted them out onto the floor one by one and the mother immediately started to lick and clean them.

Kjell Bjarne laughed and pointed: 'Let's take that one there with the tash, Elling! Look at him!'

Quite. Strange little fellow. White face, with a tiny, crooked Hitler moustache under his pink nose. However, I wasn't actually looking for a comedy cat. This day had been too long in coming. For thirty-five years I had waited for the moment when I would have my own cat, or any other warm-blooded pet, for that matter – and now that it was about to happen the last thing I wanted was pigmentary peculiarities. I did not want a cat that would make people giggle, but a member of the feline species that would look at me enigmatically when I woke up in the morning. A cat that would make me ponder the deeper questions in life. Where do we come from? Where do we go?

Then Dagny Rimstad launched into a short lecture. She repeated her claim that it would undoubtedly be better for us to have two kittens, but this time with more urgency and authority than before. Also, she advised us not to choose one of each sex, for reasons we no doubt understood. And though she was a woman herself, there was no denying that female cats were far more work than tomcats. As well we knew, tomcats did not get pregnant and castration was nothing compared with sterilizing a female cat.

We nodded and said, 'Uh huh.' Using his thumb and forefinger, Kjell Bjarne picked up the little fellow with the Hitler moustache and let him crawl around his enormous hand. 'Well, boys it is then, Mrs Rimstad,' he said. 'Or is this a miss?'

'No, it's a boy,' Mrs Rimstad said, inspecting it carefully from behind.

'You're not having us on, are you?' chuckled Kjell Bjarne. 'There isn't much to see there.'

I have to be honest and admit that I got embarrassed as Mrs Rimstad started to point and explain, whereas Kjell Bjarne followed with great interest. To determine the gender of such small kittens – they were after all no more than eight weeks old – you had to look at the position of the two holes in relation to each other. On the hims, the holes were closer together than on the hers, etc. I know it was only animals we were talking about, and two small animals at that, but I still found it embarrassing to get all of this genital information from a woman I didn't even know. I simply wasn't used to it. So I quietly slipped down onto my knees and gave all my attention to the five other fluffballs and their somewhat reserved mother. No sooner had I approached the furry family than a tiny little scrap of a thing broke loose from the group and started to suck my finger. Imagine!

'You'll have to take him now,' Mrs Rimstad said. 'He's the most active one in the litter. And he's chosen you.'

Chosen me? Chosen Elling? I wanted to whoop with joy! There certainly weren't many, man nor beast, who had made that choice over the years! Carefully, I lifted the kitten up onto my lap. I tried to give it a finger to chew again, but the little mite curled up in a ball and fell sound asleep, just lost consciousness! I could see his tiny heart pounding under the black and white fur.

'It's quite normal,' Mrs Rimstad explained, when she saw my look of dismay. 'They can even fall asleep in the middle of a game. They just recharge their batteries for a few minutes and then they're off again.'

Well. It was hardly quite normal to lie down and sleep in a stranger's lap. This was blind faith. Animals understand more than we humans know. For example, they know perfectly well who will be kind to them. As she herself had said, I was the one he had chosen. The chosen one.

Kjell Bjarne put his kitten down on the table, where it tottered about sniffing cake crumbs. 'Pepper,' he exclaimed.

We looked at him.

'His name's Pepper!'

Well, well, I thought. Perhaps I can persuade you to see reason when we're alone again. I couldn't imagine a more stupid name.

I think it would be fair to say that we caused quite a stir on the metro, on our way back into town. The kittens, which had made little fuss about leaving their mother, now miaowed and howled at all the new, unfamiliar sounds, while Kjell Bjarne and I did what we could to comfort them. Kjell Bjarne sat with the box on his knees and I leaned over to talk to them reassuringly, sticking my finger through the wire mesh as a substitute dummy. People came over all the time, young and old alike, to take a closer look at the two tiny creatures. The mewing of the little scamps immediately melted the cold front that so often develops when two or more Norwegians are forced to share an enclosed public space.

An old lady started to tell two young lads about her childhood. She came from the country, she told them, and they had had lots of different animals there. The two scallywags stopped pestering each other and listened with eyes like saucers as the lady told tales of cows and goats, and the troll-cat that stole the milk from the barn. An impeccably dressed office clerk bent over and informed us knowledgeably that the two kittens were prime examples of the Norwegian forest cat. A recognized breed, or so we were led to believe. He put two fingers to his hat in greeting as he got off the train.

As so many times before, I thought to myself: 'It takes so little. It takes so little to bring the walls we unconsciously build up around us tumbling down.' And I knew all about these walls. I had spent my entire life behind them, without being challenged by anyone other than my unenterprising mother. I had only recently, since Mother's death and my inevitable breakdown, started to chip away at the plaster. Even sitting here on the metro with my finger in a cat box would have been utterly impossible only a few months ago. I wouldn't have dared to attract so much attention. Not under any circumstances. And now I winked at the old milkmaid and let the curious boys have a look. I thought it might be good for them. Good for them to see living creatures. In a world where children think that chickens are born vacuum-packed and that God created cod in frozen rectangles, it was a joy, and quite frankly, refreshing to be able to show off these two tiny lives.

'That one's got a moustache!' the smaller boy pointed out, snorting some green snot back up his nose.

'That's Pepper,' said Kjell Bjarne.

'What's the other one called?'

'Nothing,' I said.

'Nothing?'

'Yes, nothing.'

'Looks like it too,' the bigger of the two joked. 'Just like a nothing. A great big fat zero.'

Sometimes I wish for the good old days when corporal punishment was the norm. Of course, by that I don't mean sick unnecessary violence against defenceless children. I would never, even in my wildest dreams, take a belt or anything else to the younger generation. However, I cannot deny that a good slap could have a certain educational value in cases like this. A box around the ears could well be all that was required to get a young person who has gone awry back on the straight and narrow. I can vouch for that from my own childhood. In my opinion, it was a serious problem that so many adults were prepared simply to let things ride when it came to a child's upbringing.

In the block of flats where I grew up, collective responsibility ruled. No matter where we boys roamed, unrelated mothers and aunts watched over us and kept us all in line. Mrs Lydersen was quite happy to open her kitchen window and fire a volley of verbal shots if she saw a child chewing a used condom or eating a mud pie. It made no difference to Mrs Larsen whether it was her own child or one she had never seen before; she came to the rescue regardless, to prevent strangulation by washing line on the drying green. Nor was my mother above joining in the collective chorus of reprimands intended to turn us into 'good people', as we tore around on our tricycles. There were rules and restrictions all day long, so many that it became tedious.

But enough of that. As far as I could tell, children today suffered because no-one seemed to care what they said or did. Everything was allowed. For example, here was a young mother sitting by, lazily leafing through the paper while her offspring stood and insulted a stranger's cat, and she didn't so much as bat an eyelid. A trivial matter, even I am not that hysterical, but all the same, so typical of our day and age. Neither I nor my cat was injured by the incident, but it pained me that the one who would eventually have to pay for such a quick tongue was the boy himself. Even the mildest reprimand from me now might result in some social worker or other pulling the emergency cord and reporting me to the police and the papers. Fortunately, the old milk-maid distracted the young scoundrel by saying that her name was Ovidia, which naturally released a torrent of scorn and derision. And the mother continued to read the sports pages, oblivious to the world around her. What more can I say?

We got off at Majorstuen and hurried back to our bachelors' pad in Kirkeveien. Almost in the West End. Not bad! Admittedly the flats had been built in the 1950s, but all the same we had a balcony and a shared back yard with plenty of character. When it came to our new lodgers, we agreed after much discussion that they would have to be indoor cats. It just had to be that way: the back yard might well be picturesque with all its trees and flower beds, but it was simply not possible to have a cat ladder all the way up to the second floor where we lived. Not only that, we also knew that there were other cats living down there, cats of the more undesirable kind. We had noticed one in particular, a white tomcat with a ragged right ear. We called him 'Killer'. He was a real bruiser who even managed to tip over the rubbish bins. You couldn't expose two little bundles of fur to that kind of thing, unless absolutely necessary. For the first time ever I was responsible for a life other than my own, and I intended to play my hand with extreme caution. How Kjell Bjarne felt about the responsibility I didn't know. He was not very forthcoming about his past, apart from the fact that he hated his mother and father.

We bounded up the stairs two at a time. There wasn't a sound from inside the box and I, of course, was terrified that they had died as a result of the harrowing journey. I had read in one of the library books that transportation could be very traumatic for cats. My hands were shaking as I opened the door and we burst into the hall.

But yes. They were alive. There had been no reason to worry. Pepper, who I just had to accept would actually be called Pepper, shot straight out of the box and started to pee like a fountain on the doormat. Kjell Bjarne lifted him up by the scruff of his neck and carefully put him down in the white cat litter, where he stood looking around, astonished, before starting to dig.

My own cat remained motionless, showing none of the initiative that Mrs Rimstad had mentioned. He sat as far back in the box as he could and stared at me suspiciously. I knew then and there that we would be friends for life. Because I had been exactly the same for most of my life, sceptical of anything new. Now, however, the world was opening up around me, or rather I was opening up to the world. It was a slow process, I certainly was not running to meet reality with open arms, but taking one small step at time – dragging my feet, some might even say. But moving. Definitely moving.

It turned out to be one of the best evenings I can remember. The little mite ventured out after an hour and then started to chase his brother around the flat. These boys were on top form! They climbed the curtains like monkeys, balanced on the back of chairs and stuck their little noses in everywhere there was room. Kjell Bjarne had bought a mountain of the most delicious cat food for them and it was a joy to watch them eat and defecate. Kjell Bjarne and I ignored the TV and sat and watched, wide-eyed and wondering, passing comments on their various antics. After several hours, they fell into a heap in a cake tin in the kitchen cupboard. Rolled in a ball, with their paws around each other.

'Well,' said Kjell Bjarne, 'looks like they've made themselves at home. But you've still got to give yours a name.'

'Oh, I'm in no rush,' I replied. 'Better to think about it for a while, rather than plumping for the first stupid name that comes to mind.'

Kjell Bjarne shrugged his shoulders. 'No skin off my nose.' He went to the bathroom, presumably to get ready for bed. Or rather, to pretend he was getting ready for bed. You see, I rather suspected that he was up to something, big time. The plan had been that we would each have our own room, but we quickly discovered that it was a bit lonely after having shared at Brøynes Rehabilitation Centre. We had come to appreciate our night-time chats; we had discovered that words flowed more easily between us when the lights were out and thin duvets covered our bodies. Strange, really, how things work out, isn't it? How people adapt to circumstances. When we were initially instructed to share the same room, we both loathed the idea and each other. But all's well that ends well, as they say. We became friends, which was a completely new experience, certainly for me.

All the same, there was no denying it. He smelt pretty awful at times. At Brøynes, Sister Gunn had checked behind his ears, but now Kjell Bjarne was getting very slack in terms of personal hygiene. Smelly socks and underwear that wasn't changed for weeks on end. I should really have talked to Frank about it, but it seemed a bit too personal to involve a third party in such a sensitive matter.

I went out into the kitchen and bent down to see the two small furry balls curled up and sleeping the sleep of innocents in the cake tin. I could hear that Kjell Bjarne had turned on all the taps in the bathroom. And then suddenly it was as if I could see straight through all the walls. I saw straight through his game, in fact. I marched out into the hall and wrenched open the bathroom door. And as expected – there was Kjell Bjarne, fully dressed, sitting on the toilet seat reading a Donald Duck comic. Meanwhile the hot-water tap was spewing out boiling water into the sink. He jumped up and went bright red. I didn't say a word. I just gave him a cold glare and a stern nod of the head.

Half an hour later, having first checked out the situation in the cake tin, he got into bed with his tail between his legs. He had put on a clean pair of long johns and his hair was wet. I decided not to mention the incident, if he didn't want to talk about it himself.

When I had been to the bathroom as well and all the lights were out, he said, 'It's not that bad, is it, Elling? Our own place and all that. Even a cat each. Just need a couple of women now, then . . .'

'Just carry on as you did tonight,' I said. 'Wash yourself regularly, and then it will all sort itself out. If not, there certainly won't be any girls.'

'How come?'

I didn't even bother to answer. I couldn't count all the nights I had spent explaining to him what women liked and disliked. I had covered personal hygiene so many times that there was nothing left to add. I dare say there may be some women who appreciate the smell of a pigsty, but there's a difference between smelly animals and smelly people.

He sighed. 'Wonder what time Pepper gets up in the morning?'

'Early, no doubt,' I answered. 'Where cats are concerned, you have to be ready for anything.'

He clucked quietly in the dark. 'When I saw that funny face . . . That really stupid moustache . . . Just had to be Pepper.'

'I can't think of a name for mine,' I said. It was true. I had thought and thought, but drawn a blank. It was a ridiculous situation, I was completely blocked.

'Mons is a good name.'

'No. There are two hundred thousand other tomcats with that name in this country.'

'OK, OK. You'll think of something. It's more important that we've got the cats. Bloody hell, Elling, I think we're going to have fun with those two.'

I thought so too. We lay there chuckling as we recounted the evening's antics to one another. Did he see the astonished look on Pepper's face when my cat fell on top of him from the chair? Did I see the ungainly set-to on the window sill? Finally there was no more to tell and after a pause, Kjell Bjarne said, 'Been thinking . . .'

'Come on then, spit it out.'

'Maybe we should start going out a bit more. Like Frank says. I mean, don't suppose any women'll come round if they don't know that we're here.'

Kjell Bjarne and 'women'! Though I have to admit he did have a point. Personally, I had lived nearly all my life in more or less total isolation, and it was anything but easy to change the habit of a lifetime. Just walking down Hegdehaugsveien in the morning was something of a challenge. I felt as if everyone was staring at me. Judging me, as it were. As if they were thinking, oh here comes mummy's boy from the suburbs. Because I had been a mummy's boy, there was no escaping it. The way I saw it, there had been no alternative.

'I get frightened too sometimes,' said Kjell Bjarne, as if he had read my thoughts. 'But if we go out together?'

'To a bar?'

'Maybe. Or a café. That's more the sort of place women go. And the money we get isn't bad. You only live once.'

I certainly hope so, I thought to myself. The idea of reincarnation had often worried me. Life, death, life, death for eternity. I found it hard to believe that someone like me would have anything other than a long way to go to get to nirvana. When life had been at its toughest, I had in fact longed to die. A deep, eternal sleep. It would be a bit of a shock to be met on the other side by some archangel, or a spiritual head teacher who would tell you with a sad little smile that once again, you'd failed the exam. Perhaps we should try a stay in Rwanda next time, Elling? Or what about Calcutta? Perfect places to grow up if you want to rid yourself of the material-istic urges that lie between your soul and Total Harmony.

'What d'you say then?' asked Kjell Bjarne.

'Yes, OK.' The chilling thought of reincarnation made me see that it was important to work actively on self-improvement.

'Should we go and eat at Larsen's first?' continued Kjell Bjarne. 'Noticed the other day that they had pork and gravy. And fish pudding with white sauce. Real food, nothing fancy.'

I could feel myself tensing. The old me wanted to be let out, to tell Kjell Bjarne what I thought about wasting money, swanking about in restaurants. But my stay in Brøynes and my daily sessions with

Gunn, in particular, had taught me to see things from a slightly different angle. I had become rounder at the edges and – well, though I say it myself – more curious about the world out there. It was just that . . . that people frightened me when they were given free rein. My experience from the nine long years at secondary school had scarred me. And even though, in all the years that I lived with Mother, I had shopped for her at the local shopping centre and borrowed books from the library, that had been within a safe, secure framework. They had been quick, purposeful outings, with equally swift, purposeful retreats back to the comfy chair and the radio. Just drifting around from place to place made absolutely no sense to me.

At Brøynes, this had gradually changed. Not that I found meaninglessness any more meaningful, but I had learned to appreciate just ambling around outdoors. In fact, I got into the habit of going for walks in the beautiful countryside around the centre. And on top of that, Kjell Bjarne and I had even started to take the bus down to the shops every Thursday. We would always have a steaming cup of tea and a piece of apple cake in the shopping centre. We talked men's talk and mercilessly mimicked the people sitting at the next table. Laughter and games. But then we were separated and I had to adapt to my pioneer existence in Majorstuen, all alone – if you discount Frank's incessant interference – and I completely reverted to my old self. Just thought it was best. I became a home bird once again – the hordes of people on the street scared me.

Pork and gravy? Fish pudding? Sounded like a good place. I decided to go for it. If it was too much, I could always come home. Run. As simple as that.

# 3

A hundred years before my time Edvard Munch painted a picture called An Evening on Karl Johan. I can remember there was a reproduction of it in some textbook or other when I was at school and it made an incredible impression on me, even then. The painting shows a crowd of people streaming up Karl Johan towards the Palace. Their faces are pale, almost green, and their eyes are large and blank. They look as if they have just emerged from their graves. In the empty street, walking in the opposite direction to all the others, we see a dark figure. As with so many of Munch's pictures, a feeling of loneliness overcomes me when I look at it; I feel a kind of wrench in my stomach. I suppose it must have been my first meeting with the world of Munch and for just this reason the sight of it shocked me even more. Until then I had thought that paintings were something you hung on the wall to brighten the room up a little, I had no idea they could have an effect on you.

In some strange way I could recognize myself in this picture. I knew that I was on my way down the street, away from the others, away from the main crowd. I could just feel it under my skin, so to speak. Of course, the picture made the class laugh. The jokers made fun of Munch's choice of colours and pointed out that people didn't look like that in reality. Many years later I was reading an article about Munch in the review section of Arbeiderbladet and it turned out that many of Munch's contemporaries had said the same. I could have cried when I read that, because I suddenly understood how alone he must have felt.

There were also some excerpts from the painter's diaries in the same article. One of them was about the picture I just mentioned, An Evening on Karl Johan. Munch wrote that he had been getting over an unhappy love affair. Alone and forlorn, he wandered down the street, away from company. He wrote that suddenly everything seemed so quiet around him. Reality somehow dissolved, and pale faces stared up at him.

With these words and with his painting, Munch encapsulated what I was unable to describe, but what I had felt so very often. I was acting on a different stage, that's true enough, but my experience of reality was astonishingly close to that of the great painter. It could come over me on the way to the shops, with Mother's shopping trolley in one hand and my shopping list in the other. A sense of silence would settle around me, and I had the feeling that people's facial features were distorting as I walked between the blocks of flats. I felt that they wanted to do me harm, that in some way or other they were after me. In retrospect I realize that that was exactly what was happening. There was a gang of sick boys hanging around the shopping centre who loved to force my head down into my shopping trolley.

But even in other situations, when no threats loomed, it was as if I lost all sense of my surroundings and I was paralysed with fear. Sometimes I could quite simply doubt my own existence, or, to be more precise, I felt that I was disappearing. I was dissolving. At such times I often tried to hurt myself. At least, that was what people around me thought. Even my own mother was incapable of understanding that when I whipped myself with rowan branches or slapped myself in the face, it was to regain contact with myself. I couldn't explain my actions in any sensible way; only tears or fragmented sentences came out.

The day after getting the cats, on my way to Larsen's with Kjell Bjarne, it came over me again, this sense of losing my grip on reality. My legs withered beneath me. I looked at my feet in amazement as they loyally and quite without any involvement on my part led me towards our destination. I felt as if I had cotton wool in my ears, and I could only hear Kjell Bjarne's monotonous blather in the distance. It was the usual things: women and food. I heard what he was saying well enough, but it was as though he was shouting to me from a different planet. At the same time I experienced a kind of security in having him at my side; I wasn't stricken with panic as I had been so often on other occasions. I thought to myself: here I am, walking. I can see my feet moving. My heart is beating in my chest and I am breathing in the cold February air. It's a rather strange variant of reality, but reality it is nonetheless. The lonely man in the street, the one escaping from the menacing crowd, now has one of life's simpler companions. And when this thought occurred to me I suddenly realized that I wasn't running away from anyone or anything any more. I forced myself to focus on the backs of heads and the coats of the people in front of me on the pavement, and a great calm descended over me.

In the distance I could see the beer advertisement outside Larsen's and a garish sign which I assumed displayed the menu of the day. That was where we were going, and, to my surprise, I noticed that I shared my friend Kjell Bjarne's excited anticipation. I wanted pork and gravy now; like him, I would be disappointed if it was not on the menu. At this moment I couldn't feel my stomach, I could hardly feel any physical presence, but still I was hungry. How odd. Pork. Thick gravy. I decided I would mash my potatoes in the gravy as I had done when I was a boy. Pour salt all over it, never mind my kidneys or any other internal organ for that matter. My mouth was watering at the thought of the crispy meat.

'Shit,' Kjell Bjarne said, and I noticed that the cotton-wool feeling in my ears had disappeared. 'They haven't got any pork and gravy!'

'Beef stew,' was on the menu, '55 kroner.'

I was deeply disappointed. Even with my very limited experience as a restaurant-goer, I realized that stew could be anything at all in a restaurant like this, and I doubted that the cook had been told to be extra generous with the beef. Anyway, by now I was utterly fixated on pork and gravy. All I really wanted to do was turn round and go home again, but suddenly I could hear Gunn's voice in the distance. I remembered the long intimate conversations we had had at Brøynes. 'You give up too quickly, Elling,' she used to say. And, 'You must try not to get hysterical every time you come up against an obstacle.'

Of course, to begin with, I was absolutely fuming when she spoke to me in that tone. I believed that in many ways I had managed to avoid the usual adult pitfalls. I thought that I had been able to maintain the inherent sense of right and wrong that children have, and that was why I came down like a ton of bricks on issues that many considered mere trifles. For me it was all about principles. If you gave way on trivial matters throughout the week it was a sure recipe for a troubled conscience on Sunday.

I reminded Gunn that the whole of our welfare society was based on the fact that the old Labour pioneers had fought to bring their larger visions down to the man on the street and they never flinched for a moment, however banal the debate. Wrong, she said. Politics is the art of compromise. The Norwegian Labour party would never have got to where it was if they had not had a clear sense of what mattered and what didn't. One small sacrifice one day might lead to an important victory another day. When she added that she was a member of the Labour party in Brøynes and was on the local council, that gave me something to think about. Personally, I had never been a member of anything, and, of course, I had to take her experience into account. Besides she was the first member of the Labour party I had ever met face to face. Something like that makes an impression on you. 'Be a bit more positive and you'll soon see that everything is that much easier!' were always her final words.

So now I did just that. I was a bit more positive. I put on a cheery tone, which, frankly, sounded some-what hollow, but I told Kjell Bjarne that the crucial thing was that we 'got out and met people', not what the menu had to offer. That was what Frank had been trying to bang into our heads ever since we came to Kirkeveien. 'Don't sit around sulking,' Frank said. 'It doesn't matter a toss where you go, just get your bums off the sofa! As far as I'm concerned, you can start by going to Pentecostal meetings.' Thank you very much! I could just imagine Kjell Bjarne rolling around the floor, speaking in tongues and being cured of his food addiction. We had a good laugh about that as I aired my views on this particular project. And then we stayed behind closed doors.

We went into the restaurant. We ventured in further, with Kjell Bjarne in front and me right behind. Basic decor. No knick-knacks, it was exactly as Kjell Bjarne had said. Brown furniture and red gingham tablecloths. I chose to ignore the acrid smell of smoke that hung in the air as there was also the smell of good food! And best of all: my fear of a room filled with antagonistic drunks, their psyches scarred by difficult childhoods, came to naught. Two old men sat at the back of the room, each at their own table browsing through the newspaper. Otherwise we were on our own. It went straight to my head! I assumed a carefree expression and whipped off my anorak. We chose a window table. I sat down, ran my hand through my hair and tried to yawn.

Kjell Bjarne sat down on the other side of the table. 'Are you tired?'

'Tired? No.'

'You've got your mouth open like a young chick waiting for food.'

I explained to him that I was just a little bored. I looked casually around for the head waiter, who proved to be a buxom woman with a winning smile. Would we like anything to drink? Of course, two Cokes.

'Got any pork and gravy?' Kjell Bjarne asked.

She didn't think so. She explained to us how the restaurant worked and we listened attentively. The situation was that they operated with a set menu. She pressed a menu into our hands. She went on to inform us that in addition to the set menu there was a daily special. I confirmed this, nodding towards the sign outside in the street. Exactly! Today's special was beef stew.

'When will it be pork and gravy again?' Kjell Bjarne insisted.

She didn't know. She couldn't answer. We were given to understand that she was not responsible for choosing the menu, that she simply didn't have much of a say in what went on in the kitchen.

'Just a minute,' she said. 'I'll go and ask.'

She went to ask while Kjell Bjarne and I flicked through the menu. Suddenly I felt a lump in my throat. The menu was just like my mother's home cooking! Meatballs with mushy peas. Pork sausage and sauerkraut. And smoked haddock with boiled carrots. I told Kjell Bjarne that all these traditional

Norwegian meals reminded me of my childhood, well, adulthood too, for that matter. My own mother could have put this menu together.

He grunted, and I immediately covered my embarrassment by saying that he had a really good nose for restaurants. I realized that I had put my foot in it when I used the taboo word 'mother'. I should have known better.

'I'll have sausage then,' he said, putting down the menu. 'With a lorryload of sauerkraut.' He gave a sigh of satisfaction and looked out at the people rushing by in the street. It had begun to sleet and most people's eyes were firmly trained on the wet pavements. 'Wonder where they're all going. Have you ever thought about that, Elling?'

Had I indeed! I had spent my whole life wondering where everyone was going. What their dreams and goals were. What sort of people they were, behind their masks. At times it had almost become a mania with me. In our old block of flats I could stand for hours by the sitting-room window and let my imagination run wild. Mother, who was probably in the kitchen cooking, had laughed at all this. The psychologist at Brøynes had advised me to take things easy. A lively imagination was all very well, he said, but now and then these speculations could cause a lot of trouble. For example, when fantasies became realities. And vice versa.

'There's good old Jesper Pedersen,' I said. I nodded in the direction of a large man struggling to put a cardboard box into a car boot. 'He must have bought another new alligator.'

'Alligator?' Kjell Bjarne stared at the box with enlarged eyes.

'He buys them when they're small and then feeds them up,' I said. 'And he kills them when they're fully grown. Then they're made into bags and belts and so on. Makes an absolute fortune, of course.'

'Prat!' Kjell Bjarne said.

'I don't know about that,' I said. 'There are worse jobs.'

'I mean you're the prat,' he said. 'Gunn said that you should pack all that rubbish in. It'll do your nut in!'

'You just look after your own nut,' I said. 'And I'll look after mine.'

'Where the hell do you dig this stuff up? An alligator. You expect me to believe that? Knowing you, I bet you've never even seen the bloke before.'

Our buxom friend returned. Her breasts quivered gently under her pullover, and she beamed at us.

'You were lucky there, boys! The chef has got some pork left over from Thursday.' She put two glasses of Coke in front of us.

'Does that mean that we can have pork and gravy?' Kjell Bjarne asked.

'If you want, yes.'

'What's your name?'

I aimed a kick at him under the table, but hit a table leg.

'Johanne,' she answered, without any sign of embarrassment.

'Thank you very much, Johanne,' Kjell Bjarne said, and went to shake her hand. Clearly, she drew the line there as she didn't take his hand.

'Do you know when I last had pork and gravy?'

'No, I couldn't even hazard a guess.'

'Me neither. But it certainly wasn't the day before yesterday, I can promise you that.'

She winked at him, or perhaps it was at both of us. Then she went off to get another beer for one of the old boys in the corner. Almost inaudibly, he had snapped his fingers.

'Great woman!' Kjell Bjarne said. 'I want to come here again tomorrow.'

'I'm sure you do,' I said. 'But there's absolutely no chance. Not so long as I hold the Treasury purse strings. Apart from that, I quite agree with you. Johanne is a magnificent woman.'

'At least once a week then?'

I considered that. Yes, we could afford that. Besides, the unqualified success of the last half an hour had warmed me to the idea. I liked the place, naturally I liked Johanne, and I liked the menu. The thought of doing anything as absurd as choosing a local had been completely and utterly alien to me before. The local pub or the local restaurant, a place one frequented habitually, was something I had read about in novels or seen in English television series. Now I appreciated that having just such a place, a fixed point among the vast array of places to go, could be the very solution for two men who had resolved to broaden their social horizon. There was something safe about this restaurant. We had already developed an understanding with the undisputed mistress of the house and we could undoubtedly count on her in the event of any scrapes. Her jolly winks might even turn out to be a sign that she saw us as potential sexual conquests.

Having grown wiser from previous disappointments, and with Gunn's warnings still ringing in my ears, I chose not to pursue this theme in my imagination. I was content merely to undress her and myself as quick as a flash in my mind's eye, and I caught a glimpse of her large white breasts looming up to meet me as I called 'cut'. It was time to bring this nonsense to a close as I had promised Gunn and several others. From now on I would stay close to reality, and that was that. The fact that Kjell Bjarne sat there dreaming of Johanne spreading her legs and sitting on his face was his problem.

'Wonder how Pepper and his pal are getting on,' he said, as if he had been reading my mind and was trying to cool down, to distract himself from his smutty thoughts.

Suddenly I wondered the same. Had we done the right thing, leaving them on their own? I mean, they were used to company where they came from, to Mrs Rimstad and a battalion of cats. When we left they were sleeping in the cake tin after having done their business all over the kitchen floor. But what were they doing now? Standing in the hall, howling for Kjell Bjarne and me? I could see it all in front of me – furious neighbours gathering in the stairwell, the caretaker running for a phone to contact the RSPCA.

I steeled myself. 'They'll have to get used to us being away.'

'Yes,' Kjell Bjarne said. 'And they've got each other, as old Rimstad said.'

'We can take some crackling back for them,' I whispered conspiratorially. 'That'll give them something to do this evening.'

'So long as it isn't crispy,' Kjell Bjarne said. 'If it's crispy, I'm having it.'

'OK,' I said. 'Only if it's not crispy then.'

The food arrived, brought by our big-bosomed beauty. The plates looked like two dishes on weighing scales and I was reminded of Justice. We couldn't believe our eyes. It was too good to be true. We tried to surpass each other with superlatives, and Kjell Bjarne knocked his glass over in his excitement. Delicious thick slices of pork, roasted golden brown, floury potatoes and thick gravy. We ordered iced water and launched ourselves into our food. Johanne laughed. She seemed to blossom in our company.

'Best meal I've ever had,' Kjell Bjarne said, with his mouth full.

Well, I would still plump for Mother's Christmas

roast, but never mind. This was a squire's repast for ordinary people, and there was no doubt about that. As I had planned, I mashed the potatoes in the gravy and covered them with a good layer of salt. The meat was rich and juicy. It irritated me a little that Kjell Bjarne didn't mash his potatoes in the gravy like me, but who cares. He was in a hurry, as he always was with food. Even the gravy he shovelled in double quick with his knife, a custom I always connected with my grandfather's generation and one that had always fascinated me.

I ate and purred with pleasure. I trembled with well-being. The iced water came and Johanne asked if we were enjoying the meal. Yes indeed! We would include her and the chef in our bedtime prayers, I joked. And this produced a hearty round of laughter that I shared with a woman who was a complete stranger to me. Then the old man in the corner was up again, snapping his dry, bony fingers. Johanne was off to the beer pump again. On a bad day this persistent finger-snapping would certainly have irritated me, but it was a good day. A brilliant day. An affectionate cat was waiting for me at home, and here I was gorging myself on a fantastic meal with no fancy airs and graces. I saw myself as the old man, snapping my fingers for my regular Friday meal. I liked this image.

'Frank should see us now,' Kjell Bjarne said, wrapping the crackling in his paper serviette. His plate almost looked as if it had just been washed. 'He'd have been quite chuffed.'

I took my crackling too and pushed my empty plate away. 'Quite chuffed,' I said, smiling. 'He would have preferred it if we had been sitting at a long table together with a few foreigners from a selection of exotic countries.'

'Prat,' Kjell Bjarne said. 'And this time I don't mean you.'

I had to go for a pee. There had been such a lot of pressure on my bladder and now I had to do something about it. I wasn't at all happy, because if there was one thing I was frightened of, it was going to toilets where anyone can wander in without so much as a by your leave. I couldn't really ask Kjell Bjarne to go with me because that would have been misunderstood. It was different for women. Even with the little experience I had of restaurants I could hardly fail to notice that females seemed to relish going together. What did they actually do behind the closed doors? Did they sit there having a shit while talking through the thin partitions about how awful men were? Or were they content with a couple of risqué jokes while adjusting their make-up? I didn't know and I would never find out, either. The only thing that was sure was that women liked to go to the loo together, and they always took their handbags with them, even if they only wanted to have a quick dribble. It was beyond me, but that's the way it was.

I got up and steered towards the gents' at the other end of the room. To my annoyance, I could feel the angst-ridden sense of isolation come over me again. The Munch state. At the same time I realized that I would just have to get through this expedition. That was what Frank meant when he talked about extending boundaries or even 'exploding' them. If you survived you could add another experience to those you had had before, and you were richer for that.

As I began to move my legs forward – they had gone numb again – I thought how fantastic it was that we humans were so different. The Norwegian explorer, Erling Kagge, for example, had walked all the way to the South Pole alone, while I had to summon all my strength just to cross the floor of the restaurant on my own. And I wasn't the only person to have problems like these. I knew that there were thousands of people all over Oslo who didn't even dare go to the local shop without taking a pill first, or taking a little glass of something stronger. I had read in the papers that this was a common problem, so I was in good company. And I thought: who can say which feat is greater? The anxious man or woman overcoming their own fears and simply going out into the street, into the pitiless light of day, facing piercing stares – or Erling Kagge's heroic march to the South Pole? Was he really the great hero he was made out to be? At least he must have had some peace and quiet on the way. And yet.

Like so many others in this country of ours, a country that has fostered Nansen and Amundsen, I was deeply fascinated by our modern polar explorers. I had read the old boys' polar logs and I had read Kagge's. I had been struck by the latter's openness and unprejudiced views of subjects that were seen by others as taboo in our modern society. How many of us, deep down, wondered what it was like to relieve yourself at 40° below with the unremitting Arctic winds powdering your crack with one million frozen needles of ice. Kagge not only gave us some insight into this delicate matter, he also allowed us to take part in the preparations, in the thorough planning. In fact he had to work out exactly how many pieces of toilet paper he would need on the journey. For those of us who suffer from a slightly dicky tummy, the fact that this could even be calculated is incomprehensible. To save paper, and thus weight, he realized he would have to shave his backside to reduce friction. And this was the image that was etched in my memory: Erling Kagge crouching behind a snowdrift shaving his backside, a small hand mirror trembling in the Arctic glove of his left hand!

Anyway, the thought of others' heroic feats filled my own feeble frame with courage. I strolled casually across the room and thanked my lucky stars that I had chosen the quiet existence of a stay-at-home. I might have a trunkful of problems and inhibitions, but at least I didn't need to save

toilet paper. If I felt like it, I could even grow a beard.

The toilet was fairly disgusting. It stank of stale urine. Normally I take refuge in one of the lockable cubicles even if I have nothing more serious to do than to dispose of fluids. But there was no point doing that here; one of the cubicles had a sign saying 'out of order' and the other one had no door. Someone had simply taken it with them and left. Besides, the toilet itself was so filthy that I preferred the urinal. I pulled out my old friend and was just on the point of releasing a jet into the meerschaum-coloured porcelain when the door opened behind me. Of course, I should probably add. That's how it is in this world. When you drop a slice of bread it falls butter-side down. We had been sitting with the two old boys in the restaurant for over an hour and none of us had shown the slightest inclination to go to the toilet. But now it seemed that the time had come for one of the others too and I was distracted in my endeavours, inhibited even. It had always been like that. Whenever someone watches me urinating the pipeline immediately gets blocked. Unless I'm well under way, mind you, but I wasn't. The stranger had caught me right in the middle of my run-up.

It was the old man who had snapped his fingers. A bent little gnome. I observed him from the corner of my eye while trying to ignore him so that I could get started. But no. Not a drop. He stood right beside

me, closer than was strictly necessary in my view, and then he pulled out his cannon too. How I hated situations like this! He couldn't produce a drop either and we stood there like two halfwits, each holding our sexual organ. We pretended not to notice anything and it was so embarrassing, so embarrassing. Why couldn't he have waited for a minute or two?

The seconds went by. It became even more embarrassing. But I couldn't even roll up my hosepipe as I was frightened that something terrible might happen. The need was so urgent that I thought my bladder would burst. It was simply beyond me how my psyche could hold back the flood. I had absolutely no doubt that my inhibition had psychological origins. I couldn't help noticing that the old man, unlike me, used his left hand. And that he held his penis from the top. Many men prefer this grip, I had noticed that. Each to his own, I say. I consider it more natural to hold your apparatus with your right hand, being right-handed myself, in the same way that I would hold a garden hose. Suddenly he raised his right hand and, as he impatiently jerked his crutch, he snapped two nicotine-stained fingers in one powerful movement. Then he peed like a waterfall. Whether it was the sight of his urinating torrent or it was simply my surprise at seeing him snap his fingers that did it I don't know, but in any case I instantly sprang into action as well. What a man! He relayed orders to his body in exactly the same way that he ordered Johanne to fetch him more beer. I saw him in a shop in front of me and in the bank, and I imagined how he communicated by snapping his fingers. Couldn't he speak?

'Ah well,' he said, shaking off the last few drips. 'That was all for today.'

When I went back into the restaurant a few minutes later, he had gone. Johanne had taken away the empty glass. It was just as if he had never been there. In the meantime Kjell Bjarne had ordered a cup of coffee for himself and had found a tabloid from the previous day. He sat flicking backwards and forwards through the paper as he hummed to himself and he didn't want to be interrupted. Crisis Rocks Psychiatry. Minister in Budget Row. Woman Raped in Ladies' Toilet. Suddenly I had an idea. I jumped up and strode over to the area by the toilet where I had seen a telephone. I ruthlessly dialled Frank's number and got him immediately after the first ring tone. As if he had been sitting in his office chair waiting.

'Yes?'

Was I speaking to Frank?

'Hi, Elling.'

I didn't like his casual tone. As if it were entirely normal that I would call him. It wasn't. I rang him very seldom. And only when he had asked me to. Now I felt like putting the phone down, just as I used to in the old days. He must have got wind of that because he suddenly started chatting away about Kjell Bjarne and me and our lives. What had we been up to since last time?

Last time when, might I ask?

'Last time I saw you, you muppet. Did you get the cat, or was that too difficult?'

Difficult? I had to laugh. You just had to read the paper for a while. Pick up a phone. Jump on the metro and ring the bell at a strange house. 'We took a couple while we were about it,' I explained. 'We shared Mrs Rimstad's view that that would be for the best. We got on very well with her, by the way. We were invited to coffee and cakes, and there was no shortage.'

'There you are. It's not so dangerous to do things as you imagine. Well I never. Two of them. Must be pretty lively in your sitting room then, I reckon.'

I gave a smile of triumph. Now I had him exactly where I wanted him. I told him that I really had no idea what it was like in our sitting room. Neither Kjell Bjarne nor I had been there for hours!

It suddenly went quiet for a moment at the other end of the line. 'What have you been up to then, Elling?'

My voice shook a little as I explained that Kjell Bjarne and I were at our local. At Larsen's. That we were usually at Larsen's at this time of day. 'Just had a bite to eat,' I said and forced out a yawn. 'Pork and gravy here on Fridays. That wakes up Kjell Bjarne, as you know. And it's a lot of fun. It's a bit dull for

Johanne only to have the old boys fussing around.'

'Johanne?'

'The manager,' I said, and I began to describe her in rich detail. While maintaining a sidelong glance at the counter in case she should turn up.

'Well, I'm buggered,' Frank said.

'You can say that again!' I exulted.

And banged the receiver down. I wanted to leave him dangling, with his mouth wide open.

# 4

When we came out onto the street, having paid and thanked Johanne for our meal, I felt so secure and happy that I suggested to Kjell Bjarne we should go for a stroll. A constitutional, as they say, just to mark our breakthrough, our new lives as liberated, free-range young men. We were in our prime and could go wherever we wished. Kjell Bjarne was not particularly enthusiastic but he followed me, muttering, when I started to lead the way. Past the Colosseum Cinema and then down towards Frogner Park. I caught myself whistling an old Roger Whittaker tune, a favourite from my youth. While the other boys in the class liked the Beatles and the Rolling Stones, I listened to Cliff and Roger.

I couldn't really understand Cliff Richard, who

had admitted to the world's press that he had only slept with one woman once and that he regretted it and had asked God for forgiveness. Perhaps it was in fact this sober abstinence that fascinated me, that he didn't just throw himself away, but on the contrary, dared to fly in the face of the heady rock 'n' roll circus of the Swinging Sixties. As far as I could see, he was a man of substance. A non-smoking teetotaller who boldly entered an arena full to overflowing with drugs and wanton women; who came up with the goods, a unique voice and catchy tunes, and then retreated to his hotel room with a soft drink. He deserved all the respect he got.

But it was Roger Whittaker who was my real hero! Well, 'hero' . . . perhaps it would be more accurate to say that he, as an older man (in relation to me), had represented some kind of security in my life. Puberty and teenage years are rough at the best of times, agonizing and confusing. Anxiety was my constant companion in this period, then as now. And when Anxiety came visiting, let me tell you, putting on a record by the Rolling Stones was of no help whatsoever! But it was completely different with Roger. When Roger's comforting voice sang out to me from the cassette player, I relaxed. When he whistled, tears sprang to my eyes and a shiver ran down my spine. And while my schoolmates rarely saw their idols on TV, Mother and I often snuggled down in the corner of the sofa to watch our favourite artist.

It was the 1970s, the Golden Era, and Roger

Whittaker appeared on one television show after another. Always impeccably dressed in a tweed jacket and cord trousers, his beard trimmed and his fingernails clean. Even Mother, who normally could not abide beards, had to admit that Roger's was neat and attractive. And it was. It was the most well-groomed, attractive beard imaginable.

I used to daydream as I listened to his ballads, fantasizing that the man on the screen was my father. That it was my father standing there, playing the guitar, to the sighs of the women in the audience. Mother also had a soft spot for him. She told me so. But I have to admit I was not that keen on the idea that her soft spot might keep her awake, 'soft' for him, when she had gone to bed in the evening. However, I kept my mouth shut and didn't say a word. As I said, I could understand her, though obviously I didn't share the sexual aspect of her admiration.

'What's there to do down here?' Kjell Bjarne asked as we went into Frogner Park.

'Well, we could have a look at the naked women,' I said.

'Naked women?' He looked around, confused, in the dusk. His eyes scoured the lawns that were partially covered with snow. 'Don't make me laugh!'

'See a bit of culture,' I continued, feeling a mischievous smile playing on my lips.

'Culture my arse,' said Kjell Bjarne. 'I want to go home to Pepper.'

But then Vigeland's sculptures appeared in the gloaming and I discovered, to my astonishment, that Kjell Bjarne had never visited Frogner Park before. He had probably never even heard of it. I knew that he had been taken out of a normal school and put in a special class, where they spent most of their time having the alphabet and tables beaten into them. And his home life? His home at the edge of the woods? He didn't give away much, but as far as I could tell, the drunken moonshine mutterings rarely touched on art and culture.

He stood there gawping. 'Fuck me!' he said finally, when he pulled himself together. He chortled. 'Can't be real! Can't be bloody real!'

'No, of course it's not real,' I said cryptically. 'But rather good, isn't it?' I told him a bit about the sculptor, Gustav Vigeland, and his loyal helpers, but it fell on deaf ears. He ran towards an enormous woman, who was down on all fours, and positioned himself behind her, then let his hands slide all over her ice-cold, gigantic buttocks.

'Didn't think this sort of thing was legal, Elling. Right in the middle of a park and all that.'

I gave him a brief outline of the legislation governing this area.

'Only erect penises are illegal,' I said. 'And as you can see, Vigeland is far from guilty on that score.' I pointed to a colossus of a man who was juggling a handful of children. His John Thomas looked more like a small slug that had gone to sleep under his belly.

'Fuck,' said Kjell Bjarne. 'There are hundreds of them here. Imagine . . . Shit, Elling, imagine . . .'

Yes, the thought had struck me, there's no denying it. As a boy, Mother had taken me here sometimes on our way to and from the polished gravestone in Vestre Cemetery, where my father lay buried. I'd had wild fantasies about these huge, Amazonian women coming to life, in flesh and blood, and allowing young boys to explore them. I envisaged myself cavorting on the green lawns, surrounded by mountains of laughing pink flesh, while their men remained frozen in their isolated grey-granite world.

'This is how I like 'em!' said Kjell Bjarne. 'Something to get your hands round!'

'Just a moment ago, you said "culture my arse",' I said, imitating him. 'And now you're standing there grinning with an arse in your hand.'

'Is this culture then?'

'Of the best kind,' I assured him. I started to walk back towards the main entrance. Kjell Bjarne followed me, reluctantly, as he mumbled to himself and caressed each work of art.

When we got home and opened the door to the building, something happened that gave us a fright, at least it frightened me. There was someone talking on the stairs. A stream of jabbering sounds, punctuated with strange gurgling noises. A woman. I stopped abruptly on the first step and grabbed hold of Kjell Bjarne's arm. Fortunately we were now so well attuned to each other that words were often superfluous. I sent him a questioning look: what should we do? Should we go out again and come back in an hour or two? Personally, I felt rather drawn to this option. On the other hand, it could be a damsel in distress. A beauty with a dicky pacemaker.

Kjell Bjarne had a very odd expression on his face. Despite our long friendship, I could not fathom his expression. He drew long, deep breaths and his nostrils flared.

'It smells of hooch,' he said. 'Poor quality hooch.'

'Hooch?' I whispered.

'Spirits, you idiot. Moonshine.'

There was a terrible noise above us, and shortly afterwards we heard a head bouncing down the stairs. We counted four bounces.

Kjell Bjarne closed his eyes and drew a few more deep breaths. 'OK, Elling. If it's who I think it is, you'll have to knock me out or I'll kill her.'

And with a roar he shook me off and ran up the stairs. Just like Frank.

But no, it was not Kjell Bjarne's mother who had dropped by for a visit. Luckily, it has to be said, because there was nothing to hand to help me knock Kjell Bjarne out.

In fact, it was only Reidun Nordsletten. Of course,

we had no idea what her name was as we stood there at the bottom of the stairs, holding our breath, but it turned out to be Reidun Nordsletten. She was lying head down, with her legs pointing up in the direction of the landing and her arms waving about in the air. Her long brown hair was spread out over the dirty steps, and her green eyes were struggling to focus. She was a large, solid woman with a small snub nose, out of which two thin streams of blood started to dribble. She was so drunk that she literally could not stand on her own two feet, and every time she opened her little mouth to howl, the stench of heavy spirits hit us.

Mother always said that drunken women were the most vulgar thing she could imagine. Women who stumbled around drunkenly in public were a law unto themselves. And I had always heartily agreed. We disapproved of drunkenness in any form, but drunken women were absolutely scraping the barrel.

I mean, we had got used to men crawling home along the paths at the weekend, swearing and pleading and spitting out brown tobacco juice everywhere. It was all too familiar to see some unfortunate family man being collected by the police, with dogs and flashing blue lights, after he had fired his shotgun from the balcony. These men would announce to the world that they were going to commit suicide, before they were clapped in irons and taken away. The day after they would reappear with downcast eyes, head hanging down, while their wives went shopping in sunglasses. We had got used to the unhappy group of divorced fathers who stood drinking at the entrance to the metro, but on the rare occasion that we saw a woman stumbling towards us . . . It was simply a disgrace, Mother used to say.

Of course, it was a disgrace that men, too, hit rock bottom, but it was different after all. I mean, men will be men. We are born with a stunted emotional life, we struggle to be understood. When men drink and run amok, it is usually out of sheer frustration because it takes them such a long time to find the right words. Well, that's my theory. I think that many men drink in order to achieve a kind of female intuition, a deeper understanding of reality. And then it all goes wrong when they try to tell the world what they think. The alcohol-induced perspective is distorted by jealousy and suspicion. The reasoning is understandable enough, but the actualizing goes horribly awry.

All the same, inebriated men are a part of every-day life, they're just part of the city scene. But a woman falls from a greater height and she always falls alone. I have certainly never seen a bevy of female drunks. The very thought of having to scurry past six or seven bottle-toting women in their sixties on the way down to the metro is absurd. It just does not happen in reality.

But when I stood looking at Reidun Nordsletten's

helpless condition, I noticed to my astonishment that I was ashamed. I was ashamed of my judgemental attitude. And I was astonished because I had never been ashamed of my views in all my life. I might have modified them to suit the circumstances every now and then, but I had never actually been ashamed of them before. But this person needed help and fate had sent her Kjell Bjarne and myself. It was no time to stand around philosophizing about woman's fall from grace.

We turned her round the right way and sat her up against the wall. She stared at us, bewildered, babbling away. We couldn't understand a word.

'Absolutely,' said Kjell Bjarne. 'Let's take one thing at a time. Where d'you live?'

She waved her arms around again, as if she wanted to tell us that, like a rabbit, she had a home under every bush.

'Upstairs or downstairs?' Kjell Bjarne continued. 'Upstairs or downstairs?' He kept repeating the question until she finally managed to croak 'up'.

'OK.'

And before you could say Bob's your uncle, he had her over his shoulder and was holding her in a fireman's lift. He must have seen the astonishment on my face, because he smiled grimly and said, 'I've had plenty of training, Elling. You bring her bag!' And then he staggered up the steep stairs to the next floor. I looked around, and sure enough, right by our own front door lay a brown leather bag. I lifted it up carefully and ran after Kjell Bjarne. Nervously, it has to be said. The situation could be misconstrued. If one of the other residents were to come by they could easily think that the poor woman was being attacked.

'Look in the bag!' Kjell Bjarne said, when he got to the landing. 'Find out what her name is.' He peered at the nameplates to the left and right.

I wanted to refuse, but something had come over Kjell Bjarne. He was more in control than I had ever seen him before and I just didn't dare to oppose this new authority. The woman's head was dangling over his shoulder. She had closed her eyes and appeared to be dead to the world. With shaking hands, I opened the bag. I had never opened a lady's handbag in my life, not even my mother's, and I felt like a petty criminal. A voyeur of the worst kind. The first thing I saw was a packet of menthol cigarettes and a single pink condom still in its wrapper. Naturally, I blushed to the roots of my hair. I prodded her vices to one side and held up a Visa card. One of those small stiff plastic things that the bank refused to give to Kjell Bjarne and me. Reidun Nordsletten, it said, and on the back, a bright young woman smiled up at me from a good amateur photograph.

I reported the woman's identity as well as I could, but noticed that my voice was trembling.

'Well find the key, for fuck's sake!' Kjell Bjarne barked. 'It's the door to the left.'

Were there no limits? I rummaged around in the make-up and loose tampons and felt more and more unwell. Finally, I found a key ring in one of the side pockets. We rang the bell and I mumbled a silent prayer that someone would open the door for us, so we could just hand her over without any fuss. But nothing happened.

'Open the door,' Kjell Bjarne instructed.

'We can't do that,' I said.

'So you think we should just leave her here on the landing, eh?' he said, irritated. 'Open the bloody door!'

I did as he said and followed him nervously into someone else's home. In my fearful state of mind I could see what would happen if she had a husband or boyfriend, or even a mother who was at home but asleep. They would shout at us, maybe beat us up, and no doubt report us to the police because this must constitute forced entry, even if we had not broken down the door. I felt very sick and anxious. To my knowledge, I had never done anything illegal in my life, and now I had ended up on the wrong side of the law due to a set of unforeseen dramatic circumstances. I had just wanted to go to an unpretentious restaurant to have pork and gravy with my friend and flatmate and then later to show him some of Oslo's cultural heritage, and now here I stood, peering into the sitting room of a complete stranger.

And very nice it was too, I noticed through the

haze of my discomfort. The layout of the flat appeared to be identical to our own, only she had different decor. Whereas Kjell Bjarne and I had gone for a more minimalist style in terms of furniture and ornaments, Reidun Nordsletten had chosen the opposite. The flat looked more like a furniture warehouse, with deep red and pink as the dominant colours, the walls covered in posters, paintings of crying children and roaring stags, and there were shelves upon shelves of dolls and bric-a-brac. She obviously collected owls of all shapes and sizes. There were small porcelain owls, owls cast in metal and plastic, leather owls and great horned owls made of fabric, with embroidered eyes and brown felt beaks. On top of the television there was a small barn owl with electric yellow eyes that blinked at us every second – probably from Hong Kong.

Kjell Bjarne flipped Reidun Nordsletten onto a couch and straightened his back. She lay there on one side, with her face turned towards us, quietly snoring.

Then we saw it.

Her sweater had ridden up and we could see her tummy. The white, soft skin shone in the dusky room: it was a big, round tummy. Nature took its course and I got a powerful erection. For a short, evil moment I saw myself in the role of abuser: I saw the abuser exploit the situation, saw him go down on his knees and lick round the sunken navel with his tongue. But, as I said, it only lasted a moment. I still had an erection, but I banished the image of the abuser into the depths of the stinking sewers of my subconscious.

I shot a glance at Kjell Bjarne. He stood there and swallowed, the blinking owl's eyes casting a yellow sheen on his face. Grey, yellow, grey. He was a strong man, but Reidun Nordsletten was also a heavy young woman and the sweat formed in pearls on his forehead.

'Bloody hell,' he said quietly. 'She's up the duff.'

My sexual organ immediately shrank to nearly nothing. Just collapsed, automatically, as it were. I sank into the sofa and Kjell Bjarne followed my example. We sat there side by side, with our eyes glued to Reidun Nordsletten's tummy.

'It can't be true,' I whispered. 'It's probably just fat.'

'It's fat as well,' he said. 'But an astronaut is floating inside the fat. That's for sure.'

He was right. I could see that as well now. And I felt myself shrivelling the moment I acknowledged it. What kind of wretched misery was this? Wasn't the world harsh and difficult enough, without you having to be poisoned by your mother's blood before you even pushed your way towards the bright light and loud noise?

Astronaut? I thought to myself. For once Kjell Bjarne had evoked a beautiful image. I remembered the TV reports from my childhood. American astronauts dancing in space, in the endless universe. In the blue-white light of the moon they spun around weightlessly, with stiff, comical movements, always attached to the spaceship by cables and pipes, umbilical cords to life itself. These pictures made a great impression on me, emotionally. Other people thought how incredible the new technology was; I thought how moving it all was. Even then I had been aware of the dual symbolism to which Kjell Bjarne referred, but that he was unlikely to understand fully.

I had seen a foetus, a new person, floating around in its mother's womb, in some colour photographs in a science magazine – and the little mite had already learned to put its thumb in its mouth. I had torn out these pictures and filed them away, along with all the other things that I came across in papers and magazines. I would take them out every now and then, and I was always awe-struck when I looked at them. Because where abortionists only saw a jelly mass, a rather disgusting 'thing' that could be removed without too much fuss, I saw a complete person. How absurd that a new individual could be created from next to nothing, with the magical conception taking place after the nocturnal romps of mothers and fathers, giggling under the duvet in a winter-dark room, or to jubilant shouts from scented bushes and thickets. Yes, it is magical! The sperms' determined journey towards the waiting egg, an egg as big as a globe. And then, the selected sperm slips into the soft centre of the ovum. The chosen one! The winner.

I had often comforted myself with this thought when life was against me. That I was really a winner, a victor, despite the defeats I had to concede every day. In keen competition with millions of other sperm, it was that little scamp Elling who was first over the line, and who could raise life's trophy above his head and join the human race. And I applied this logic beyond the limits of my own ego and interests. There was a boy of my own age in our neighbourhood who had been born deaf, blind and retarded, a more dreadful fate it is hard to imagine. But when I watched him on the lawn outside in summer, his heavy head lolling to one side, I knew that he was the living proof that he had won his race. He had beaten potential physicists, athletes, artists and intellectuals hands down! And when it boiled down to it, who could know what kind of abstract images rolled in front of his inner vision?

'Just hope she hasn't hurt the baby,' said Kjell Bjarne. 'She went down the stairs arse over tit.'

Thus ended my philosophical meanderings. He was right. I immediately began to worry. What should we do? What if the fall on the stairs brought on a miscarriage? Could we just leave her now and hope for the best? Should we call a doctor? I was reluctant to do this as it would cause such a stir. On the other hand, Kjell Bjarne and I had been given instructions, in Frank's words, 'to take responsibility'. Not to run away from problems and challenges, as we had tended to do throughout our whole lives.

What if a premature birth had already started? I could imagine the terrifying scene: Kjell Bjarne and I would have to roll up our sleeves and open our arms to welcome a new global citizen. It would be so typical that the first time we came into contact with a woman's naked bits would be at precisely the opposite end of the process from that experienced by all other men. Not a body trembling with desire, but one trembling with ignorance and fear that something might go wrong. I had to pull myself together so that my imagination didn't run away with me, force myself to be practical in all the confusion. She was lying on her back when we found her and I was sure that it was her head that we had heard banging down the stairs. Definitely not her soft belly. Her breathing was fine and regular.

'I know what we'll do,' I whispered. 'We'll go down to our flat and then phone her in a couple of hours, just to make sure she's all right.' I pointed to the telephone, which was on a small table beside a squadron of porcelain owls.

Kjell Bjarne shook his head. 'You go and give the boys some food. I'm staying here until she wakes up.'

'You can't do that!' I hissed. 'You'll frighten the life out of her!' I could just imagine Reidun Nordsletten waking up from her alcohol-induced coma and seeing a complete stranger sitting on the sofa staring at her. An enormous desperado with a bristly chin and wiry black hairs on the backs of his hands. What Kjell Bjarne did not know, and naturally I was never going to tell him, was that despite his mild-mannered nature, his appearance could be quite scary.

'Never frightened anyone except myself,' said Kjell Bjarne.

I stood up and noticed that I was shaking. 'If you don't come down with me immediately, I'll phone Frank.'

He shrugged. 'Ring the President of America for all I care. I'm staying.'

I was beside myself and just wanted to cry. Give in. And we had had such a nice time earlier on in the evening. The visit to Larsen's restaurant had been a singular success. Our little cultural excursion afterwards likewise. And now this! As a result of our kindness, we had entered a total stranger's home, become enmeshed in a hopeless situation, and now Kjell Bjarne refused to budge. I was scared that the police might get involved. A real to-do. I was scared that we might lose our new home. That was what Frank threatened if we acted up.

I just had to leave. Get out. Not even ten bull-dozers could budge Kjell Bjarne when he had his mind set on something like now, so I turned and left without saying a word.

I was halfway down the stairs when I saw through his ruse. In a moment of revelation, I saw the situation for what it was. Kjell Bjarne wanted to sell himself as the man on the white horse! The knight in shining armour – friend to all pregnant damsels. I realized that he had set out his stall. If it all went wrong, he would be thrown out and reported to the police and the process would then run its course. But if, on the other hand, the drunken woman realized that she was dealing with a genuine, everyday hero, things could develop in a completely different and more favourable direction.

I had never thought of Kjell Bjarne as cunning before, but I simply had to admit that this was a side I had not seen hitherto. Behind the somewhat simple facade lurked a calculating mind that swiftly assessed situations, so they could be manipulated to his advantage. Fair enough. He could do what he liked. I wasn't going to ruin his game, unless he came crawling back to me looking for sympathy when the whole thing went pear-shaped. Then I would give him the cold shoulder. And if things did develop in the way that pig upstairs was no doubt sitting up there dreaming about, I would have to assess the situation carefully before making a move. I simply could not disregard the fact that he might have to choose between my friendship and this woman's love. I may be slow, even reserved to begin with, but when I do commit myself to something, for example to a friendship, then I do it with all my heart. And, logically enough, I expect my commitment to be reciprocated.

But, if our lives had taken a turn for the worse that

afternoon, everything was forgotten the moment I opened the door into our flat. I was greeted like a returning god! The two little fellows had definitely recognized my steps on the stairs and were waiting in the hall, calling to me in their plaintive voices. I kicked the door shut behind me and fell to my knees, babbling away to them and stroking the two delightful creatures.

They climbed all over me, miaowing, as I rolled onto my back and Pepper started to bite me on the nose with his sharp little teeth. Overcome with joy, I rummaged around in my coat pocket and found the serviette with the bits of crackling. They stood on my chest, quivering with anticipation, as I unwrapped their gift. And once they had each got hold of a piece of crackling, they immediately dragged it into the sitting room, making endearing attempts to hiss at each other and bristle their fur.

I remained in the hall on my back, gasping for breath from pure joy and gratitude. With a welcoming party like that at home, going out was not a problem. No matter where I went, to Larsen's restaurant, the shops, or just for a walk, I would always know that the two small brothers were sitting and waiting for Daddy to come home. I would never let them down. I vowed never to return from one of my expeditions empty-handed.

# 5

It was a strange night. Or to be more precise, it was the strangest night of my life. I'm not used to sitting up all night and the oddest thoughts ran through my mind. At first I was anxious, but that's not really surprising. I was sitting in the armchair and worrying that Kjell Bjarne's foolish behaviour might jeopardize the secure existence we were in the process of building. I was worried that Frank and the others at Oslo City Council might say enough was enough. We gave you plenty of opportunities, but you abused them, you spurned our generosity. What I feared most was that the pregnant woman's husband, lover or partner would let himself in with his own key. Catastrophe would then be inevitable. Even though we lived in difficult times and the morality of our day was shabby, I assumed that it was not yet the rule that women brought up children on their own in this country. I thought Reidun must have a man. At any rate, it was clear that up until a few months ago she had shared a deep intimacy with a person of the opposite sex. She had allowed this person into the temple of her soul, which is what the human body is, and she had celebrated Mass with him there.

The boys went to sleep early on a jumper that Kjell Bjarne had thrown onto the floor by the wood burner and I sat there listening for the sound of footsteps on the stairs, or ominous signs from the floor above. Howling and shrieking and the regular thud of a blunt object. I didn't dare put on the TV. I just sat rigid in the armchair and allowed my fears free rein, so free in fact that in the end I had to rush to the toilet and empty my bowels. In a funny way, that helped a little.

As tiredness gradually made inroads and dulled my senses, I slipped into a state of near-indifference. It was too late to ring Frank; there was simply nothing I could do without moving heaven and earth. And I didn't want to do that. Besides, slowly I began to realize that I had done enough worrying in my life. More than enough. And this worrying had never done me any good. When I looked at the two small cats who had rolled themselves up into little balls, when I thought of their blind faith that life would treat them well, I was ashamed of my own disquiet. A few brief years, I thought, that's all we have here on earth. Then we die. The more we squirm, the more it hurts. All my life I had been fascinated by, and had looked up to, the people who actually dared to break out, who let life carry them along from adventure to adventure. It had always been painfully clear to me that I was not one of them.

Now I noticed, to my dispassionate surprise, that I was relaxing. It was well past two o'clock. Well, well, my boy, so you are sitting there with a grin on your face in the middle of the night? I was in fact sitting there grinning. Yes, I was grinning. In one corner of my inner eye I could see Kjell Bjarne's huge shadow towering over Reidun Nordsletten in the flat above me. In another corner, I could see my anxieties and my sense of responsibility dissolving into nothing. I said to myself that I had been responsible enough in my life and now it was time to let go. In my imagination I jumped into a large Dodge and put my foot down. A mental image of the North American continent lay spread out before me, full of opportunities and surprises. I was zooming along the highway of my own senses without paying any attention to speed limits or radio reports of weather and road conditions.

I had never taken drugs in my life but I thought that this semi-dreamlike state must be akin to what unfortunate addicts clung to. Flickering images and this enormous, beautiful feeling of freedom. How many American films had I seen where the main protagonists broke out of poverty and despair, out of defunct marriages and the grind of work, and, with the gas pedal pressed down to the floor, simply roared off into the future! Always on the move, the odd blonde on the way, anonymous hotel rooms in sleepy towns in the Midwest. I was sitting in my own armchair in a flat in Kirkeveien, Oslo, but I had the same feeling that these freewheelers must have had.

For once I wasn't fantasizing, this time I was me, nurturing the devil-may-care attitude in myself. A few minutes earlier I had been weighed down by fears of the moment and of what the future might bring. Now I was almost welcoming confrontations and challenges. A few brief years, I reminded myself. You've lived over half of your life, perhaps you have only days left, so what can actually hurt you, I mean really hurt you? Eviction for illegally entering a neighbour's flat? Well, so what? I'd already been thrown out of a flat and it didn't kill me. The police had led me away into a waiting patrol car as the neighbours went into a huddle, excitedly talking over each other. I couldn't remember very much about that incident, just isolated fragments of detail, but Eriksen, from Social Services, had later told me that when I was evicted I departed with a certain style. I had tossed my head and bared my teeth at the authorities before fainting.

Sitting there now, half asleep in the dark room, it

88

became suddenly clear to me that this was the part of my personality that I had to rediscover. I simply wanted to be a colourful character. Well, in fact, I already felt I was quite a character, a mischievous rogue. Not your common or garden villain, of course, not the run-of-the-mill trigger-happy gangster or someone like that. No, a free and easy spirit, someone who scribbles down a prose poem on the restaurant bill to give the waitress food for thought, before stumbling out of the restaurant and taking another draught from the goblet of life. Imbibing the sun and wind, the dancing pollen and the gentle summer rain. All these years I had been like a bud waiting to open, but now that was over! Some poet or other had said that it hurts when buds burst open. I didn't believe a word of it, or, to be more precise, I knew that it wasn't true. I knew that it hurt to be in bud. To unfold, on the other hand . . .

I sat bolt upright in my chair, suddenly wide awake and clear-headed. I stood up and went to the window. It was as if all my senses were more receptive than usual, as if the room around me, the flat, the street outside took on new, sharper contours. A car slipped by, down towards Frogner Park. The crunching of tyres on frozen asphalt sounded in my auditory canals. What was it I had just been thinking about? I conjured the image up from inside myself, the image of Elling spontaneously scribbling down a poem, a minor work of genius, on a restaurant bill. And then the words came to me. Yes, that is how I would express it, that the words came to me.

We found her on the stairs.
Her hair,
a black raven's wing that the wind had blown
onto the unwashed lino floor.
We laid her on her bed
and lo: the angels had made her with child.

I felt faint! I staggered into the kitchen and scribbled the poem down onto an old shopping list. Afterwards I stood there shaking – then came the tears. Beautiful, tranquil tears. I had made poetry. Restlessly, I walked to and fro across the sitting-room floor, reading the poem to myself in a half-whisper over and over again. Slowly it dawned on me: it was a touch of genius, a true gift from God. Was there more where this came from? I hardly dared hope.

From time to time I had dreamt about becoming a writer. In my dreams I had seen myself as a kind of nineteenth-century shining beacon in the literary world. But what had appealed to me most was actually being an author. Apart from a few personal notes and a number of audacious reader's letters, I hadn't done a lot with the pen. Poems had never particularly interested me. Well, the interest was there now. A touch of inspiration from something that was me, but greater than me. A product of the human miracle. It was something no-one can describe, perhaps something that is not meant to be described.

I made myself a pot of tea and returned to my chair. The cats were still asleep on Kjell Bjarne's jumper. I contemplated my hands holding the mug; my feet in my old slippers; the window frame with the joyless Christmas decoration. Everything was as it was, and yet . . . A revolution had taken place in this room. I saw my whole life with all its problems and its suffering in a completely new light. I had walked this earth for almost forty years without realizing that I was a poet! Was it any wonder that there had been misunderstandings before when the poetry, my own language, had lain dormant within me?

I closed my eyes and began to delve for more poetry inside myself, but I found nothing. I must have fallen asleep, for the next thing I remembered was that Kjell Bjarne was standing on the floor in front of me, yawning like a hippo and scratching his back. I was tired, on the very brink of unconsciousness, but I could not restrain my curiosity. I demanded a report.

And was completely ignored. He behaved as if he were alone with the cats. He went down on all fours and burrowed his nose into Pepper's tummy!

I had another stab and asked him to tell me what had happened.

He stood up and began to get undressed, throwing his clothes off all around him. 'Why didn't you go to bed?'

'Because I was sitting here waiting for you!' I snapped. 'To come and help you as soon as I could, if anything should happen.' Sooner or later I would probably decide to tell him about my poetry, but this certainly wasn't an opportune moment.

He just looked at me stupidly. Yes, really stupidly. 'Happen? What could have happened?'

I asked him if for one tiny little moment he had entertained the idea that there might have been some unpleasantness if the woman's lover had turned up and found a strange man in her flat.

No. I had the impression that he hadn't been thinking about anything. That he had just sat there staring into the dark.

'Well,' I said. 'It was a good job you got out before she woke up, anyway.'

'Why's that? She was bloody awake!' He kicked off his trousers and went into the kitchen.

'And she didn't raise the alarm?' I shouted after him. 'She must have been frightened out of her wits finding a hairy orang-utan in her own home.'

He drank milk straight from the carton and dried his mouth with the back of his hairy hand. 'I told her what happened. I found her on the stairs. I was frightened she would choke on her own spew, if she spewed.'

'And?'

'And what?'

'She must have said something, for Christ's sake.'

Now I was swearing, too. 'On top of that, we found her, not you.'

'Said she didn't drink that much normally. That's why she was in such a state.'

'And she wasn't angry that we had let ourselves into her flat?'

'Didn't say anything about that, no.'

I withdrew into myself again. The woman must be as daft as a brush. Didn't she read newspapers? Didn't she listen to the radio? Or watch TV? Last summer there had been a series of vicious rapes in town. A disturbed youth from Sunnmøre had clambered into the bedrooms of single women through the open windows. He had raped five women before the police caught him. He had threatened them with all sorts. The oldest of his victims had been nearly ninety. It was absolutely unthinkable! And here was Reidun Nordsletten sleeping off a skinful, and she wasn't even surprised to find Kjell Bjarne in her room when she woke up!

'I refuse to believe that!' I said. 'I refuse to believe that you didn't even get an earful!'

'You can believe what you like. I'm off to bed. I've got to fix a few things for her tomorrow. Or later today.'

'Fix what?' I asked, following him.

'Mind your own business,' he countered. He went behind the wardrobe to his corner, and threw himself on his bed. I could see his eyes in the half-light. He was on his back staring up at the ceiling. He was staring up at Reidun Nordsletten.

I wasn't going to give up so easily. 'Fix what then?' I repeated.

'Nothing. Fix a tap.'

'That's right!' I said as sarcastically as I could. 'Reidun Nordsletten wakes up, finds a stranger in her room, and the first thing she thinks about is getting the intruder to come back later in the day to repair her tap!'

'She didn't say anything about the tap. It was just dripping the whole time. Thought I was going nuts.'

'Oh great! I suppose you took her key with you as well, didn't you. So that you can come and go while performing your heroic deeds whether she's at home or not?'

He didn't answer. He turned to face the wall and pretended he couldn't hear.

'You're in love!' I jeered. 'And I promised Frank I would tell him if you lost control.' I ran out into the kitchen and smashed a cup. And then another. I lifted up the bread bin and shook it so that the crumbs flew out.

Then he was there. I could feel his enormous right hand slowly twisting my right ear round until I was bent double and begging for mercy. He didn't say a word, but led me into the bedroom and didn't let my ear go until I was lying under the duvet with all my clothes on.

Afterwards I quietly got undressed without leaving my bed. My ear was glowing.

# 6

Sure enough. It was just as I thought. Now that Kjell Bjarne had taken the bull by the horns and embarked on what he imagined was a blossoming relationship, he had no intention of letting go. That very afternoon he emptied out his toolbox to find a new washer for Reidun Nordsletten's dripping tap. And then when he found one and was sitting with it in his hand, he got a dreamy faraway look in his eyes, as if he was sitting there looking at a small gold ring and not at some stupid rubber thing. And without him saying a word, without so much as even glancing at me, I knew that he would kill me if I threatened to tell Frank. Some things you just understand intuitively.

But when he disappeared out of the door the

minute we heard some hesitant steps above our heads, I sat there, aghast. Because I had never seen him like this before. We had always agreed that the world was menacing; that was why we stuck together, at Brøynes Rehabilitation Centre and now here in Oslo. Something was happening to both of us. I felt that it was all moving a bit fast, really. Nevertheless, I was sitting in my own home with a cat on my lap and a poem in my pocket, and really had nothing to grumble about.

Above me, I heard that Reidun Nordsletten's light steps had now been joined by Kjell Bjarne's plodding gait. I could even hear the steps moving from the sitting room into the kitchen. I tried to imagine them. All my life I had been so good at imagining every situation possible, but now I found that I couldn't. I couldn't quite picture Kjell Bjarne and Reidun Nordsletten together up there in the kitchen. What were they talking about? Would Kjell Bjarne be just as monosyllabic as he normally was with me, or would he show off with witticisms and eloquent phrases, now that he had a captive female audience? Was she doing more than just listening? Was there already something between them? No. If that was the case I would have noticed. There is a limit.

When he came back down, whistling, with his toolbox under his arm, I became preoccupied with the paper. If he thought that I was sitting here with a thousand questions burning on the tip of my tongue, he shouldn't hold his breath. I had no intention of speaking to him whatsoever. I just glanced over at him lethargically before diving back into my article again. How ridiculous! The Christian Democrats wanted to cut import duties on cars! It was going to get colder, it said somewhere else. Well, well. You learn something all the time.

What now? Quarter of an hour passed. Half an hour passed. I kept an eye on the time, constantly looking down at my watch, but Kjell Bjarne did not say a word. He sat at the kitchen table, fiddling about with something in his toolbox. OK, I thought. Fair enough. I knew him well by now. He was sitting there, waiting for me to ask for a report so that he could have the pleasure of telling me to mind my own business. Fine. If there was one thing I was good at minding, that I minded by instinct, it was my own business. He could keep his stupid secret to himself about what had been said and done in Reidun Nordsletten's flat.

When we went to bed that evening, neither of us had said a word about it. We had only exchanged some passing comments about the crust on top of the liver pâté.

Some peaceful days followed when harmony ruled. Kjell Bjarne came out of his shell again, and he seemed to be lighter, more alert than he had been for a long time. And even though Reidun Nordsletten was in some way omnipresent, like a poltergeist, we heard her above us at all times of day and night, we did not talk about her or about what had happened. No. We allowed goodwill to prevail between us and avoided the topic as best we could. We had had one conflict and we had worked it out between us. Exactly as Frank prescribed. He used to say, 'Get it off your chest and move on.' Of course, I did notice that Kjell Bjarne often froze in a certain position with his head cocked to one side when there was a noise from upstairs, but I was not so mean as to point it out. When all was said and done, I had nothing against Reidun Nordsletten. Quite the contrary, in fact. It had been me who took the initiative in the small rescue operation we had undertaken. I just didn't like the boat to be rocked. I did not want events to run away with us, when we were so obviously heading towards a new dawn in our lives.

The third room in the flat, which had been empty for some time since Kjell Bjarne moved into my bed-room, caused us some consternation. One day neither of us knew what we should do with it, the next day we would argue because we both had very definite opinions about what we should do with it. A luxury problem of huge proportions, obviously. There were plenty of people living under bridges in this town and here we were bickering about what we should do with the spare room. Finally we seemed to have reached an agreement without having really even broached the subject. I don't remember who first mentioned the word, but one word led to another and before too many words were said, apologies for my wordiness, we had agreed to use the empty room as both a library and a workshop.

I had cherished the idea of having my own library for a long time, but Kjell Bjarne had objected to the project for the reason that he didn't like reading anything other than men's magazines, and anyway, I didn't really have enough books to fill more than one wine box. My point was that I had always cherished the dream of building up a collection of books. All my life I had been obsessed by various projects, and collecting books, preferably cheap books arbitrarily acquired from second-hand book-shops and jumble sales, seemed very appealing to me. Naturally, I could put up a bookshelf or two in the sitting room, but the thought of being able to say to Kjell Bjarne, 'I'll be in the library if anyone wants me' was particularly appealing. It was fairly suspect, I admit, it being the sort of thing the English upper classes would say, but I liked the sentence. To say anything else would be less than truthful. Anyway, I thought that Kjell Bjarne's idea of putting the workbench and the lathe that he yearned for in there was utterly idiotic. Not least because a lathe would mean noise and nuisance. We were saving up for a video player and we had a long way to go.

But now we agreed that if he was happy to have

only the workbench for his bits and bobs, I would be satisfied to line half the room with my library. We could even organize things in the spare room so there was some sort of room divider between us. Shelving for books, for example. We would each have our own little area and I was already looking forward to starting my search for the requisite armchair at all the flea markets. I quite clearly had a new project. Suddenly, as we were standing there in the empty room, making plans and taking measurements, the doorbell rang.

Let me put it this way: it was unusual for our doorbell to ring. Frank was the only person who came to see us and he always phoned before he came. In other words, there was every reason to be suspicious. I was about to suggest that we should just ignore the whole thing when the doorbell rang again. Persistently and impatiently. Kjell Bjarne grunted and moved towards the door.

As I have said before, he had no intention of letting go. His antennae were not exactly the most sensitive, but he must have guessed that it was Reidun Nordsletten who had her finger on our bell out there in the corridor. Personally, I decided not to show myself. I positioned myself by the door frame and listened. Kjell Bjarne's deep rumble and a high female voice that was almost inaudible. I listened with both my hands cupped behind my ears and my mouth open, but it was impossible to catch the words. Then the front door shut again with a bang and I was alone. Kjell Bjarne had simply left the flat without so much as a goodbye.

The good mood that I had been in was, naturally, destroyed. Splintered and spread to the wind. I ran to the kitchen window to see if they were leaving the building, but there wasn't a living soul to be seen in the back yard. I stood there and pondered on the power women have over men. There is a lot of whingeing and whining about lack of equality and poor pay, but the truth is, unfortunately, that women have men wrapped around their little fingers. As far as I could make out, you could almost say women have absolute power, due to men's basic sex drive. In Kjell Bjarne's case it was obviously extra basic as he was a slave to his sex drive in the same way that a robot is controlled by electrical impulses. If Reidun Nordsletten was of the calculating type, and I had no reason to believe that she wasn't, she would be able to exploit Kjell Bjarne's gullibility in the most grotesque way. And there would be nothing that I, his only friend in this world, could do. Any sign of female calculation, however, would be met on my part with animosity – of that I was absolutely certain.

Where had they gone? They hadn't appeared down in the back yard and there wasn't a sound from upstairs. I tiptoed out into the hallway and put my ear to the door. Silence reigned there as well. Complete silence. For one reason or another, I got it into my head that I had to hold my breath, and when

I finally spluttered for air, I heard noises on the stairs. Laughter and steps. They were coming up and crossed the landing outside our door. And continued on up the stairs. Once again it was impossible to catch the words, though I could have sworn Kjell Bjarne mentioned my name. Elling, he said. Accompanied by fine words and followed by laughter.

Well, it was noted, as they say. Stored at the back of my mind. And contrary to expectations, I was neither upset nor disturbed. Unwittingly, he had handed me a card that I could use against him, in some future quarrel. Was that what he meant by being underhand? Wasn't he the one who wanted honesty and loyalty? The same man who slandered his only friend in order to gain favour with a pregnant woman with alcohol problems!

Shortly afterwards he came storming back down the stairs and I quickly withdrew into the sitting room where I started doing knee bends, with my hands behind my neck.

'Had to help Reidun with a sack of birchwood from the cellar,' he stated, without being prompted.

Aha, glasnost. A new openness. Kjell Bjarne started to inform me about the labyrinth of love without me even putting on the pressure. I ignored him. Continued knee-bending.

He head-butted the wall and made the whole house shake. 'She said she'd cook for us tomorrow evening!'

'Hang on a moment,' I said. 'Before you beat your-self to death. She said she'd cook for us?'

'Yeah. She said that I could take you along with me.'

'Thank you very much,' I said. I didn't even try to curb the bitterness that flavoured my words. 'But I'm not in the habit of letting myself be "taken along" anywhere. And in any case, I'm busy tomorrow.'

'Busy?'

'Yes, I'm going to a meeting.'

He let out a coarse, hideous laugh. 'You expect me to believe that!'

'I don't expect you to believe anything,' I retorted. 'Please send her my regards.'

'What sort of meeting are you talking about?'

I explained that it was actually none of his business. Just as it was none of my business if he allowed himself to be exploited by a casual passer-by.

He shook his head. 'Shall we have a game of ludo and see if it puts you in a better mood?'

'No,' I said. 'I'm going to watch TV.' I grabbed the remote control.

And so the evening passed. One dreadful programme after the other.

There was no way round it. I had given myself a not insignificant problem. I had lied and said that I was going to a meeting. I had never been to a meeting in all my life. It wasn't actually that surprising that Kjell Bjarne had laughed in my face. To tell the truth, I did exactly the same thing the next morning. I laughed in my own face with the help of the mirror in the bathroom. Scorned my own deceitfulness. Of course, I didn't actually have to go to any meeting, but I would have to find something to do with myself. My angst returned like an old friend at the very thought. It made the skin under my fingernails tingle. I could wander the streets for a few hours, I supposed. A walking target for unprovoked violence. If the papers were to be believed, the situation in the country's capital was now so awful that being out in public places was a gamble in itself. There were people out there whose hobby it was to maim innocent passers-by. They blinded you without batting an eyelid and relished kicking you in the face when you were down.

In the taxi queues and in front of the city's fast-food kiosks, people were being executed. Without a word, individuals, scarred by a difficult childhood, pulled out loaded guns and shot the person next to them right in the face. And it was in this insanity that I now would have to walk alone. All the same, the thought of the alternative was unbearable. I was absolutely certain that I was not wanted in the flat upstairs, that Reidun Nordsletten had felt obliged to invite me. And I didn't want to get on the wrong side of anyone. On principle. The two lovebirds could coo in peace without me being there.

Kjell Bjarne left me to my own devices. He did not try in any way to make me change my mind. That hurt me. I felt that he could at least have put some pressure on me, so that I would have the opportunity to use some of the retorts that I'd stewed up during the night. But no. Not a word. He sat listening to the radio all day, as he alternated between tidying his toolbox and eating slices of bread and raspberry jam. In a way, I didn't benefit much from my lie, as he didn't even pester me for details about the meeting I'd talked about. But that's just the way he was – self-centred in the extreme. In his mind he was probably well into Reidun Nordsletten's panties. With his mouth full of mutton and cabbage stew.

I studied the newspaper in minute detail, searching for a meeting or event, something that might be of interest to me. A safe place to go, a place where you could kill a couple of hours in the back row without being forced to actively participate. The cinema was out of the question. I only went to the cinema with Kjell Bjarne and Frank. A safety buffer on each side, if you like. Sitting beside a complete stranger for an hour and a half had never been my idea of fun. I mean, you're stuck there. And then all of a sudden there's an unsolicited hand on your thigh. Or somewhere else for that matter. The anonymity that darkness provides allows some people to step over the line.

Pop concerts? Niet. Nada. Not even Cliff or Roger

could tempt me to a place where the volume was well over the pain threshold and where the hippest of the hip Oslo-ites swanned around in black clothes. Swilling beer and taking illegal drugs. Conversations in G minor.

But then my eye caught a small advert at the very bottom of the page. Poetry reading, it said. Haakon Willum and Cecilie Kornes reading their own poems. At Nordraak Café.

I was so happy. So very excited! Because this really appealed to me. My own poem was still burning a hole in my pocket; no-one was aware of it yet, but the town had a new poet. This was an opportunity to meet other people in the same line of business. Of course, I wouldn't let the cat out the bag; as far as I was concerned, anonymity was absolutely essential for my further work. I would be the silent man in the back row. The one that no-one knew. The one who did not belong there, but who just turned up, listened and left. Who was he? Did he write himself? Why did he only smile patronizingly during the obligatory post-show discussion? Why was he the only one who did not have a question for the poets? A number of women would undoubtedly wonder.

I was convinced that the audience at a poetry reading would be of the gentle-natured variety, the sort of people who, like me, managed to observe all the details in the rich tapestry of life. Sensitive souls, gathered together in a forum where random violence and quarrelling were inconceivable. Each and every one had come to listen. To meditate on the words of a couple of poets, whom I for one had never heard of, but who most certainly wanted to open their hearts.

The reading was due to start at eight and as I am not the type of person who saunters in at the last minute, I started to get ready around six. I was dreading it, I admit quite openly, but I said to myself that I just had to go through with this. If all went well, as it had with the meal at Larsen's, it would be a major coup. I could imagine the satisfied smile on Frank's face when I told him that I had dropped in on a poetry evening at Nordraak's. I would keep quiet about my own poem safe in my pocket, for the time being.

As I put on my coat, I noticed Kjell Bjarne's dusty sunglasses lying on the shelf under the mirror. I put them on and I liked what I saw. The slightly mysterious impression that lingered with me from my previous mental images was enhanced. It was actually dark outside and there was snow and sleet in the air, but so what. The sunglasses gave me character. And they created a distance between me and the rest of the world that I felt certain I would need. They made me cool and at the same time protected me. If I let my hair grow for a couple of months and then lightly tousled it, I would look a bit like Bob Dylan.

After spending three hours thoroughly tidying up

his toolbox, Kjell Bjarne had stopped and was watching TV. He was engrossed in a wildlife programme, in which the life and times of the otter were being discussed in detail.

'I'm off now,' I called.

'Those sunglasses are mine,' he said. 'And anyway, it's the middle of winter.'

'You can't wear your sunglasses when you're having dinner with Reidun Nordsletten,' I said.

'Where're you going?'

'Just down to Nordraak Café for an hour or two,' I said, and successfully managed to make the name sound familiar. 'There's an important meeting about modern Norwegian poetry there this evening.'

'You're raving mad,' he said. 'That's for sure.'

'Goodbye,' I said and turned on my heel.

'Elling?' He followed me out into the hall. 'Is there . . . Have you really thought about this?'

Well of course I hadn't, so I didn't really know what to answer. And in any case, I got a big lump in my throat when I felt the care and concern that radiated from him. He stood there fumbling with his sausage fingers and then carried on, 'Could drop the whole bloody dinner, you know. If you want me to come with . . .'

You had to know the man to understand what sort of sacrifice this was. Tears sprang to my eyes and I was grateful for the dark sunglasses between him and me. I shook my head and grabbed his hand. It was a long time since we had been so close and I truly and deeply wanted him to have a lovely evening with Reidun Nordsletten. I pulled myself away, opened the door and ran down the stairs.

Outside, it was freezing cold and the sleet that had been driving for most of the day had now been replaced by gently falling snow. The streets and pavements were already covered by a thin layer and the postboxes, telephone boxes and parked cars had been given funny hats. For a moment I stood outside the house and looked up at the sky. The snowflakes danced through the air towards me and some of them landed on Kjell Bjarne's sunglasses. For some reason it put me in a good mood. This, and the certainty that despite our daily feuds, I had a friend for life in the form of that big oaf upstairs in the flat. I started to walk towards Hegdehaugsveien and noticed, to my astonishment, that my old enemies Dizziness and Discomfort had been blown away. I walked with a light step and with my hands deep in the warmth of my coat pockets. Despite being in a public place, I moved with the greatest of ease and greedily gulped in the cold air.

But that is not to say that it was easy to 'enter' when I reached the yellow facade of Nordraak Café. The proud old building lay in the shadow of the towering SAS hotel and I suddenly felt that the situation was threatening. I went round to the court-yard where I knew the entrance to be. I had read somewhere that there were tables outside in the summer. A soft light shone from the windows onto the snow-covered courtyard, but my anxiety just mounted. Behind the panes of glass there were moving shadows of people, a mass of people, and the sound of laughing and talking reached my ears.

My heart started to pound with a heavy doomsday beat; I could feel the reverberation on the inside of my eardrums. But I simply couldn't give up. I felt a delightful defiance swelling inside me, a quality I have always had in rich supply, but which often prevented me from having a social life. I had used my defiance as a shield, as protection against unpleasant intrusions into my personal space. But now I turned it around and used it to take action. I wanted to go in and I would! Even if it was going to kill me, I wanted to take part in this poetry evening. Three times I put all my angst and inhibitions behind me and strode resolutely towards the closed door. And three times I turned around when I reached my destination and allowed myself to be driven back to loitering in the courtyard.

People came and went, but no-one noticed me. Perhaps it was this that helped me. The fact that people obviously registered that I was there, but didn't really see me. I was a shadow in the yard, an anonymous figure that no-one knew anything about, and that most people were not bothered about. I felt that this perspective gave me some freedom and instilled fresh courage in me. Whatever, the fact is that after a quarter of an hour I gritted my teeth, marched over the frozen asphalt and tore open the door.

And I was inside, sharing the easy-going atmosphere with other people who were complete strangers to me. There was no reason to think that they had any designs on me, for better or for worse. I was simply the man in the sunglasses. A man without a name, but with a good winter coat, snow in his hair and a secret poem in his pocket.

The room was not nearly as full as I had feared. So far, the number of people was almost bearable. A hard core had sat down near the microphone at the front, presumably regulars or friends and acquaintances of the two poets in question. Glasses of wine and amber beer sparkled in the light, but I went to the bar and asked for a lemonade. For a moment I felt a bit silly because of the sunglasses, but then the young man behind the bar gave me my drink and put the money in the till without changing his expression. He didn't say a word, but he made it clear to me that this was a place for people with strong personalities and images. I had an urge to lean casually against the bar and nonchalantly pick my teeth with my fingernail. And I did it! I stood there and belonged, exuding a mysterious inner peace. Every now and then I would take a sip of my drink which I had carelessly placed on the bar beside me. The lemonade was delicious, sharp and sweet at the same time.

I was one of them now. One of the people who

belonged at Nordraak's. Each time the door opened and new people came in, perhaps having overcome worse fears than I had, they saw the same thing: a cool character at the bar. An unshaven guy in a worn winter coat. The glass of lemonade? I presumed that they drew their own conclusions. They were looking at a man who'd been around the block so many times that his liver simply couldn't take any more. Now it was a matter of lemonade or death and he had already diced with death.

I started to observe the people around me more carefully. They were a motley bunch. A couple of pretty blondes having fun with a clean-shaven man. His scalp shone in the spotlight. He was wearing thick-rimmed square glasses and every time he took a swig of beer, you could see his fillings. It was as if he had caught a hail of bullets with his teeth. But all the same, popular with the ladies. Could this be the poet of the evening standing in front of me? Haakon Willum in person? It was clearly the case that women in these artistic circles did not just look for outer beauty, but on the contrary, looked behind a man's exterior to cherish the qualities that were to be found here. In a more conventional environment, that man wouldn't have stood a chance. At least, not the obvious double portion of good fortune he had here. The thought that I could perhaps manoeuvre myself into a similar position if I really had a breakthrough with my own poetry, filled my heart with warm expectations.

A youngster in a black leather jacket stood smoking a cigar whilst conversing with an older woman. I liked the mix of sexes and different generations. I noted the cigar. When I was young I had smoked a bit at weekends and even though I was now undoubtedly seen as a non-smoker, there was no getting away from the fact that it smelt quite good, and it looked quite masculine. The cigar gave the young man an air of indulgent elegance. It was as if he was tasting his own words before letting them slip from his mouth, loosely wrapped in blue-grey smoke. I could see myself lighting up a long, thin cigar next time Frank suggested something for our benefit. I would blow a couple of lazy smoke rings in his face before clearing my throat and rejecting his suggestions outright. Sorry, I was now completely in control of my own social-integration programme. I would give the matter of smoking some thought. After all, it wasn't necessary to inhale.

People streamed in through the door all the time. The room inside was getting very full. To my surprise, however, I realized that panicking was not an issue. I simply decided to stay exactly where I was. At the bar. I could hear the poetry readings just as well and didn't need to find a place in the heaving mass. If I moved half a metre up the bar I could even see Haakon Willum and Cecilie Kornes through the open door. But also, I was struck by a rather good line that I could later serve up to Kjell

Bjarne, maybe even to others, should I talk to them. 'I propped up the bar,' I would say. Then they could think what they liked.

There was some banging on the microphone and then a somewhat strained female voice called for attention. I slipped into position and gave her my full attention. It was a woman in her fifties. She did not have breasts, but instead had a flushed red neck and darting eyes. Poor person! She welcomed us all before launching into a harangue about Haakon Willum and Cecilie Kornes, their distinctions and their merits. It was completely over the top and immediately I was on my guard. All this bragging seemed totally unnecessary to me. Prizes. Piles of publications. Translations into Russian and Mongolian.

If it wasn't for the fact that poets in general are constantly broke, I might have thought that the two rascals had slipped her a fat backhander. In fact, I felt some animosity towards them now. I could hardly imagine that their poetry was any good when it had to be packaged in superlatives in advance. The whole thing stank. It reeked of cultural mafia, of Parnassian elitism. I had read about things like this in the newspaper. Angry articles by hardworking writers who never got anywhere because they came from Northern Norway or were women, or for one reason or another did not warrant the attention of the tabloids.

And even before Cecilie Kornes, to deafening

applause, walked onto the stage, I had decided. Chosen my corner. I would be the spokesman for the misunderstood. I would never be bought, never be trumpeted by a neurotic librarian, or whatever she was. I would look for my new friends in dark corners where ruthless conspiracy theories were hatched. In fact, I decided that I didn't even want to be published. Slope from publishing house to publishing house where know-it-alls sat with their fat pay packets, throwing crumbs from their table. My poems, because now I knew there would be more, would be found scratched on toilet doors, written in felt pen on banisters, they would reach their readers where they least expected it. Short, sharp responses to everyday greyness. Carefully calculated verbal bombs that would blast a hole in the walls of superficiality that surrounded us all and robbed us of our vitality. I was all a-quiver and the first thing I was going to do on my way home was buy a packet of cheap cigars.

But back to Cecilie Kornes, who nodded her head in thanks for the applause. She certainly did not have me to thank, I thought, because my hands had remained demonstratively inactive the whole time. To put it bluntly, Cecilie Kornes was a bulimic anorexic: a young woman with the body of a small boy. The whole thing was a tragedy. I felt deeply sorry for her. I imagined how she threw up in secret and wrote poems about her wretchedness after-wards. And, from what I could make out, I had just about hit the nail on the head. Her latest book was called Twisted Intestinal Obstruction and the title certainly gave me some associations, as meaningless as it was.

First she described how the work had come about, that it had been a painful process that had taken several years of her life. And it had not been properly resolved until she fell ill with malaria somewhere in Indo-China. It was the simple way of life and good humour of the villagers that had opened the doors into the secret chambers of her inner self. In her feverish dreams she had seen the constant striving for status in the Western world in a new light, and that light was cold and hard, and ice-blue. Then she cleared her throat and allowed the silence to settle before pressing on in her grating, high voice. I imagined that her vocal cords had become entangled with her malaria-scourged intestines and were twisting and turning inside her.

She reminded me of a stick insect being buffeted by the wind, who could be blown away at any moment, vanish into thin air in front of our very eyes. And her poems! Sick hallucinations! Disconnected sentences that seemed to pull in opposite directions, a ship that had sprung a leak with water pouring in from all sides, whilst the decking curled up under the pressure. Cecilie Kornes was totally without talent. A neurotic nothing who needed help, which she wouldn't get from her publishers, nor here at Nordraak Café. She needed psychiatric treatment and fast. It was urgent. If I wasn't mistaken, it was a matter of life and death.

But people clapped. Lulled her into believing that she was one of the greatest things the nation had seen on the literary front for the past couple of decades, yet not one of her poems had any substance whatsoever! I felt completely overwhelmed. What we had witnessed was part of an unhappy story about illness and I was the only one who had truly understood this! She would leave the place and head home utterly convinced that she had given us something great, due to the unseeing and unhearing audience that had totally misunderstood her, though politely so.

What Cecilie Kornes needed was not applause and grave nods. What she needed was an audience who, in a friendly but firm way, took away her poetry book and slowly rocked her to sleep every time she wanted to say something about the uncorrupted people of Indo-China and the savage conditions in the West. An audience who held her and carefully stroked her hair every time she felt the urge to recite another bout of nonsense. A silent, attentive audience who could relieve her of her intestinal obstruction and give her back her belief in herself as an average person with no bothersome talents or poetic vision. Cecilie Kornes had found the wrong calling in life. She should have been a gardener. She should have eaten fresh carrots and felt the sun and fresh air on her face. She should have had a child or two, so she didn't have so much time to think about her rotting intestines.

But if Cecilie Kornes' performance had been difficult to swallow, well, embarrassing in fact, it was positively intelligent in relation to what Haakon Willum had to offer. My guess that the man with the Yul Brynner haircut and tortoiseshell glasses was the male poet of the evening proved to be wrong. Once again to thunderous applause, a little homosexual in red leather trousers leapt onto the stage. With his hands above his head, one of which was holding a crumpled copy of his poetry collection, he started to make grinding movements at the audience! He thrust his leather-clad pelvis towards us and started screaming into the room in a rock 'n' roll manner. He wanted to know how we were. If we were happy. And in response to this stupid, wholly inappropriate question, some people actually shouted 'yes'! It was unbelievable!

Fortunately he was so eager to get started that he did not waste any time with perambulatory stories of suffering, I'll give him that. With a dramatic movement of the left arm he silenced all noise in the room and then wrapped himself round the micro-phone in a way that can only be described as pornographic. Some people laughed. I simply turned away and looked in the other direction. This was cheap. Vulgar. And while Willum declaimed his base poetry, the main content of which was all about what two men could do, in purely technical terms, to each other as a form of sexual practice, I stood at the bar and studied my glass of lemonade.

The librarian's glowing praise was still fresh in my mind and I found the whole situation depressing. She had talked about Willum's 'refreshing and direct form'. Well. Obviously, he was relatively direct when he described how he thrust his entire lower arm up the rectum of a 'blond imp from Patmos'. But was that refreshing? Was that poetry? What did he actually want? To provoke us? Well, really, we were hardly living in the nineteenth century. Even I, who wasn't that interested in sex, at least, not in sexual deviants, knew something about it.

In one of Kjell Bjarne's dirty mags, I had read about a club in New York where the special attraction was a man with a shaven head covered in different oils, who actually managed to press his whole head up another man's rectum. And I had just thought, oh well. That's progress. The picture of the headless man, with two rubber tubes coming out of his nostrils so he could breathe clean air, became, for me, an image of the age in which we live.

Once upon a time in the distant past we had unsteadily raised ourselves up on two legs and grabbed for a stick to support ourselves. Our journey into the future, to fulfil man's potential, could begin. And now, luckily, we had actually achieved this. We had invented the nuclear bomb, we had landed on the moon, and, finally, we had learnt how to stick our heads up our neighbour's arse. The prospects had never been better.

People howled with laughter. This was poetry for the people. All the heterosexual teacher trainees laughed extra loud, just to show that they weren't prudes. But in a dramatic pause, when Haakon Willum held back in order to really make a meal out of some horrible point, I heard a sound that I recognized. The sound of a thumb clicking against a middle finger. And before the emancipated laughter was once again released like ejaculated sperm, I had turned around and my eye caught the old man from Larsen's. Like me, he was standing at the bar, drinking beer.

And then he nodded to me. As if we were old acquaintances. I was so astonished that I nodded back. And the minute I'd done that, a good feeling started to grow inside me. Because we might well be strangers to one another, but we were linked by the secret bonds that exist between men who share the same local. Admittedly I had only been to Larsen's once, but I must have made an impression on him. He hadn't forgotten me, and he had recognized me despite the sunglasses. This made me happy. I was starting to collect quite a bag of tricks to pull out the next time Frank decided to stick his nose into my business. And that wasn't far off. A matter of days.

He leaned towards me and said, confidentially: 'A lot of internal medicine today, isn't there?'

I released a short snort of laughter.

'But the strange thing is,' he continued, 'digestion is important. That's what you realize as you get older.'

I pulled myself together. Some flushed listeners had turned to look at me. I hadn't laughed in synch with the others. I wanted to say something to the old man, something friendly, preferably intelligent, but the words had clammed up inside. I knew that this moment was important, a gift that mustn't be broken by just blurting out some rubbish there and then. I was frightened that I might ruin something that could change my future. Because sometimes things happen that make me believe in fate, believe that there is an underlying meaning in everything. A person sails into your private bay. OK. But a person contains an entire universe. That is why it is important how you welcome them. You have to guide them onto your shores with great care.

Some time passed without either of us saying a thing. And most important of all, without the silence feeling awkward. When I think about it, I had revealed myself in that short burst of laughter. It said more than any words could say about how I felt about the situation.

Haakon Willum ended with a poem about a blow job and was almost knocked flat by the applause. He lurched down from the stage and made straight for a glass of red wine. The atmosphere was electric and I assume that most of the people in there were ashamed of their limp heterosexual endeavours in the bedroom.

The old man snapped his fingers again. An entire routine this time.

I had to say something. I understood. The time had quite simply come. 'Well, well,' I said. 'That's that.'

'Shhh,' he said. 'The poets will be here soon. The poets always come after the clowns.'

That was deep, I thought. I wasn't quite sure what he meant though. But I pushed the boat out and said that this had been a major disappointment for me, in fact it had made me angry. I emptied my glass and got ready to go in case he didn't agree with me.

He snapped his fingers and finished his drink as well. 'Come on,' he said. 'Let's find a better planet.'

I never cease to be amazed by myself. There was always something new happening. If anyone had told me that I would follow a stranger out into the night, I would have laughed scornfully at them. Or I would have been furious. But here I was, doing it. I was trotting after the old man through the door.

He buttoned up his coat and pulled up his collar. 'Alphonse,' he said. 'Alphonse Jørgensen. My parents' fault, they were completely mad.'

And then there I was, shaking his hand.

I told him my name.

He nodded. 'Let's have a drink at Broker's. I'll pay.' He shot me a canny look. 'Just one thing though, we won't tell anyone that we met here.'

And then we laughed. We were roaring with laughter in the courtyard of Nordraak Café!

On the way up Hegdehaugsveien, it started to dawn on me that I had perhaps found the pot at the end of the rainbow, that maybe I had found a friend, all on my own. Indeed, as we passed block after block without anything being said, I sensed that I had found someone I had subconsciously been looking for all my life. A person who had been around considerably longer than myself, a person who I could go to for advice when things got bad. All my life I had been a fatherless child, with the constant sense of loss that that entailed. Now I saw an opportunity. And what sparked precisely this hope in me, what made me believe that there was something significant in this experience, was the quality of the silence between us. Every now and then he would snap his fingers – it was a strange habit of his – every now and then I would cough, but apart from that we left each other in peace. We walked along in comfortable silence and the fresh snow crunched under our winter shoes. Cars glided silently past on the road.

Broker's? The name meant nothing to me. But when we arrived at the place in question on Bogstadveien, I realized that I must have passed this café a thousand times without noticing it. That was really rather natural. My interest in cafés and bars was still in its infancy. In fact, not long ago I had been extremely negative about such 'watering holes'. As far as alcohol was concerned, I maintained my old position. I did not drink, full stop. But in terms of cafés and public places, I was definitely getting better. Frank was right, this was where people met, where new contacts were made, and I was actually entering the premises with the living proof of this. Alphonse Jørgensen, perhaps my new friend-to-be.

There were a lot of people inside, but as neither of us smoked, we had plenty of tables to choose from in the non-smoking section. There was no-one sitting there. I was so relieved that I decided to delay my cigar project. Obviously, if I didn't smoke I could always reckon on being able to find a seat in places like this. The paradox was that I would then probably not come into contact with other people, but who cares. There was also something known as 'going out with good friends'.

'Do you go to Nordraak's often?' Alphonse Jørgensen asked, snapping his fingers to get the waiter's attention.

I told him the truth, that until now I had lived a quiet, sedate life and that I didn't go anywhere often. At Brøynes I had learnt a good deal about the disadvantages of starting a friendship with lies and exaggeration. I had told Kjell Bjarne a pack of lies and certainly had to pay for it. But more about that later.

Alphonse Jørgensen nodded and I had the impression that he understood my situation. Just in case this impression was wrong, I added a couple of sentences about my mother who had passed away a few years earlier, and about my father who had died in a work-related accident when I was just a foetus. That was the way it was. He could imagine. But now, it was all about Kjell Bjarne and me in a flat in Kirkeveien that the council had given to us. I deftly avoided mentioning the existence of Frank, but obviously told him about the cats.

The waiter came. Alphonse Jørgensen looked at me questioningly when I ordered lemonade, but fortunately didn't comment. He plumped for a glass of red wine. And even though he didn't remark on my drinking habits, I felt it was necessary to hint that I had left my days of alcohol behind me.

'That's good,' he said. 'I personally drank far too much when I was young. I hope it doesn't bother you if I have a small glass?'

Of course not! I assured him that I had absolute control. I had stopped drinking and that was that. It was unthinkable that I should have a relapse after all these years. He who has experienced delirium tremens does not forget it in haste! I didn't want to, I really did not want to, but before I knew it I had launched into a long story about how I had lain on the couch at home and downed neat spirits. I had ripped the wedding ring from Mother's finger and pawned it. Tried to sell her body to my unsavoury friends. That was how my life had been. There was no more to be said. I was ashamed, but who could change the past?

Had I gone too far? No, he only nodded sagely and then he said, 'Look up.'

I looked up.

'That is one of the most beautiful ceilings in Oslo. The whole interior is listed.'

Indeed it was a beautiful ceiling. It was in fact the most beautiful ceiling I had ever seen. Green glass panels with a lovely painted pattern. I didn't quite understand what this ceiling had to do with my claimed debauchery, but never mind. The ceiling was exquisite. As long as we sat here in this café, we were also protected, in a way, by the Director General of Historic Monuments. What a strange idea.

'There is too little beauty in the world,' he continued. 'That is why so many people take refuge in alcohol or in any sort of drug or pill.'

Precisely. That was the connection. Neat. Nearly a bit too elegant. Was he a homo? Wasn't that the way that homosexuals spoke? I forced the thought from my mind, because with regard to my fear of homosexuals, I had been severely reprimanded at Brøynes Rehabilitation Centre. This nonsense had to stop, they had told me, or there would be no flat for me in Oslo, either with or without Kjell Bjarne. Anything that whiffed of obsessive thinking, not to mention compulsive behaviour, had to be weeded out. The psychologist had even given me a lewd smile when he asked why I was so obsessed with homosexual men. In an indirect way, he insinuated that my healthy facade perhaps concealed a minor perversion. I was furious of course, but he held his ground. Stop this nonsense.

The drinks came. Lemonade for me and red wine for Alphonse Jørgensen. He tasted the first mouthful and then gave a friendly nod to the waiter. A wine connoisseur, I thought. A man who knew about architecture and fine wines. A man of the world.

'It was awful down there today,' he said, once the waiter had gone. 'Worse than normal. I cannot fathom why vulgarity should be so highly rated.'

I took a risk and said that it was a sign of the times. I personally believed that there were signs of moral decay everywhere. I gave him a résumé of the last film that I had seen with Kjell Bjarne and Frank. The one where Anneke von der Lippe had shown her white buttocks when coupling with the pathetic poet. Aha, there it was again. A superficial poet was one of the main characters. I was fired up now, because I thought I saw a pattern running through it all. Poets, those who were supposed to be a gauge of our times, to help us steer a steady course as it were, had abrogated their responsibility.

It turned out that I'd struck a lucky vein and we had a heated and fruitful discussion. The words flowed between us like warm honey. We heartily agreed on most things. Newspapers were getting worse and worse and more and more expensive every day. The radio and TV were increasingly focused on celebrity and superficiality. We returned to the subject of Nordraak Café and ripped the two poets to shreds. Alphonse Jørgensen was more careful in his choice of words than I was, but all the same, he was an elderly gentleman and probably not as used to suggesting radical solutions as I was. Not that that made any difference. I did not mean it literally when I said that they should be forced to eat their own tongues.

Which Norwegian poets did I appreciate the most? I couldn't answer. If I started to lie now, I could find myself well out of my depth before I knew it. So I told the truth. That I didn't know much about poetry. That I was new to the scene. And that was why I had been so terribly disappointed by Haakon Willum and Cecilie Kornes. They had robbed me of the illusion of beauty and purity, they had dragged everything into the gutter.

Well, he felt there were still some good poets in this country. Even among the younger ones. He mentioned some names that I had never heard of before. My own poem was burning in my pocket, but I managed to control myself. My anonymity had to be protected in the poetic project that was gradually taking shape in my mind.

Time flew. I had always had enormous problems communicating with strangers, but with Alphonse Jørgensen it was completely different. He gave me the impression that he understood what loneliness was; in fact, he even said so himself. He had been a widower for over twenty years.

Eleven o'clock came and went. I started to worry that Kjell Bjarne might start to worry. I think that Alphonse Jørgensen assumed that my short glances at my watch were indeed the signal they were intended to be. Anyway, he snapped his fingers at the waiter. It had been a lovely evening, but now it was over. He paid for me as well, as he promised, and I thanked him warmly. He said that it had been a pleasure – he sat on his own so much and he was bored with talking to his reflection in his beer glass, as he put it. Beautifully expressed. There was great sadness in that sentence. I wanted to do something for him, I wanted to give him something, a little present, but I only had some change and the keys to the flat in my pockets. My telephone number, I thought. That was something!

I gave Alphonse Jørgensen my telephone number.

It was the first time that I had ever invited someone into my personal world.

Kjell Bjarne had been forced on me. Frank had walked right in and made himself at home.

I stood outside Broker's and watched him disappear down Hjelmsgate, the street where he lived. A hunched-back figure beneath the stars.

On the way home, I bought a hot dog. For the boys.

Kjell Bjarne was standing brushing his teeth in the kitchen when I got home – a bad habit he had recently acquired, though why I don't know. More than once I had had to have words with him about the hardened lumps of toothpaste in the sink, but he was not an easy man to change. Surely, as everyone knew, it was more natural to brush your teeth in the bathroom where the toothbrush and toothpaste were kept?

But this was not the time and the place for everyday gripes. I tossed the sausage to the cats, peeled off my coat and flopped into the sofa.

'They shat on the floor again,' Kjell Bjarne informed me, his mouth full of toothpaste.

I shrugged it off. Children will be children. Even animals must be allowed to be children. I was a clandestine poet who tussled with existential questions. I had dealt with enough trivialities in my life. Petty, I had been. A pedant. Well, that was over now. Finished. Kjell Bjarne would have to deal with petty bourgeois matters on his own.

I made myself comfortable, with my head resting on a cushion and my hands clasped behind my head. 'You are anally obsessed,' I said. And instantly I thought of Haakon Willum's poems. 'Tell me about your evening.'

He gargled and rinsed out his glass. 'What a woman!' Well, I knew that. He wandered off into the bathroom, his braces dangling behind him.

'What sort of a résumé is that of an evening with a young lady?' I shouted after him. I felt the urge to challenge his damned reticence. 'Come on!' I continued to chide. 'Full report! What did you eat?

What sort of wine did she have? Did she say anything about her boyfriend?'

'No boyfriend!' he called back. 'And if the bastard comes here, he won't stand much of a chance!'

I roared with laughter. This was pure bachelor paradise! We had found the tone for the night now.

'I see! So she's pregnant but has no boyfriend. And if he comes here, he'll have to answer to you. Doesn't that sound a bit stupid to you?'

He came into the sitting room. He had peeled off his vest and it was now orang-utan time. The hairy play of muscle could begin. He clenched his right hand and flexed his biceps. 'Dago bastard. Got her pregnant then buggered off.'

How shocking! I had to control myself so I wouldn't laugh. But I had heard this reaction before in all sorts of corny contexts. I noticed that the cynic in me was taking the upper hand. The beat poet was taking over. I still hadn't taken off the sunglasses and bitterly regretted that I hadn't remembered to get some cigars from Seven-Eleven.

Kjell Bjarne sat down and stayed there staring in fascination at the muscles in his forearm, as they popped up and then sank back according to whether he was flexing or relaxing them. Eventually he shook himself and looked over at me. 'Did you agree on the poems?'

'Agree on the poems?'

'Weren't you going to discuss poems down there?'

'Later. It's your turn first.'

A faraway look came into his eyes and a broad grin spread across his face. I realized that he was replaying the evening in that great heavy head of his. 'Aaw, I dunno . . .'

'Come on!' I encouraged. I had been drilled in this by both Gunn and Frank. (Get him to say something, don't let him just go around fretting about things.) 'What did you eat?'

'Hen. With some lemon stuff. And rice.'

'Chicken,' I corrected. 'With lemon sauce and delicious rice.'

'It was a broiler!' he said aggressively.

'OK. And the conversation flowed pleasantly and easily?'

'What d'you mean?'

'You talked to each other, didn't you? You didn't just sit there with your mouth full of fowl the whole time? Did you ask her about the baby's father, or did she tell you about how he had left her in the lurch, unprompted?'

'Didn't ask her anything. She's a cleaner at the big hospital. That's where she met him, she said.'

'Good, good,' I said. 'And you told her all about your lovely family, if I'm not mistaken?'

He didn't answer.

'Did you tell her that you hate your mother?'

'Can't remember.'

'Dessert?'

'Some pudding thing. Bloody delicious.'

'Best you've ever tasted, perhaps?'

He looked at me suspiciously and I thought it was best not to push it. But I couldn't resist all the same. There was one thing I just had to get clear. He owed me that much at least.

'Do you remember the first evening you came to town?' I said. 'The evening that Frank said that we needed to get better at talking about our feelings? That we had to get used to really talking to each other?'

He looked everywhere but at me.

'Do you remember?'

'Didn't really get what he was talking about.'

'Yes, you did. And now I really want to know what sort of feelings you have for Reidun Nordsletten!'

He had to rub his temples with his fists now. I couldn't expect anything else. He shut his eyes and rubbed and rubbed.

'Stop it,' I said, when he showed no signs of stopping. 'I withdraw my question.'

He stopped. Sat there staring vacantly ahead. 'She said that . . . She said that she liked me.'

I whistled meaningfully. 'And you?'

'Me?'

'Yes, what did you say?'

'Nothing, don't think. Didn't know what to say.' He looked at me helplessly. 'Should I have said something?'

'I don't know,' I said. 'I'm not sure. For once you may actually have earned some points by keeping quiet. It's quite possible that that is why she likes you. Because you are who you are.'

Nicely put, really. In my heart of hearts I had to praise myself. But Kjell Bjarne had so definitely earned my support. I had in no way forgotten his gesture earlier that evening, when he offered to cancel the whole date for my sake. That went deep. I decided to do everything in my power to ensure that a relationship blossomed between Kjell Bjarne and Reidun Nordsletten. Yes, I would give everything. But discreetly. I would work in the wings. The first task was to give him encouragement. So as to get this incredibly slow man moving.

'Did you arrange to meet again?' I prodded.

'What d'you mean? She lives upstairs.' He tossed his head towards the ceiling.

I stood up and took off the sunglasses. 'You have to make an effort, Kjell Bjarne. You can't just wait and see what happens.'

He looked at me, at a loss.

'It was very kind of her to cook for you,' I said. 'And now it's your turn.'

Kjell Bjarne nodded. 'No problem, I can make her a meal.'

I took the plunge. 'Take her out! Our benefit money will be coming soon.'

'Right. Larsen's maybe?'

'No,' I said. 'Too masculine. Too rough. Larsen's is more the sort of place for raucous male laughter and arm-wrestling.'

'Arm-wrestling?'

'Forget it. Why not invite her to Peppe's Pizza? Yes, Peppe's Pizza would be a good place! Candles on the table. And it's always more intimate when you share a meal. You can eat your way into each other's hearts, as it were!' I could see their hands accidentally touching as they reached for the last slice with ham and melted cheese. Half intentionally, half unintentionally.

'OK. But we'll go to Larsen's on Friday?'

'It's a deal,' I said. 'If we can afford it. Yes, and we could round off the evening with a drink at Broker's.'

'What's that?'

'Oh, just a place that I've started to frequent.'

'Were there any women at your poetry thing?'

'Plenty,' I said. 'But you stick to Reidun Nordsletten. I can safely say that the circles that I have started to move in are not for you. Not really for me, either, but I do have to keep up with what's going on in poetry.' I gave him a brief summary of the two poets' terrible performances.

He shook his head. 'And you've got to listen to that stuff?'

'Unfortunately,' I said. 'I have to keep myself up to date.'

I hadn't thought I would, but I dropped the bombshell now after all. 'You see, I have started to write poems myself!'

'Jesus! Let's hear one!'

'No way José. Not yet. And you mustn't tell a soul. Especially not Frank!'

'What are they about?'

I shook my head. 'There's no point, Kjell Bjarne. When the time is ripe, you will hear them. And not before.'

'You don't write about me, do you?'

'Men with hairy backs, you mean? No, you can be sure of that. I leave that sort of poetry to Haakon Willum.'

'The jerk with the poof poems?'

'Relax,' I said. 'He doesn't know you even exist.'

He grunted.

'Oh, before I forget. If a man phones to get hold of me, it's probably Alphonse Jørgensen.' I slipped swiftly into the bathroom and started to get ready for bed.

# 7

Spring came early. At the beginning of March the temperature suddenly leapt up; the days were longer with lots of sunshine, roofs were dripping and there was the happy sound of babbling water in the city's gutters. I have never had a particularly good relationship with spring – the dark season was always closer to my heart – yet now I noticed that this too had changed. As I began to let go of things from the past with greater frequency and greater daring, I could see the symbolism of town and country suddenly sloughing off its winter-worn skin. My writing was coming along rather slowly and I was not putting myself under any pressure. I was just grateful when now and then I hit on a couple of good lines. I wasn't in any hurry. I went on long walks, on my own and together with Kjell Bjarne. Every Friday we went out for a meal at Larsen's. I always expected to see Alphonse Jørgensen, but he was never there. That worried me.

Another thing that worried me was Kjell Bjarne's total paralysis when it came to matters Reidun Nordsletten. In the evenings, with his head cocked and a furtive smile on his face, he listened to her steps, but when I hinted he should make a tiny move in her direction, he withdrew inside himself. Or, to be more precise, he withdrew to his 'work-shop', as he called it, where he was well on the way to making a shelving unit to act as a partition between the two halves of the room. The situation was threatening to become an impasse after such a promising start. I recalled the incredible energy he had shown when we found Reidun lying on the stairs, and I understood him less and less.

It was a Saturday, the end of the month. Kjell Bjarne had gone shopping and I was relaxing over a game of patience and listening to the programme Critics' Forum on the radio. They slaughtered books on this programme and the blood flowed; I often had a really good laugh. I saw myself as a critic, too. There were a few things that needed to be said about Haakon Willum's new collection of poems . . .

There was a ring at the door. It startled me and I dropped the cards. I would never get used to this. Unexpected loud noises scare the wits out of me. They make me think of sudden death. Of a heart that stops beating. The switch of life being turned off. I didn't find it very amusing imagining who could be standing on the other side of the locked door.

I stood up anyway, as I realized that this too – casually opening your front door to a Stranger – was part of the New Times. With great determination I had cracked one phobia or aversion after the other, I had come to terms with the telephone and dangerous streets, now it was the Door's turn. Walking through the hallway I thought that it would be a good idea to set up a small training programme. I would ask Kjell Bjarne and Frank to ring the door-bell without telling me in advance. Any time of day. So that I could get this one under my belt, too. I grabbed my sunglasses from under the hall mirror, put them on and opened the door.

Reidun Nordsletten. It was Reidun Nordsletten. Through my dark glasses her face looked pale. Milky blue. Her breasts heaved and sank beneath her blouse; she must have run down the stairs.

'Are you Elling?' Her round button of a nose moved in a funny way as she spoke, taking little jumps as it were, and I had a terrible urge to squeeze it between my thumb and first finger. Just to feel its consistency. I imagined it was probably a little squidgy. Like a penis.

'My name is indeed Elling,' I reproved.

'May I have a brief word with you? Can I come in for a moment?'

Even worse! I could feel my hands beginning to sweat. 'Kjell Bjarne has gone shopping,' I said.

'Yes, yes I know,' she responded, without a pause. 'I saw him going.'

'Oh, my God!' I thought. This can't be true! I'm in a French film, without a film director. One of those awful love triangles. She takes up with Kjell Bjarne so that she can get closer to me. Now I understood why she had surreptitiously slipped my name in a subordinate clause that time she had invited Kjell Bjarne to a meal. It was a precaution, of course, it was immensely important not to arouse suspicions. When I didn't go, when I chose the poetry evening instead and Kjell Bjarne went on his own, my absence had only increased her desire. And since then: silence. Kjell Bjarne's paralysis. She can't stand it any longer. Blind instinct has driven her out of her den and down the stairs. Her fantasies have got the upper hand in that little head of hers. She saw me together with other women, saw other women nestling in my arms, where she felt she belonged. The baby would be here soon, she needed security, warmth and affection.

However, I would have to disappoint her. I probably could learn to love this woman, even though my first impression had been underwhelming. But to cheat on my good friend Kjell Bjarne, to go behind his back, was out of the question. Even if I had to go through life in excruciating celibacy, I would stand firm in this matter. Under no circumstances would I allow myself to be pressurized into a relationship that was based on infidelity and a betrayal of Kjell Bjarne. The morality of the issue was one thing. Quite another was the fact that Kjell Bjarne would batter me to pulp the day he discovered the sordid love that existed between Reidun and me.

I was quite used to dealing with the most shocking of secrets, indeed I had kept secrets that were so dreadful, so confidential, that I would be killed if they ever became public knowledge. But Reidun Nordsletten was a woman, with all that that entails, with innate qualities such as ingenuousness and the urge to talk. Besides, I didn't even know her. I barely knew who she was.

So, no. She wasn't coming into my home. A confrontation early on was better than having to have an argument with her when she had begun to feel at home. At the same time I was reluctant to have a scene on my own doormat, so I rejected her request in a friendly but firm manner and gave her a warm parting smile.

'Please!' she said as I went to close the door. 'I must speak to you about Kjell Bjarne. And you know him best, don't you.'

What was it now? She only wanted to talk with me about Kjell Bjarne? It was unfair of me, I could see that, but I had the acute and painful feeling that she had hoodwinked me. I felt my lower lip beginning to tremble; it does that sometimes when

I'm under pressure. I didn't feel like talking with her about Kjell Bjarne. Nevertheless, I discerned a certain curiosity developing. There was absolutely no doubt that I could be considered an expert on the subject of Kjell Bjarne. I could have written a dissertation about him with one hand behind my back. But what information about this somewhat slow-witted man would interest a young pregnant woman? It was the prospect of getting an answer to this question that finally persuaded me to let her in. I was far from happy with this situation; in fact, the thought of what could happen if Kjell Bjarne came home and misinterpreted the whole thing filled me with nausea, but I could see no alternative.

She stood in the middle of the sitting-room floor and looked around her, as if surprised by the masculine sobriety of the room. The bare, white walls. The withered houseplants. It went through my mind that this was probably what her own flat looked like before she moved in with her collection of knick-knacks. With her army of owls and pewter Viking longboats.

Then she caught sight of the kittens rolled up in a corner of the sofa, and immediately sank down onto her knees. What could be more natural!

'Lor!' she exclaimed in a child's voice. 'Aren't they cute! What are their names?'

'Pepper,' I said. 'And Elmer.'

Yes, I christened my kitten then and there, with-out a second thought. I had a brief vision of the round head of my favourite comic figure, the long-suffering Elmer Fudd. I was right behind him in the fight against all the Daffys and impudent rabbits of the world. Right from when I was a small boy I had intuitively understood that Elmer's vegetable patch, forever under attack, was to be seen as a symbol of man's private domain and personal identity. I had intuited that Elmer Fudd was actually fighting for his life, not just a couple of bunches of carrots. I had experienced this struggle at first hand in the school playground.

I repressed these awful images. No point dwelling on the past when the heat of the moment demands that you play the role of host. I invited her to take a seat, next to Pepper and Elmer if she wanted, and then I asked her if she would like a glass of milk.

'Milk?'

'Yes, milk. Fresh Norwegian milk.' I made it apparent that I was au fait with her condition and added that young bones were in the process of developing. So a bit of calcium wouldn't go amiss, would it?

'Did Kjell Bjarne tell you? That I'm pregnant?'

Fortunately she didn't seem very hostile, merely curious in a female sort of way.

'He hinted at it,' I said. 'He was extremely discreet.' I didn't breathe a word about the Spanish scoundrel.

'Yes, I would like some milk please,' she said. 'In fact I am a little thirsty.'

I went out into the kitchen and filled a large glass. 'I hope you'll understand that I cannot tell you everything about Kjell Bjarne just like that,' I shouted out to her.

'Why's that?'

I gave her the glass and she drank deeply.

'Because certain areas demand confidentiality in a friendship between two men,' I instructed her.

She didn't grasp a word of this, I could see that, and my confidence began to grow that these two were a good match. They were made for each other, so to speak.

'I just think he's odd,' she said and giggled.

'I think I would rather use the English expression "odd one out",' I said with panache. 'One of a kind.'

She sent me an ingenuous look. She had a pretty milk moustache. 'I think you said that very nicely. Yes, that's what he is. One of a kind. I think he's sweet. How did you get to know each other?'

I leaned against the door frame. I didn't want to sit down, not even in the armchair on the other side of the table. I thought that would be too intimate. It could send out the wrong signals. 'We were both very stressed,' I said. 'We were simply drowning in work over a lengthy period. Independently of each other, we had accepted an offer of a recreational sojourn in natural surroundings. In a kind of secluded country hotel, you might say.'

'Sounds exciting,' she said. 'I can't even afford to stay at a hotel.'

'It soon gets boring,' I assured her. 'After six months there are no surprises on the buffet counter. You miss your own fridge. Your own bed.'

'How was it you . . . got so stressed?'

'At the time I was working on a very stressful archiving job,' I said, which was true. I could still remember the piles of newspapers. The smell of glue. Scissors on the table. The nineteen files containing newspaper articles about the then Norwegian Prime Minister, Gro Harlem Brundtland. Another time. Another life.

'And Kjell Bjarne?'

I shook my head and explained that she would have to take that up with him. 'When we met we were both determined to start a new life,' I continued. 'The past was not that important for us. We've put a tough year behind us now, and it looks as if spring is bursting out all over.'

'Spring bursting out?'

'Yes. Just like in the song.'

'Oh, yes.'

I liked her. There wasn't much spark about her, but she didn't pretend there was. We were talking about a simple soul here; the flashes of wit were few and far between. She would have been easy meat for the Barber of Seville.

'I don't know,' she said. 'He's so quiet somehow. Doesn't say a word.'

'A meditative nature,' I added generously. I saw no reason to go any deeper into Kjell Bjarne's meditative periods. I was worried that if I told her the truth – that what he meditated about most was how he could get into bed with a willing woman and how he could exterminate his own family without going to prison for it – it would scare her off. Anyway, it would give a false image of the man. Despite everything, Kjell Bjarne was someone with enormous qualities.

She took a deep breath and out it came. 'Do you think he likes me?'

'No,' I said, deadpan. I went over to the window and delighted in her bewilderment. I let the seconds tick by before turning round abruptly and pointing my trembling finger at her. 'I think Kjell Bjarne loves you, Reidun Nordsletten!'

She blushed bright red. Almost burgundy, I would say. Her hands fidgeted around in the warm cat fur, and she swallowed and swallowed.

I had the upper hand now. And I enjoyed it, I openly confess. I found her blushes incredibly attractive. In this respect I regarded myself as more or less the last of the Mohicans. A representative of a dying breed, a throwback from the time when concepts like modesty and honesty did not have negative connotations.

'Has he said anything?' She was staring at her feet.

'Let me put it like this,' I said. 'He sits here in the evening listening to your footsteps.' In my thoughts I added: with a stupid smirk on his face.

'But he doesn't say anything?'

'No, he doesn't say anything.' I explained to her how still waters ran deep, though I didn't get the impression that she understood any of this imagery. And perhaps that was just as well since still waters can be shallow, too.

'He's a big clod,' I said to make it a little easier. 'A great big, good-natured clod.' I felt I had sufficient evidence to say that.

All at once I was sure of myself. Confident. Here was someone who was even more insecure than me. I would never have thought it possible. How on earth had she managed to become pregnant? Had she been raped? The very thought hurt. I had mental images of this nasty Spaniard pouring sweet liqueurs down her and making up to her, then out of the blue he brutally grabs her throat and takes out his throbbing member. Revolting it was. Disgusting. I hoped he would turn up one evening on the stairs so that Kjell Bjarne could squash his face on the unwashed lino floor. I didn't go in much for violence, but if this show ever hit the road, I wanted to be a spectator and cheer Kjell Bjarne on.

'I don't know what to do,' she said. She sent me a begging look. 'Do you think I should do anything?'

'I think you should leave it to me,' I said. 'Let me think about it.'

What was I saying? What on earth was I letting myself in for? I mean it's one thing to 'explode boundaries' and it's quite another thing to blow up your own life. I was taking chances now. I was interfering in the innermost emotional lives of two people, walking into a minefield of tenderness and desire. I had never asked anyone to rely on me in my life.

'I'll find a solution somehow,' I proclaimed as if someone was talking through me. My own voice sounded completely alien, my words seemingly accompanied by a metallic echo.

'Thank you,' she said. 'That's kind of you. I knew you were a kind person. I could see it in your face.'

OK. She wasn't exactly the first person to draw that conclusion. My own mother had also mentioned that I gave off an aura of harmony and goodness, especially when she observed me sleeping. In her opinion, man's innermost being was revealed in the mask that sleep created. And why not? Now my good intentions broke through during waking hours, in bright daylight. And they were good. Almost noble. I was working selflessly in the service of love, without any personal gain, exactly the opposite.

If this 'matchmaking' succeeded I could even end up losing my best friend. He would probably choose to spend more of his time with Reidun and value our close friendship less. My act of altruism could lead me directly into a new spell of loneliness. Alphonse Jørgensen hadn't rung after all, so I didn't have anyone up my sleeve, either. And as for Frank, Oslo City Council paid him to interfere in my life. I had learnt to accept this relationship, but genuine friendship was totally out of the question.

'I think it's best if you go now,' I said. 'Kjell Bjarne could be here any moment. The situation could be misconstrued.'

'Mamma mia,' she said. 'Is he so jealous?'

'It wouldn't do to challenge him on this point,' I ventured.

She put down the empty glass and stood up.

'Perhaps we could do something together? All three of us.'

'Yes,' I said. 'Perhaps.' I was beginning to feel uneasy. My warm sense of security was receding. I listened for the sound of Kjell Bjarne's key in the lock. 'As I said, I'll give this matter some thought.'

She thanked me. And then she kissed me on the cheek! Two fleshy lips pressing against my stubble!

Misty-eyed, I watched her disappear into the hall. The sound of the door opening and closing.

Just one or two minutes later Kjell Bjarne was there. I felt guilty for some reason or other. As if Reidun Nordsletten and I had been caressing each other's naked body. I joined the two sleeping cats on the sofa and played with the empty glass that I hadn't had time to clear away. Not long before, a pregnant woman's delicate fingers had run across the smooth surface of the glass. Now it was my turn.

'Mince was on offer,' Kjell Bjarne said. 'So it's meatballs this weekend. I bought two kilos.' He lurched into the kitchen with his plastic bags, still wearing his coat and boots. I used to tell him off for leaving boot prints all over the flat, but this time I kept quiet. Instead I praised him for his foray into the frozen-food section of the supermarket. Two kilos of minced meat. That would make at least 400 meatballs if you mixed in breadcrumbs in the usual way.

'You bought the odd potato or two as well, I take it?' I asked.

He crammed the fridge full. 'Instant mash. And stewed prunes for dessert, to keep the system working. I've had a few problems dumping just recently.'

Exactly. I was becoming more and more certain that his reticence towards Reidun Nordsletten had been a blessing. A report about the functioning of your bowels was hardly likely to inspire intimacy in a developing relationship between a man and a woman. That he told me about it and not her was complete chance, I was quite sure of that. He didn't say a lot, but what he did say, he would say to anyone.

'Oh yes,' I said. 'I was just sitting here relaxing with a glass of milk.' I felt I had to say something. Explain why I was sitting with an empty glass in my hands.

He didn't answer. He was studying the instructions for instant mash and had the packet right under his nose.

'I'll take care of that,' I offered magnanimously. 'If you do the meatballs, I'll sort out the mashed potatoes.' I had tried to explain to him the difference between litres and decilitres a hundred times, but without any success.

'Fine.' He threw the packet down and put the plastic bags of mince into a pan of warm water so that the meat could thaw.

'I'm afraid I've given you some bad advice,' I said. 'With respect to Reidun Nordsletten.'

'What advice?'

'You were talking about taking her to Larsen's. I thought it was too masculine there. But now I'm not at all sure.'

He stood quite still, staring at the walls, with his arms hanging down by his sides. His hands were dripping water onto the floor. 'You mean we should take her with us to Larsen's after all?'

'It's not such a stupid idea,' I said.

'And you'd come, too?'

'Of course. But only if you want, naturally.'

He wrinkled up his eyes again and began hyperventilating.

'Take it easy,' I said. 'I can go and listen to poofters' poetry instead, if you like.'

'I've been racking my brains,' he said, without opening his eyes. 'I don't know what to talk to her about. That's the thing.' He banged his right fist down on the worktop so hard that the glasses and cutlery underneath rattled.

'I can see that,' I said.

Half an hour later the telephone rang. I was

tidying up my underwear in one of the drawers, so Kjell Bjarne took the call. I heard him give a series of monosyllabic grunts before putting the receiver down on the table.

'It's for you!'

'Frank?' I whispered.

He shook his head and padded back into the kitchen. 'Some bloke or other. Alf something.'

It was Alphonse Jørgensen! As soon as I heard his voice on the line I knew something was the matter. He was breathing heavily and sounded a long way away. He wanted to know if he was interrupting anything. If I was very busy at the moment. In fact I was, I was tidying up my drawers, but something held me back. I lied and said that I was bored out of my senses.

There was a long pause, the kind I could remember all too well from the old days, and then he said, 'I wondered if you could help me a little. I'm completely at sea. I don't know what to do. I must have fallen. Don't ask me how it happened because I can't remember a thing. I feel bruised all over. I'm sitting on the floor and I can't get up.'

'Stay where you are!' I said. 'I'm already on my way!'

'It's just that . . . the door's locked. Perhaps I can crawl there . . . and pass you the key through the letterbox.'

'Have you broken any bones?'

'I'm not really sure. It feels a bit like that. My right

ankle is all black and blue. I don't want to be any bother but . . .'

I interrupted him. What are good friends for, I said. Then, having ascertained his house number, I rang off.

Two minutes later Kjell Bjarne and I were on our way out. Majorstuen's New Emergency Services Team. Pregnant women, old people, ring day or night, we were always ready.

'What kind of bloke is he?' Kjell Bjarne asked while doing up his parka.

'Just someone I know,' I said. 'We have a couple of beers together now and then.'

There was the pungent smell of boiled cabbage and cat piss on the stairs. In addition, it was dark and I was glad that Kjell Bjarne had volunteered to come along. We were faced with a situation which, at worst, might require us to ring for the police and an ambulance, and for the moment I wasn't up to that.

We found his name on one of the doors on the first floor. Strange. This was a parallel situation to the one we found ourselves in some time before, but the other way round. This time the patient lay helpless inside his own flat behind a locked door.

I crouched down and opened the letterbox with my finger. 'Mr Jørgensen?' I used his surname out of respect for the difficult situation and because I really didn't know how he liked to be addressed. In any case, it seemed unnatural to me to shout

'Alphonse', however often he had called me Elling.

I could hear him breathing in the dark. The sounds of dragging movements across the floor.

'Yes, I'm here, Elling. It's so stupid! Wait a minute and I'll give you the key.'

The next moment a shiny key landed on the door-mat. I grabbed it and opened up.

Alphonse Jørgensen was sitting on the floor in the hall. Behind him there was a long, dark corridor. Kjell Bjarne switched on the light and it became a lot less scary.

'We'll have to get you to a doctor,' I said, after I had composed myself.

'Yup!' Kjell Bjarne said.

'Yes, I'm sure you're right,' Alphonse Jørgensen said. 'But first of all I need to go to the loo.'

'I'll help you,' Kjell Bjarne said. 'Just tell me where it is.' And before I knew it he had gently lifted Alphonse Jørgensen up in his strong arms as though the old man were a sick child. He carried him down the corridor and disappeared into the room Jørgensen indicated. I thought: there he goes again, carrying people. Kjell Bjarne carries. He had carried me in his time, after a bad breakdown, the time I managed to ruin a brand new suit. And only a short while ago he had carried Reidun Nordsletten with such expertise that it became clear to me that he had also carried his hated mother. Now he was carrying Alphonse Jørgensen. That was the way it was, Kjell Bjarne carried the people he met. Weird.

Then I saw all the books. There were books every-where. There was shelving from floor to ceiling on both sides of the corridor. You couldn't slide a piece of paper between any of the books anywhere. The shelves were simply crammed. I had never seen so many books in one place, except at the library. I wandered down the narrow corridor and let my right hand glide over the faded, worn spines. Through a fine layer of dust I could make out writers' names and book titles I had never heard of. I was in another world. I was in Alphonse Jørgensen's world.

I went into the sitting room, a large dark room with the curtains drawn. Here, too, there were books from floor to ceiling. Thousands of them. An old wooden ladder led up to the top shelf; I could see the two hooks on top of it so that it could be hooked onto the edge of the shelf. Alphonse Jørgensen lived in a library. My own dream of a reading corner at home paled into insignificance by comparison. I walked around the large dark room in wonder.

Kjell Bjarne came in. I heard him behind me.

'Jesus! Bloody hell!' He stood there gawping at the crowded shelves.

'How is he?' I asked.

'Sitting on the bog,' Kjell Bjarne said.

'We'll have to get him to casualty,' I said. I shivered at the thought, for this was a challenge that went way beyond my experience.

'I'll put him in the chair over there when he's

finished in the bog,' Kjell Bjarne said. 'He can ring himself, can't he?'

What a relief! After all, he had two healthy arms and a head that functioned perfectly well. I hadn't thought of that. But why hadn't he simply called casualty himself instead of ringing me? Friendship, I thought. The most natural thing in the world was to ring his good friend Elling first. To consult him about the problem. A warming thought, to be relied on.

They didn't want to send an ambulance from casualty unless the injury was life-threatening, and Alphonse Jørgensen did have someone to help him, didn't he? So all three of us went in a taxi. The driver was in total agreement with me that the welfare state was on the point of collapse. How much money had Jørgensen paid in tax during his lifetime? Quite a lot, I imagined. 'Take a taxi,' the voice had said at the other end of the line. So Kjell Bjarne carried the old man down the stairs and stood holding him until the car arrived. At casualty I gave several members of staff a good ear-bashing. I'm a rather unassuming sort of person, but injustice infuriates me. I even threatened to go to the tabloid, Verdens Gang, but Alphonse Jørgensen asked me to moderate my language and calm down. It was my impression that he didn't approve of the newspaper.

However, justice prevailed. In the middle of all the misery and my righteous anger, providence smiled down on us. He hadn't broken his leg. It was a bad sprain, so bad that Alphonse Jørgensen's right foot bore a great similarity to a multicoloured football. He was given an elasticated bandage and a crutch so that he could get to the toilet under his own steam – and then we were out into stark reality again. The waiting-room had filled up with the results of everyday violence. A woman was crying with her head in her hands, blood dripping onto the floor. A young boy was sitting and hyperventilating as the colour of his face alternated between red and ashen grey.

I shivered and looked away. I was glad that I had been helped to get rid of my former habit of living other people's lives. In the old days I would have imagined how this woman came home to a husband after a long night's infidelity, to be met with a pair of clenched fists. I would have tortured myself over the young boy's stroke. Like him I would have been paralysed on one side and lost most of my powers of speech. Everyone would have thought I was mentally retarded. I would have sat at home dribbling and snivelling for long periods.

When we had returned to Alphonse Jørgensen's flat, we put him in an armchair and pushed a stool under his injured foot. I opened the curtains and the spring sunlight flooded in, revealing a ton of dust lying everywhere like a fine grey-white powder.

But Kjell Bjarne didn't have an eye for this detail. 'I've had it,' he said. 'If I don't get something to eat quickly I'll die.'

'Now you're talking,' said Alphonse Jørgensen. 'I haven't had anything to eat since yesterday, and I haven't got a bean in the house.'

'I'll go home and get the mince,' Kjell Bjarne said. 'Then we can make something here. I can go shopping on the way back.'

Good idea. Alphonse Jørgensen gave Kjell Bjarne two hundred kroner and Kjell Bjarne made for the door. It sounded like a landslide as he ran down the stairs.

'What energy,' Alphonse Jørgensen said. 'He's quite a man, isn't he?'

I nodded. 'Where on earth did you get so many books?'

He leaned back in his chair and surveyed the walls around him as if it were the first time he'd noticed the crowded shelves. 'They just fluttered in. Help yourself! You can borrow anything you like. Doesn't matter whether you return them either. I'm old. I'll die soon. I've made up my mind that I'll read everything by Hamsun again, and then that's the end of all that crap.'

I told him about my little reading snug and how I wanted to fulfil an old dream. My own library, with an armchair and a reading lamp. I even showed him an old newspaper advert I'd kept in my wallet. An electric fire for 369 kroner with mock glowing coals in robust plastic. No other option, of course, but anyway. My feeling was it would make the place a bit cosier. What did he think?

He shook his head. 'Shame you can't have a real fire. I've got enough fuel. But, as I said, help yourself.'

I didn't know what to say. I was completely over-whelmed. And not just a little surprised by the disrespectful tone he used to talk about literature. We sat in silence until Kjell Bjarne returned with bulging shopping bags and went to work in the kitchen. Soon there was the wonderful smell of fried onions and meatballs. I played my part; my speciality, so to speak, was instant mashed potatoes with a dash of nutmeg. The dash was important. You have to dot the i's and cross the t's!

We ate. Kjell Bjarne had made a mountain of meatballs and all three of us laid into them. Alphonse seemed suddenly distant, almost dis-missive, which made me nervous and I ended up telling one wild story about Brøynes after the other. He did burst into laughter, though, when I told him about the time Kjell Bjarne had been tempted into buying a mail-order 'surprise packet'. Four hundred kroner it had cost him. Two plastic cake slicers, one fountain pen which didn't work and a pocket calculator, the kind you can get on offer, two for 19.50. Plus some other junk we couldn't even make sense of. I can certainly say that the company kept their word! Kjell Bjarne was so 'surprised' that he was not far off smashing Brøynes to matchwood.

'I can't stand people who tell porkies!' he said. 'I

go bananas!' He stuffed a whole meatball into his mouth in one go, it was his sixth.

'Well, no-one had actually promised you anything,' I reminded him.

'There were pictures of fishing rods, transistor radios and CDs in the paper,' he objected, with his mouth full of food. 'And electric tin openers.'

'What were you going to do with an electric tin opener in Brøynes?' I teased. 'We had our food served every day, didn't we? For the year I was there I didn't see one single tin.'

'Wanted to see what the thingy looked like on the inside,' he replied, piling up a new load of potato mash.

'He's pretty good with his hands,' I explained to Alphonse Jørgensen. 'Very good, actually. When you look at his two fists you wouldn't believe they would be much good at anything apart from killing hippos.'

Kjell Bjarne chuckled and sent Jørgensen a complicit look.

'He took the wall clock in the lounge up at Brøynes to pieces,' I went on. 'There was just a pile of brass components all over the floor. But, my goodness, he put them all together again.'

'Goodness me,' Jørgensen said. 'And then it worked?'

'No,' Kjell Bjarne said. 'But it didn't work before I pulled it apart, either.'

'What about car engines?' Jørgensen said. 'Can you fix them?'

'What type of car engine?'

'Don't ask me. But it's got eight cylinders. It's an old Buick. 1952 model.'

Kjell Bjarne was out of his chair. 'Where is it?'

'Sit down,' Jørgensen said. 'It's in the garage in the yard. But there's no light down there. Come another time and you can have the key. I haven't used the car for years, but if you can knock some life into it, it would be nice to go for a spin some time this spring. What do you think, boys?'

Kjell Bjarne didn't answer. He had the cheesiest grin on his face that I had ever seen in my life.

I smiled and was quiet, too. I could see the whole thing in front of me. I didn't have a clue about cars, but even I knew that a 1952 Buick must be a bit of a gem. I wanted to sit in the front. I would roll the window down and watch the changing countryside through Kjell Bjarne's sunglasses. I wanted to be the beat poet, on my way towards new adventures with my crazy, crazy friends! I could see us so clearly, slamming the doors of the car and moseying into wayside inns and gas stations. The ageing, slightly disillusioned literary guru, the young poet and Kjell Bjarne as the representative of raw, natural power.

'I'll get that old crate going,' he said as he got up for the stewed prunes. 'Even if I have to rebuild it from scratch!'

# 8

Kjell Bjarne had come to Oslo some time in the middle of January. It was a rainy evening with sleet in the air and a bitter wind blowing straight off the fjord. He took the train from Brøynes on his own, and Frank and I went to Oslo Central Station at around half past eight in the evening to meet him. It had been a long struggle to get to this point. For over half a year we had made enormous efforts to convince various people in authority that we belonged together and that if the council was going to give us a flat, it was logical that we should share, rather than each of us living alone. Gunn had supported us and that was comfort indeed when the prospects were at their bleakest. Our case took so many bureaucratic turns that it makes me dizzy even to think about it. And I didn't really understand what was going on either; it was like fighting an invisible monster.

Kjell Bjarne and I had found each other naturally; we had learned to appreciate our night-time chats. In a way we were pulling the same load, and this bond was actually something as valuable as our lives. Once I had made it absolutely clear that there was not even a hint of homosexuality in the friendship, I jumped in with both feet. We were, in fact, so heterosexual that it was enough to drive you mad. I, for my part, was deeply and unhappily in love with Gunn, but she was married and refused to leave her husband's side. She did not dare to take the leap into my embrace even though she might well have wanted to. Kjell Bjarne was after any woman, as long as she had the requisite body parts and orifices provided by nature and two growths that could, with a little goodwill, be called breasts.

I had lied outrageously to him about my own exploits with women, painting a picture of myself as a combination of a super-virile sailor and a mean biker. In reality, I had not even sat on the back of a moped and my sexual organs were utterly untouched by a woman's hand. Furthermore I had never been to sea apart from when I went on a couple of shopping trips to Denmark, which I would rather forget. But all the same, evening after evening I told him about the women who pursued me everywhere. Out of sheer politeness, I felt obliged to gloss over all the moaning and sighing and Kjell Bjarne listened to me wide-eyed and open-mouthed, and believed every word. These nightly tales gradually become a near obsession for me, and I didn't see any harm in the game.

Kjell Bjarne was as virginal as I was, and, as he lacked imagination, he positively begged me for details and colourful stories. I think that he was actually happy when I took him to a brothel in New Orleans where the black ladies of the night were so impressed by my acrobatic abilities that they omitted to ask me for payment. I told him ever-changing variations of the story of how I'd had oral sex while manoeuvring a large motorbike at one hundred and fifty km/h through the centre of Drammen.

The only problem was that Kjell Bjarne opened his big mouth. I'm sure that it wasn't done with ill intent, but whatever the reason, he mentioned the various imaginary escapades to Gunn. And she was angry. Furious, in fact. She claimed that these 'disgusting fantasies' were part and parcel of the 'wild imagination' that she had taken months to rid me of. An exaggeration, of course, but never mind. I told myself that that was just the way women were. They exaggerated. The imagination that she was talking about stemmed from nothing more than a healthy interest in the people around me. I was interested in who they were, where they came from and what they were doing with their short time on this earth. But I didn't say anything. My stay at Brøynes had taught me to keep quiet. In any case, it was not worth trying to discuss things with Gunn when she was in that frame of mind. Men and women have very different perceptions of concepts such as logic and common sense. At least, in my experience.

'This nonsense must stop, straight away,' she said. 'And the two of you sharing a flat is out of the question unless you apologize to Kjell Bjarne and tell him that all your disgusting stories are not true.'

I can tell you that hurt!

I refused. I lay down on the floor and refused. Never on my life!

But for once she was not open to discussion. This was something she was really passionate about. She immediately went into the lounge where Kjell Bjarne had parked himself in front of the television and hauled him back into her office.

'Sit down, Kjell Bjarne!' she said. 'Elling has something to say to you.'

I could hear him sitting down somewhere behind me. I lay perfectly still and studied Gunn's feet. Small, sweet feet, each one inside a white Scholl sandal.

'Come on!' she said. She stamped her right foot on the floor. 'Get up and get started.'

I certainly was not going to get up. I would stay lying on the floor for the rest of my life. I might wriggle into a corner, but I would never stand up.

'What's the matter?' Kjell Bjarne asked. 'Have you got a sore tummy?'

'He's got a sore conscience,' said Gunn. 'You see, he's lied to you.'

'Fibbed? 'Bout what?'

'Everything that you told me about during our meeting this morning,' Gunn said ruthlessly.

It was quiet for a moment. Then Kjell Bjarne coughed and said, 'So you've not been to sea then, Elling?'

'Not really,' I said.

'Not at all,' said Gunn. 'And he has never been a member of Hells Angels, either.'

An uncomfortable silence fell over the room. I had absolutely no idea how Kjell Bjarne would react to these revelations.

'And the women?' he asked after a while, in a husky voice.

'I made them up because I needed a friend!' I screamed.

'Rubbish,' Gunn said. 'You made them up because you're disgusting. Now you apologize to Kjell Bjarne and we'll forget the whole thing.'

'Sorry,' I whispered.

'No problem,' said Kjell Bjarne.


When we went to bed that night, we lay there for a long time without saying a word. The ticking of the alarm clock on the desk was the only sound between us. And the wind in the trees outside. Over half an hour passed before he eventually broke the silence.

'Those women down in Borneo . . .' He hesitated, as if he were frightened I might have gone to sleep.

'Just lies, all of it,' I sobbed.

'Doesn't bother me,' Kjell Bjarne said.

And so I told him about the ladies in Borneo one more time. I have never felt so relieved in my life.

On the evening that Kjell Bjarne was due to arrive in Oslo from Brøynes, Frank and I positioned ourselves on the platform, right by the exit, to look out for him. Frank had helped me to prepare the flat. A bed from the Salvation Army shop, new bed linen, a wardrobe and everything was ready. We had prepared a stew together so that all we had to do was warm it up when we got home. The platform was teeming with people and we did not dare to make a move towards the train in case Kjell Bjarne managed to slip past us. He had been dreading this trip, I knew, and I couldn't begin to think what might happen if he got lost and started wandering around in the enormous station. I didn't even like to think of myself in that situation.

Then I caught sight of him. Far down the platform amid the mass of people. He towered at least a head above everyone else, I had completely forgotten that he was so big. He was wearing a coat and woolly hat, as was his wont.

Frank coughed. 'Don't say anything, Elling. Let me guess which one he is!'

Of course, Frank hit the bull's eye. A few seconds later he was shaking hands with Kjell Bjarne.

'Welcome to the country estate,' I joked.

His eyes wandered up the post giro building. 'Well, I suppose this'll do.'

'Good journey?' Frank enquired. He tried to be helpful and offered to carry one of Kjell Bjarne's bags, but Kjell Bjarne just shook his head and started to walk.

'Dark all the way. So I just saw my own stupid face in the window the whole journey. Can you get hot dogs anywhere round here?'

'Frank and I have made enough stew to feed an army at home!' I said.

'Great. But I want a sausage first. Or I'll die.'

And he got what he wanted. Three hot dogs with all the garnishes. Frank paid. Or perhaps it was Oslo City Council.

When we got home I showed him round the flat, while Frank pretended he wasn't there. The newly decorated bathroom. The kitchen. His bedroom facing out onto the street.

He sat down on the bed to test it. 'Am I going to sleep here?'

'Yes,' I said. 'It will be fine.'

'What about you?'

I showed him my room. The bed. The wardrobe. The picture of my mother on the wall. He nodded and didn't say another word that evening. Not until Frank had left. He wouldn't even answer direct questions, but ate a ton of food. He didn't even say 'Goodbye' when Frank got ready to go.

Frank manoeuvred me discreetly out into the hall. And as he put on his jacket, he whispered, 'You ring me immediately if there are any problems!'

I promised I would. When I went back into the sitting room, Kjell Bjarne was sitting rubbing his temples with his fists. 'What is it?' I said.

He looked at me unhappily.

I threw up my hands in despair. 'Well, I can't carry your bed on my own.'

So we moved all his things into my room and put the cupboard between the two beds.

To begin with we had kept ourselves to ourselves, despite Frank's constant nagging that we should be sociable. We watched TV and played around with the sex phone lines, or we just sat quietly and listened to all the new sounds: the gurgling from strange toilets, footsteps on the stairs, a loud argument. To be fair, Kjell Bjarne went out to buy food nearly every day, after all he had his motives. But I saw the beads of sweat on his forehead when he came back. It was tough. His expeditions to the supermarket took it out of him. Sometimes he came back empty-handed and upset. The checkout queue had been too long. I comforted him and understood; it was exactly the same for me sometimes. If the checkout queue was too long, the palms of my hands would start to sweat and I'd suddenly have to throw up and go to the toilet. Even if I didn't feel sick and had just been. Strange, but that's the way I am.

Frank would come and visit every second Thursday, bursting at the seams with good ideas and constructive plans. Surely I could go and do the shopping as well? We just had to get out there and get to know the area. Hup two three! He forced me to go down to the kiosk to buy a bag of peanuts for him and Kjell Bjarne!

After a while we started to like the combination of film and pizza. We were more relaxed when Frank was around, it was true, even if we were full of ill will towards him to begin with.

However, what really broke down the barriers between us was an invitation to dinner. Lamb. At Frank's place, his home. It was also on this occasion that I was able to see Frank's office, with the telephone on the desk. To tell the truth, it was there and then that a New Sense of Security came into my life, or at least the seed that was later to grow and transform me into a balanced, discontented underground poet with a small circle of friends.

Frank did not make it easy for us. It was difficult to get to where he lived, somewhere out in Asker. He was honest about that. But no. He blankly refused to pick us up in Kirkeveien and he wouldn't even discuss meeting us at Asker station. We would have to do a bit of orienteering and if we got lost, we'd just have to ask the way. He made it clear that if we were not able to find his house by eight o'clock, he would have to reassess our new-found freedom in Kirkeveien. I got the impression that it was a question of confidence for Oslo City Council. If we got lost, the possibility of a dishonourable retreat to Brøynes Rehabilitation Centre might be on the cards.

My, did we sweat! First of all, we forced each other to go into a bookshop to buy a map of Oslo and the surrounding areas. For two days we sat and studied the winding roads out in Asker and the location of the street where Frank lived in relation to the railway station. All the time I imagined Frank sitting somewhere in this dreadful labyrinth, smugly stroking his moustache. Once we had marked out a possible route with a red ballpoint pen, we started on the train timetables. We could make neither head nor tail of them, but then I had the bright idea that we could just jump on the first train going south. I couldn't imagine that any of them would not stop in Asker. And we could double-check by asking at the counter when we bought our tickets.

Everything went far better than anticipated. Once we were sitting on the suburban train to Asker, we realized that the hardest part was getting started. Frank was right. Neither of us had enough initiative. When I bought the tickets at Nationaltheatret station, everything went smoothly and the conversation between the man behind the counter and myself flowed easily. Did we require a single ticket or a return? I insisted that we only needed a single ticket. I explained to him that Frank had promised to drive us back to town in his car, and that there was no reason to doubt what Frank had said. And while I was at it, I told him in confidence that Frank was employed by Oslo City Council. I made it clear to him that Frank was extremely well connected, so he needn't think that he could hood-wink us. All in a jokey manner, obviously. I was on top form.

And did the NSB employee know his way round the residential areas in Asker, I continued. I thought that I might as well ask this gentleman as any other person. For all I knew, the man might be from Asker. Asker, he might have said. Yes, it was my old stomping ground. My whole family can be traced back to Asker. Right back to the Iron Age, we've always lived in Asker. But no. In fact, it was my distinct impression that he had never even been to Asker, that he didn't even know where it was, and then I became slightly suspicious. I whipped out the tickets again and studied them carefully. In the end, he actually had to ask me to move. There were other people behind me who wanted to buy tickets as well. And didn't I have to catch a train? What a comedian.

It was half past three and outside the train

windows the countryside and civilization rushed past. We had given ourselves plenty of time, even though Frank maintained that he lived only a quarter of an hour's walk from the station. But you never know, once you get lost, four hours can pass in the blinking of an eye. And I have always staked my honour on being punctual. To be fair, Kjell Bjarne did say that the half past three train was far too early, but I did not even deign to give him a reply. What Kjell Bjarne knew about travelling and sensible planning was simply not worth commenting on.

I spent the entire journey sitting tensely with the tickets in my hand. I just could not relax, even though it said Asker on both the front of the train and the tickets. I had to have confirmation from the conductor before I could lean back and enjoy the journey. Because it is a fact that in this country a lot of place names are used more than once. Vik, for example. Or Vangen. I knew of two Håøys. As the train accelerated, carrying us further and further from the city and its relative security, I became more and more certain that something was wrong. That we were on our way to Asker in Jæren or Asker in Telemark.

The people around me sat with closed expressions behind newspapers and book covers and I did not dare to ask them for confirmation that this was the train to Asker, the correct Asker. And the conductor didn't come! He just never showed up! I mean really! You buy tickets that cost a fortune in good faith and then the conductor can't even be bothered to come round and check them! Kjell Bjarne, who until now had been sitting opposite me looking at his feet, must have noticed my agitation, because he suddenly asked why I was sitting there fidgeting the whole time. I explained the situation: I needed confirmation and it appeared that the conductor had forgotten us.

Then a young boy who was sitting next to Kjell Bjarne piped up. He explained that the carriage was intended for people with monthly travel passes, an arrangement that I had never even heard of before. I showed him my ticket. Was I to understand that this was not valid? No, no, that wasn't the case, either. It was just that there would be no ticket inspection in this carriage. If there was an inspection, it was to check that everyone had valid monthly passes.

'Yes, but we don't have valid monthly passes!' I shouted.

'OK, don't worry,' he said. There was hardly ever an inspection and in any case, I did have a ticket. I could just explain the situation if that became necessary.

That was not good enough for me. I stood up to go into another carriage and Kjell Bjarne stood up too. When I shouted, people started to notice us. And now they were staring. They put down their books and papers and stared at us. Have a good old stare, I thought to myself. Adieu to you all! Only to discover that the door into the next carriage was locked. So there we were. I ran like lightning through the carriage to try the door at the other end, but this was of course locked as well. We were caught in a trap, devised by some horrible bureaucrat or other. Presumably to assure himself of the 4-million-kroner safety net that he could demand if he didn't do his job properly and was sacked.

The rest of the journey was a nightmare. When we reached Asker station, I tottered out with Kjell Bjarne at my heels. The ticket, which I had clutched and fiddled with in my sweaty hands, was now no more than a damp piece of paper, as good as illegible. I had lost my appetite and did not want to visit anyone. I just wanted to be left in peace. All my life I had just wanted to be left in peace, but this wish was obviously like a red rag to a bull for everyone else. I was so upset that I was shaking.

It was quite the opposite with Kjell Bjarne. He had already put the whole thing behind him and now he wanted a hot dog. Fine. As long as Kjell Bjarne got food, the world could do what it liked. I found myself wishing that nature could have given me such simple needs as well. How many sleepless nights could I have been spared, if I had been blessed with a simpler mind? Thousands! I had spent days and nights formulating biting remarks, retorts that I should have made in such and such a situation, when I had been treated unfairly. To no avail, obviously, but I just couldn't help it. Right now I could feel it brewing inside me again. I could see myself in the stationmaster's office, venting my spleen about the new arrangement with conductor-less carriages. I would produce my ticket. Look! I could do that journey again if I wanted. No wonder the state railway system was in such financial difficulty.

Kjell Bjarne went on and on until he got his hot dog. I paid and bought myself a packet of eucalyptus lozenges at the same time. Frank had told us that he lived with a certain Janne and I wanted to greet her with fresh breath. Her standing as Frank's girlfriend did of course mean that she was unavailable, but I wanted to have some ground on Kjell Bjarne all the same. He would greet her with the stench of raw onion and mustard, and I would have breath as fresh as a lozenge factory in the country.

It was laughably simple to find Frank's house. Everything had looked so difficult on the map, but for once reality proved to be a doddle. All our preparations had been a waste of time.

Well. What now? There we stood, looking at 'Janne and Frank' on a ceramic nameplate, and it was only twenty past four. We were invited for eight o'clock. Kjell Bjarne was of the opinion that it didn't matter and before I could stop him, he rang the bell. Long and hard. No response, luckily. There was no-one at home; it was a relief, actually, even though I knew we had a long, cold wait ahead of us. We sat down on the steps and I sucked my eucalyptus lozenges. Kjell Bjarne put his hand out at regular intervals, but I looked the other way. He had had his sausage and the lozenges were mine. I started to feel a bit sick after a while, but there was nothing to be done. My breath had to be kept fresh, no matter what. I was actually toying with the idea of whispering something in Janne's ear if the opportunity arose, and then I wanted my breath to touch her auditory canal like frost. I wanted to be remembered as the eucalyptus man.

They did not come back until a quarter to seven! I felt sick and unwell and my mouth was more than a little raw. My gums had even started to bleed. Kjell Bjarne had taken to walking round and round the building to keep warm. A small family stood with their noses to the glass in the kitchen window of a neighbouring flat, timing his rounds. The children cheered and waved their tiny hands, but Kjell Bjarne was deep in his own thoughts and didn't notice a thing.

Frank and Janne swung into the yard and parked by the rubbish bins. Frank was first out of the car and he looked, confused, from me to the back of Kjell Bjarne's coat disappearing through the neighbour's hedge. The neighbour's children waved and waved.

'Jesus,' Frank said. 'When did you get here? Elling! You look like a marble statue!'

Thank you very much! I felt like one too. A rather coarsely hewn one at that, if the truth be told. I tried to get up from the freezing step, to greet them, but my legs buckled under me. I fell forward into the snow and at the same time, threw up. A green dribble, an exclamation mark of shame. I gave up and rolled over onto my side. For the hundred and fortieth time I had made a fool of myself. I had been sitting here for over two hours, imagining my first meeting with Frank's Janne. I had wanted to greet her with a little ironic smile and maybe a couple of witty remarks about Frank's free-style moustache, build some kind of waggish alliance with her. I had imagined that she would immediately pick up on it, that we would find our ground and have a bit of friendly banter about her partner. And now, here I was lying like an overturned marble fountain.

'Bloody hell, Frank! That's pure bile!'

Her voice was not at all how I had thought it would be. High and sharp. I could forget the honeyed purring that I had imagined.

'Calm down, Janne!' Frank said. 'Just open the door!'

Then he guided me in while Janne waited outside to intercept Kjell Bjarne.

Unlikely though it may sound, it actually turned out to be a very pleasant evening. Already on the way to the bathroom, I caught a whiff of the delightful smell of lamb roasting gently in the oven. A few minutes later I was lying in an unfamiliar bath with warm water up to my chin. Out in the hall I could hear Janne giving Frank a piece of her mind for not having picked us up in Oslo, and Kjell Bjarne chuckling in the background. She was on our side. That awful voice of hers now came into its own. Once I was warm again, I got out of the bath and rubbed some of Frank and Janne's toothpaste onto my teeth. Then I got dressed and went out to quench the flames of conflict. We were to blame, as well. We could have refused, stayed at home.

The lamb tasted delicious! I had never eaten anything like it. Even the paella that I had eaten on a package holiday to Benidorm paled into insignificance. Light pink lamb meat, so tender that you could have eaten it with your bare gums, dotted with garlic and with lots of rosemary ground in. Floury potatoes and gravy. I was glad that I had emptied my stomach of the lozenges and other stuff, so that I could really fill myself. Both Janne and Frank tried to strike up a conversation with Kjell Bjarne, but he didn't say a word until only the bone remained, yellowy-white on his plate, stripped of every fibre of meat.

'What a meal!' I said and burped garlic. I was so full that I had to undo the top button on my trousers.

'Best I've ever eaten,' Kjell Bjarne said. I noticed that he glanced over towards the kitchen, in case there was another piece of lamb lying there. Was the oven still on?

Janne was chuffed, I could see that. She was the gourmet cook. 'Espresso, boys?'

We said, 'Yes, please.' With so much food in me, the tannic acid would somehow be neutralized.

'Frank!'

'On my way!' Frank played the whipped hound and padded out into the kitchen.

'He's really very kind,' Janne said. 'You just have to put him in his place when you think he's being too bossy.'

'He decided what colour our sitting room was going to be,' Kjell Bjarne told her.

'I heard about that,' she said. 'But dark orange can be quite depressing in the long run.'

'Let's just forget it,' I said generously. I did not want to force her into a conflict of loyalty with her partner, but I had no intention of forgetting it. This just wasn't the right time.

'And he says it's our fault that we don't know any women,' Kjell Bjarne continued.

'Well, now you know me,' said Janne. 'It's maybe not the same, but it's a start.'

'What d'you do when you're not with Frank?' Kjell Bjarne was really making up for his prolonged silence.

'I sit in the welfare office in Bærum and refuse to write out cheques.' She smiled.

Of course! I thought. Frank and Janne met each other at college. Some time in the Seventies, I would guess, as they were a good bit older than Kjell Bjarne and me. I could just see them. Purple shawls and sensible shoes. Frank with flared trousers and sideburns. I started to laugh out loud. I couldn't help it. Frank looked so stupid!

Naturally the others wanted to know what I was sitting there splitting my sides about. Even Frank appeared in the doorway and stood there smiling uncertainly.

So I told them the truth, the naked truth. I said I had just dropped by the social studies department at the university in the Seventies, and I'd met Frank there. With sideburns.

'Idiot!' said Frank and retreated back to the espresso machine.

But Janne giggled and said that it was true. Wasn't it strange how something that was the height of fashion one year could be utterly derisible some years later? And she pointed at my stripy sweater! Well. I have always been good at taking jokes, but I still couldn't help pointing out that some clothes were in fact timeless due to their simple elegance. Other clothes, such as terylene trousers for example, survive because they simply never wear out. Fine. But enough said on the subject, though Frank did advise me to let the latter piece of clothing remain in the cupboard should I ever have a date with someone of the opposite sex.

'You've got no idea about fashion,' Janne said. 'Old clothes like that are really hip again with the cool crowd. Peau de pêche jackets and nylon shirts. String vests and the lot. The more horrible the better. They call it nerd.'

'The world's gone mad,' Frank said, putting an espresso down in front of each of us and a small dessert bowl with ice-cream and red sauce.

Nerd? I thought. Was I a nerd? The thought appealed to me. I came to the conclusion that I was possibly a hip nerd, without even realizing it.

'Good sauce!' Kjell Bjarne said.

'Yes, I'm actually quite proud of it myself,' Janne said. 'It's elderberry juice with berries from our own garden.'

Kjell Bjarne nodded. 'D'you have a lot of bottles?'

'Kjell Bjarne!' I hissed.

But Janne just laughed and said of course Kjell Bjarne could have a bottle of elderberry juice to take home. No problem at all!

Later on we played ludo for a couple of hours and listened to Abba's greatest hits. A 'cool' evening, as Kjell Bjarne put it in the car on the way home.

But it wasn't so cool after we said goodbye to Frank. We were about to open the door to our building when Kjell Bjarne managed to slip on a patch of ice and pulled me down with him. The bottle fell under us and before we knew it, we were lying there flailing around in juice and broken glass. Our hands were covered in small cuts that were bleeding profusely and when Kjell Bjarne managed to pull me to my feet, we realized that we had mixed blood without even thinking about it. We were blood brothers, to put it simply. The thought of

AIDS terrified us for the first hour or so, but once we had put plasters on and had calmed down a bit, we came to the conclusion that the chances were minimal. After all, there had to be some advantages to living as an involuntary celibate! But it bothered me for a while after the accident, knowing that some of Kjell Bjarne's bodily fluids were now pounding through my veins. There was something terribly intimate about it, almost sexual. However, as the days passed, I settled down. I was a part of him and he was a part of me. Even fate had designed it to be so. We were blood brothers now.

# 9

I carved the poem about Reidun's tummy into the new toilet door at Larsen's. I pushed Kjell Bjarne's Sixties sunglasses up onto my head and concentrated on working with the penknife that my mother had given me for my confirmation. I hadn't shaved for three days and whenever I took a break I ran a rasping right hand over my stubble. I was starting to like myself more and more now. I liked what I was doing. Earlier in the day I had been Marjorie the Matchmaker, now I was Carl the Carver. With stubble, with tousled hair, with sunglasses on my head. I carved my poetry deep into the white hardboard. Recently I'd been thinking again about the conversation we'd had some months earlier at Frank and Janne's place. I had dug out my terylene slacks and bought some lemon-yellow socks. I was wearing a dark green nylon shirt buttoned up to the neck. I was the person I had been before all the bad things happened. I was a mummy's boy once again, but now I was a newer and more dangerous version of a mummy's boy. I was Elling, the nerd poet, the face-less underground artist.

Well. So far I hadn't got any further than this one poem. The poem about the angels' impregnation of Reidun Nordsletten. Art was like that, however. Pegasus didn't swish his tail every day and only very seldom took to wing. I had enough time, I could wait. I was still noting down occasional sentences and kept the notes in my bedside drawer. One day I would be able to put them together to create small gems, of that I was convinced. About the poem I was carving into the toilet door I could add that it was probably on everyone's lips in this part of town. I had written it out several hundred times and had distributed the slips of paper all over Majorstuen. In directories in telephone boxes. Teased into toilet rolls in public conveniences, as a surprise. But in the main I had focused on two local supermarkets: Prix and Rema 1000.

As my fears gradually subsided I followed Frank's instructions and now did my share of the shopping. I rediscovered the secure, happy young boy who used to do the shopping for his mother. These days, however, I was armed with poetry, hot from the press. I made a sport out of sticking copies of the poem between products on the shelves. I went in as a kind of thief in reverse and enriched the lives of my fellow human beings. An exhausted woman drags herself in on legs riddled with pain. She has lost her husband and her children don't ring any more. Her back hurts, she has already had a hysterectomy, and she's had a lung removed. Then – in between two vacuum-packed salami sausages – she finds a handwritten poem. A small glimpse of light in her dark grey everyday routine.

Or what about the hard-working industrial magnate who pops in for a deep-frozen lobster? He too takes a few lines of poetry with him on his way, frozen to the plastic packaging. The next time a tabloid journalist rings him to ask what reading material he has on his bedside table, he won't need to give them any guff about Hamsun and Ibsen. He can tell the truth. He has a glass of water on his bed-side table. And next to the glass of water is a poem that came into his hands in the strangest of ways. He reads the poem every night before he goes to sleep, in fact it's become a sort of ritual for him, a bit like bedtime prayers when he was a child. Who wrote the poem? It's a mystery. Someone who signs himself 'E'.

The story about a poem frozen to a lobster in the frozen-food section in a supermarket was just perfect for tabloids. I was fantasizing more and more about going for the big one, smuggling a poem or ten into a sealed packet, instant soup for example, but so far I hadn't had the courage. And yet I was painfully aware that taking an action like this would really expand my readership, in fact I would become famous nationwide overnight. I could just see the front-page headlines in Verdens Gang and the furious search for 'E' in the production halls of Toro instant-soup factories.

How many volumes of poems did an average poet sell in Norway? I had no idea, but I would guess at about forty if this person hadn't fallen out with all his friends before publication. I already had a much larger readership. Actually, it was only my own mind that set limits on how far I could go. I could take the tram and conquer other areas of town. I could take the train to, let's say, Holmestrand and after a two-hour 'shopping' spree I would be on everyone's lips.

I felt so happy and free as I stood there carving the poem with my knife. Excited and curious about what the future would bring. I had days that were as black as pitch as well, of course. Days when all the old sludge rose up inside me again, days when I stayed in bed, afraid of light and sound. I told myself that all artists go through this – artistic talent resides in a sensitive soul. Things had been considerably better for me since I'd realized that a fear of life was the price you had to pay for talent.

The crucial thing was that I had a project again, I thought to myself. I had ever been a project man. Idleness had always been my greatest enemy. In my youth I had collected every conceivable thing from stamps to tin-can labels, bottle tops and the paper that oranges were wrapped in. As an adult I developed an interest in politics and psychology, and this led to a comprehensive collection of everything that had anything to do with the former prime minister, Gro Harlem Brundtland, such as photos and interviews from the newspaper. Then there was – I suppose I dare say it – a not insignificant archive of all the misdeeds and comings and goings of my neighbours. I knew them better than they knew themselves as I observed them from my neutral viewpoint behind the curtains in my room.

During my enforced stay at Brøynes Rehabilitation Centre all this material was taken from me. For over a year I had to listen to them telling me that these projects were not good for me. Collecting stamps, yes! Gro Harlem Brundtland and neighbours with varying degrees of madness, no, no, no! And I obeyed. I obeyed them because I understood the language of power. I sat watching TV and went on long walks, always with an inner certainty that one fine day it would be my turn again. And the night, that wonderful night, when the poem came to me I knew that everything was breaking loose again. Now that I was writing a kind of poetry journal I noted down every move I made in my well-intentioned guerrilla warfare. The whereabouts of every single copy of the poem that I carefully hid was recorded in minute detail the very same evening.

I finished carving and swept up the debris on the floor. I put it down the toilet and flushed it. Then I went out and washed my hands.

I checked the time. A quarter past three. It was all beautifully timed. We had synchronized our watches and unless she had been run over by a tram or had got cold feet, Reidun would be in position now. I had thought everything through in rigorous detail and had come to the conclusion that it would be easiest for Kjell Bjarne to relate to her if he was under the impression that their meeting had all been a matter of chance. Not that he had shown much initiative recently, because he hadn't! He had clearly forgotten or repressed the fact that I had advised him to invite Reidun to Larsen's.

I knew that Reidun was on late shift this week, so I rang her at ten as soon as Kjell Bjarne had gone out to buy bread and milk. Was it not the case that she felt a certain attraction for Kjell Bjarne? Yes, she had to confess that she did. I outlined my plan to her in all its simplicity. At five minutes past three I would get up from the table and go to the toilet. I would stay there until a quarter past. In the meantime she was to seize the opportunity and pretend to be surprised to see him. I thought it would be best if I were in the toilet when she came in so that Kjell Bjarne got a bit of practice at being alone with her. At any rate, he would have to find a way to greet her. Anyway, I still had a job to finish where I was. I had asked him to wait for me before he ordered so that we could eat together.

I almost cartwheeled with joy when I emerged into the restaurant and saw that she was already there. She had even got herself dressed up. She was wearing a pink angora sweater and tartan slacks. She'd hung her light blue quilt jacket round the back of her chair and sat puffing nervously at a filter cigarette and fidgeting with the menu. Staring at Kjell Bjarne all the while. And Kjell Bjarne was staring at his hands. Oh hell, I thought. Yes, I was swearing to myself. Somehow or other I had to put an end to his helplessness. Was this the man who actually went round claiming that he would sell his soul to the devil for one single 'pussy hair'? It certainly didn't look like it. He looked like a homosexual lumberjack whom some trickster had lured into a whorehouse.

'Well, I never,' I said in a loud and obviously false voice, slipping youthfully onto the chair. 'Fancy seeing you here!' I pushed the ashtray across to her.

She smiled nervously, briefly raising her eyes to the heavens. She obviously wanted me to rein in a little. Not to overdo it.

'Kjell Bjarne!' I said. 'Reidun Nordsletten's here. She came while you were nodding off.'

'Don't be so mean, Elling,' Reidun said, laughing.

Even Kjell Bjarne smiled a little.

'Let's have something to eat,' I said jovially. 'Boys pay. No, no protests.' There weren't any, anyway, and I began to wonder if she was a brick short of a load when it came to normal courtesies. She could have protested a little. Never mind. It was her day. After all I was the one who had dreamt the whole thing up.

Kjell Bjarne cleared his throat and said, 'I think it'll have to be lamb stew.'

'Oh, yes!' Reidun Nordsletten said. 'I'll have that, too!'

For myself I ordered smoked haddock with carrots. I wouldn't have minded lamb stew either, but I wanted to distance myself from their choice. I wanted them to have something in common.

'How's the young 'un?' Kjell Bjarne asked out of the blue. He even looked right up at her for a few seconds. Now I really hadn't expected this bold move. I had come to terms with the fact that I would have to take the lead in the conversation.

'Absolutely great,' Reidun said. 'I'm due at the beginning of June.' She was positively glowing. Glowing with new life and grinning from ear to ear because Kjell Bjarne had ventured out onto the ice. 'It's a good time to come into the world.'

Kjell Bjarne gave a weighty nod of his head. 'And the dago? Heard anything from him?'

She shook her head. 'I don't want to hear from him, either. I don't think he's even in Norway.'

'Give us a ring if he bothers you!' I chipped in audaciously. 'Isn't that right, Kjell Bjarne?'

'Just let him try!' Kjell Bjarne muttered. It

sounded as though it was his fervent hope that the Spaniard would try it on.

Reidun giggled. 'He wouldn't get very far with you, would he!'

He cleared his throat. 'Nice girls don't grow on trees. When you meet one you have to treat her properly. The bloke must be off his rocker!'

He was simply masterful now. One sentence pouring out after the other. And what sentences! It was a pure declaration of love. I almost felt superfluous. Reidun cooed and thanked him for the 'compliment'. 'Is that the right word?' she asked, and everything in the garden was rosy. Her tiny potato nose shook with ardour. At the same time I could recognize my own ingenuity. It was my suggestion that she should ring us if the child's father should turn up with unsolicited demands and suggestions. In that way I had made it possible for Kjell Bjarne to take on the role of protector – and I knew that was a role that suited him down to the ground. In fact it was a shame, a great shame, that this Spaniard wasn't following Reidun like a shadow. It was in situations like these that Kjell Bjarne could clearly show his feelings for her – feelings that he found so difficult to express in words – by beating the fellow to pulp. On the other hand, I found it difficult to conjure up a situation in which Reidun Nordsletten's life or honour would be in danger. Nor could I imagine that there would be too many competitors for Reidun's hand.

The meal arrived and Kjell Bjarne withdrew into himself again. Reidun and I resumed our conversation. She told me that she came from Bøler. Although she didn't go into any detail about her life up until now, it was clear that her passage to this table in the restaurant had been steep and tortuous. Her time at school had been something of a nightmare, she informed me. She didn't even complete year eight; she was quite open about that.

'You can talk to him about that!' I said, giving Kjell Bjarne a friendly nudge in the ribs.

'Special school,' he said, with his mouth full of food. 'They thought I was an idiot.'

'He learnt to read when he got his first porno magazine.' I said, in the hushed confidential tones that are used between good friends. 'That's when he realized that reading was a necessity.'

Then I delivered a long harangue about how terrible they were at motivating us when we went to school. And before very long all three of us were sitting there hating society. Each in our own way, we had all been conspicuously different from the average person, and, each in our own way, we had all had a taste of the whip. But when Reidun Nordsletten more than hinted that it was the Labour party's fault, that was where I drew the line. She should just leave the political analysis to me. Which she did. I pointed out that it wasn't the social democratic party platform that was at fault, it was some of the rotten planks within it. And the rotten planks were smuggled onto the building site by workers in the pay of the KGB and the CIA! She couldn't make head or tail of that, as she said, so I let it go.

'Great lamb stew!' Kjell Bjarne said, pushing his plate away as he dried his mouth with the back of his hand.

'Fantastic!' Reidun said. 'But they're very large portions. I can't manage more than half.'

'Give it to me then!' Kjell Bjarne said. She passed him the rest of her meal and Kjell Bjarne plunged into action again.

'There are no limits to what Kjell Bjarne can eat,' I explained. 'Once at Brøynes he ate four plates of roast pork. With potatoes and cabbage and all the trimmings. There was someone on cover duty that day, and he didn't know that Kjell Bjarne was supposed to be on a diet.'

Kjell Bjarne chuckled. 'You just have to make sure you dump regularly and the whole thing runs like greased lightning.'

Reidun giggled. 'You're disgusting, Kjell Bjarne!'

He looked at her with genuine surprise in his eyes. 'Disgusting?'

'Nooo, I just mean that . . .'

'It's just that you don't sit and talk about that sort of thing when ladies are present,' I remonstrated. 'Or even when they're not, by the way.'

'Fine.' He pushed plate number two away from him. 'But now I really have to go to the bog.' He smiled. 'I mean, I just have to go and wash my hands!'

Kjell Bjarne was joking! I had never experienced that before. Reidun Nordsletten and I burst out into hearty, liberating laughter.

'The cubicle at the back!' I shouted after him in the hope that he would discover the anonymous poem and perhaps comment on it when he returned.

'He's so sweet!' Reidun confessed when he was out of earshot. Her eyes hung on his broad shoulders.

'Listen,' I said, my voice suddenly becoming very confidential. 'It's going really well but Kjell Bjarne and I have got to go and meet someone now. I think you should join us.'

'Oooh, I don't know. Who is it?'

I told her about Alphonse Jørgensen and his sprained foot. And about the Buick that Kjell Bjarne had promised to have a look at. I had rung Alphonse that day and said we were going to come.

'My goodness!' she said. 'The poor man. And here we are, all three of us, stuffing ourselves instead of making him a meal. Men!'

'He's got a fridge full of meatballs from the last time we were there,' I said. 'I assume that he's got enough to take him through to midsummer. Anyway, it wouldn't have been natural to take you with us to Alphonse's place before we "bumped into you" here. Now it's natural,' I said with a complicit smile.

'You're a sly one, Elling!'

Well. Yes. Probably I was. All my life I had enjoyed staging things. Making things happen, like now. Preferably without taking part myself. When I was a child I had always been a cunning little devil in this respect. From my vantage point on the edge of my gaggle of friends in the playground, I had thrived on giving the others ideas which they then adopted as their own. I never made anyone do anything bad. It was always the 'what if' scenario. What if someone glued the drawer of Pettersen's desk with superglue? What if someone hoisted the head teacher's bike up the flagpole? What if. Someone. There was always someone who did it, and no-one could remember where the idea came from. They didn't see me. They weren't aware of the source of the anonymous voice. They were only really ever aware of me when they decided it was time to clean the urinals using my closely cropped hair as a brush. A couple of times a month, or so.

That was a long time ago and a different game. Right now the game was called 'Anonymous Poet in the Service of Love'. Actually, I was extremely surprised that I hadn't been overcome by jealousy when all this between Kjell Bjarne and Reidun had flared up. Not because I had considered Reidun Nordsletten an attractive woman at any point in the proceedings, but because Kjell Bjarne was possibly on the threshold of experiencing something that I would unfortunately have to accept I would remain excluded from for a long, long time. But, no. I remained loyal to my blood brother, even though all my efforts could only lead me into a new period of loneliness.

When I really thought about it I was quite moved by my own actions. There was no point denying it: I had been a selfish person. You become like that when you grow up without friends and with a family that is limited to one rather unenterprising mother. I mean, how can you learn to think of others when 'others' simply exist in a kind of haze outside the sitting-room windows? Semi-real? No. It's more like delivering long monologues to the mirror.

'You're so strange sometimes,' said Reidun. 'You almost seem to vanish into your own world.'

'Yes,' I said. 'Do you wonder what on earth I'm doing there?'

She laughed.

'What's happened to your boyfriend, by the way?' I went on. 'Has he locked himself in, I wonder?'

'Don't tease, Elling! Don't joke about that!'

'I've never been more serious,' I said. 'I can feel the passionate tension between you. It's almost unbearable to be sitting near you. I don't understand why you don't simply jump on each other.'

'It's not that easy, you know! At least not for him. After all, I'm pregnant and all that.'

'And all that?'

'I just mean that perhaps it's not all that romantic.'

I looked at her askance. 'Do you have the impression that Kjell Bjarne is the romantic type?'

'Perhaps not. Well, yes, deep down, I do. Not everyone can express themselves like you, can they? In any case, I think he's so sweet!'

I went quiet. I really didn't know what to say.

'Hey.'

'Yes.'

'Has he been around much? With women, and the like.'

I couldn't restrain a brief, strangled burst of laughter, but I pulled myself together quickly. I thought of answering that it was mostly 'the like' with him, but instead I dodged the question. 'Well, there's much and much. It depends what you mean by "much".'

'I've been with three men,' she said. 'I wasn't really up for it with any of them. It just sort of happened. Wasn't anything special.'

I had to stop her now. I simply didn't want to hear any of the intimate details that she was suddenly revealing. If she absolutely had to talk about that sort of thing, then she should do it with Kjell Bjarne. What was she saying anyway? That it 'just happened'? I could just imagine it! Reidun Nordsletten, bent over her bucket at the hospital. The erect male member that appeared from nowhere and slid up inside her most intimate place. What absolute bunkum! Either you are raped or you surrender yourself willingly. There are no other options.

Luckily Kjell Bjarne came back at that moment and I didn't have to put her in her place. I tried to tell from his face whether he had read my poem, but he was looking impassive. As usual, I have to say.

We found Alphonse Jørgensen in considerably better spirits than when we had left him. The swelling round his foot had gone down and he was limping around his flat with the help of a handy little stick he had found somewhere in the chaos. He greeted Reidun Nordsletten courteously, he even kissed her on the hand and Reidun blushed becomingly, with a furtive glance over to Kjell Bjarne. However, Kjell Bjarne had his back to us and was rummaging through his toolbox, which we had picked up from home on our way. He was absent-mindedly whistling 'The Bridge on the River Kwai', and seemed to be absolutely in his element.

'It has certainly been a long time since I've had a lady visiting me,' Alphonse Jørgensen said.

'I can see that,' Reidun said, running a finger along the edge of one of the bookshelves.

'Oh well, I'll soon be the same age as the dust and then … Please sit down! Would you like a cup of coffee?'

'Nope,' Kjell Bjarne said. 'It's car time.'

'Yes, of course,' Alphonse Jørgensen said, winking at me. 'I'll just find the garage key. And the car keys, naturally. But I think you'd better take Elling down with you. It's so tight in the garage that you won't be able to work in there and it'll take two of you to push the car into the yard.'

'That I'd like to see,' Kjell Bjarne said. 'He'll just get under my feet. No, it's best Elling stays here.'

He was showing off now. At my expense on top of that. Had that happened a year ago I would have gone for him, but I just let it drop. Anyway, I wasn't in the mood for pushing a car. I caught myself hoping that he would do himself an injury, perhaps slip a disc. Now that would teach him a lesson in humility.

'I'll come down with you!' Reidun said. 'I'll make the coffee first and then I'll come down.' She slipped into Alphonse Jørgensen's kitchen as if it were her own.

'Tea for me, please!' I called.

Kjell Bjarne grunted something or other and disappeared out through the front door with the toolbox under his arm.

'There are some overalls down there,' Alphonse Jørgensen shouted after him. 'Put them on so you don't ruin your clothes!'

'He didn't hear,' I said.

'No,' said Reidun. 'But I did. Are you aware that moss is beginning to grow on the dirty dishes out here, Mr Jørgensen?'

'Just leave them!'

'I'll do them now while the water's boiling.'

He fell back into his armchair. 'OK, OK. But you can stop all that Jørgensen rubbish right away, both of you! Call me Alphonse. Or Alf. Most people who know me call me just Alf.'

'I think Alphonse has more style,' Reidun said. 'There are not many people with that name. There's something south European about it.'

'Southern European,' I corrected.

'Same difference. I'm sure you understood what I meant.'

'How we use the language is not "same difference",' I said. 'If we're sloppy, the whole language will die out.'

'Well, that's perhaps not such a bad thing,' Alphonse said. 'By the way, I've dug out a couple of books for you.' He got up and limped into an adjacent room.

I went to the window and looked down into the back yard. Sure enough, Kjell Bjarne had managed to manoeuvre the enormous car into the yard and now he was fiddling around with the car bonnet. The gentle rays of the evening sun fell across the yard, causing the bare patch on his head to glow. A couple of minutes before I had been furious with him, but now the last trace of anger left me. Yes, this simple, everyday image moved me. A man with incipient baldness bending over a car bonnet. It must be the blood. It must be the blood we shared, I thought, and all the long conversations we had at night in our room at Brøynes. We'd become a part of each other's lives and nothing would change that. Not even the budding relationship between him and Reidun would be able to shake the fact that we were partners. We had something that could never be destroyed.

I heard Reidun opening the kitchen window and a second later her voice echoed around the yard.

'Put the overalls on, Kjell Bjarne, or you'll ruin your nice sweater!'

He straightened up, stood still and looked up at her in surprise. Then he smiled, raised a hand and plodded into the dark garage.

Yes, I thought. This is how it's going to be. What I am seeing now is a glimpse of the future. Here I am, in the sitting room of my friend Alphonse Jørgensen, known to his friends as Alf. Reidun Nordsletten is pottering around in the kitchen and there is the smell of freshly brewed coffee and soapy water. Down in the yard Kjell Bjarne is messing about with a car. If he got it to go perhaps all four of us could go out for a drive, as Alphonse had hinted. All five of us, to be more precise. We mustn't forget the little astronaut.

Why not indeed! I thought. Why not! Alphonse and I were given a mug each, of coffee and tea, and Reidun took the coffee pot and two mugs down to the yard.

'Is Kjell Bjarne the father of the child?' Alphonse asked when we were on our own.

'No, not at all!' I assured him. I explained the

situation to him, told him about the scoundrel from Spain and the little push start I was giving their relationship.

'How noble of you,' he said acidly. 'I think you can leave them to their own devices now.'

'Yes,' I said. 'You're probably right.'

# 10

Anyone who has tried to open a soup packet without ripping the actual packaging to bits will have had the same experience as me. It is impossible. I had bought ten packets of Toro pea soup, but I ruined them, one after the other. I tried to steam the packets open, with no success. I attacked them with a razor blade and surgical precision, but achieved nothing more than a cut on my finger and another ruined soup packet. We ate split-pea soup with sausage for days and Kjell Bjarne started to wonder if we had overrun our budget again. Then I gave up.

It was immensely important that Kjell Bjarne did not get wind of my poetry project, because there was no point in relying on him to keep quiet. He was indeed a man of few words, a master of the monosyllable, but all the same he was not good at keeping secrets, if he had someone to tell them to. And now he did. Reidun Nordsletten had got him really geared up that afternoon in Alphonse's back yard. She had won her way to his heart with freshly brewed coffee and Kjell Bjarne had puffed out his chest and pointed at the engine and said this and that. I had no idea that he could do things with broken car engines, but eventually it was revealed that they'd had a tractor and a rundown Bedford on the farm in Maridal where he came from. He had, of course, not said anything to me about that. Every time we'd touched on Kjell Bjarne's past in the course of our many nocturnal conversations, silence would fall in his part of the room. His parents should have been hanged without trial or legal recourse. That was all he had to say about his background.

At first I had been offended, it would be untrue to say otherwise. And slightly dismissive of Reidun Nordsletten as well. I felt things were going a bit too fast. Already the next day she was walking around with a knowing expression on her face. She knew things about Kjell Bjarne that I had no idea about. And she let me know this through hints and half-finished sentences. Words like 'Maridal' and 'Bedford' vibrated in the air. She had been initiated.

But I shook off the discomfort. I thought to myself that if they had their own things, well so did I. I had my poem and a pile of books that I had placed in neat order on my new bookshelf. I still hadn't got hold of a comfortable armchair – I wanted to wait until I found the right one – but I had put a kitchen stool in my corner and was more than happy with that. The artificial fire to create the ultimate cosiness could wait until the autumn storms set in. And there I sat. Upright on my stool. And read Olaf Bull and Herman Wildenvey. They had definitely worked in a different section of the poetry garden from me, but some of the poems weren't bad. I did not like Jan Erik Vold, however. It was too much cock-a-doodle-do for me. Basically I thought he was a silly fool, but I faced stiff opposition there from Alphonse. Well, well. Horses for courses, as they say. One evening I did in fact walk out on him in anger after a harrowing discussion about Nils Kvilekvål's books, but I quickly phoned him and apologized, having first conferred with Frank.

I had to give up on the soup packets in the end. It simply was not possible to slip a poem in among the dried peas without the customer noticing that some-one had tampered with the packet. Tins were also out of the question – I didn't even try. Well, it was a defeat. Of course I knew that you had to do some-thing quite major to get on the front page of the tabloids. And it certainly was not enough just to distribute some pieces of paper as I had until now.

But then I had an idea. It wasn't as clever as the idea of using soup packets and tins as packaging for my poem, but it was at least possible. I went down to the supermarket and bought a box with twin packets of sauerkraut. Two separate sachets of ready-made sauerkraut in a sealed cardboard box. Kjell Bjarne was at home, so I smuggled it into my reading corner where I set about the laborious task of opening the box with a razor blade. It was more difficult than I had thought, but I realized immediately that it was within the realm of the feasible.

When I was nearly halfway there, Kjell Bjarne came thundering in. Naturally, I might add. I just managed to hide the razor blade under my right buttock.

'Jesus,' he said.

'What do you want?' I said. 'Can't you see that I'm busy?'

'Are you sitting here reading a sauerkraut box?' In confusion, he looked at the sauerkraut box, then at the books on the shelf and then back at the sauerkraut.

'Yes, I am.'

'Why?'

I had to defuse the situation immediately, otherwise the image of me with a box of sauerkraut in my hand would be for ever fixed in his memory. And if he thought my behaviour was too odd, he might tell Alphonse and Reidun about it and then they would remember when the news broke in the press. It would pull the plug on my project and make me a laughing stock. So I fed him a couple of semi-white lies about my intentions to take the whole issue of additives more seriously in the future. We were no longer just going to eat things without first checking what ingredients were contained in the food. For example, how did he feel about E211? Did he realize that he sat and guzzled large amounts of carbohydrates almost every day?

'The most important thing is that it tastes good!' was his opinion. 'I'm going down to Alphonse's now.'

Fortunately. He was no longer thinking about the sauerkraut packet, I could see that. 'Do you think that you'll ever get that car on the road again?'

'Course. Just need some parts. Alphonse said he'd advertise for them in the paper. You coming?'

'I'll come down later,' I said. 'What about Reidun?'

'What about her?'

'Is she coming with you?' I asked patiently.

'She's there already. Making food for him, she said.'

So that's the way it was. It was all getting very cosy now. But why not? We had all sat brooding in our corners for long enough. Kjell Bjarne and I with the sex phone lines and remote control. Reidun with a child in her belly and a flat full of dead owls. Alphonse in his library, a library he was no longer that interested in. And in any case, I thought, because I could now visualize Reidun down in Alphonse's kitchen, the child would need a grandfather. She had openly told us that her father had taken his own life. He had hanged himself from a pear tree just outside Copenhagen, whatever he was doing there.

'Kjell Bjarne?'

'What?'

'The two of us have eaten, haven't we?'

'Yeah.' He looked bothered. Of course I had seen through his plan.

'So eat some more then!' I said in a tremulous voice. 'And eat an extra portion for me! This is not Brøynes!'

His face lit up. In fact, he was truly happy. 'And you won't say anything to Frank?'

'Of course not. I have decided to limit my contact with him to business only from now on. We have friends enough! But Kjell Bjarne – promise me to be a bit careful with the carbohydrates. Do you promise?'

He nodded. 'I'll ask Alphonse.'

'No,' I said. 'You don't need to do that. I was just joking really.'

He pretended that he had got the point and forced out a chuckle. 'OK, mate! See you later, crocodile!'

An hour and a half later I had achieved what I set out to do. I had managed to open the box with a razor blade, without damaging the cardboard. I had sliced finely through the glue. I carefully pulled one of the sachets of sauerkraut out and attached the poem to it with Sellotape. Then I carefully sealed up the box again with some of Kjell Bjarne's wood glue. It was perfect. It was impossible to see that anyone had tampered with the packaging. 'Poem Found in Sauerkraut Box!' I could see the headlines. It was possible that I might not manage to get the whole of the front page, but I felt certain that the editor would sacrifice at least a couple of columns to this bizarre phenomenon. That was, of course, dependent on the person who bought the sauerkraut having their wits about them and contacting the press. It was abundantly clear to me that the consumer was the weak link.

However, I did not intend to give up after only one packet. The chance of sudden, anonymous fame would increase with every packet of sauerkraut I was able to smuggle back into the shop. That was the part of the project that I dreaded the most, actually getting the packets back into the shop, but somehow or other I managed to galvanize myself. I also decided to stick only to sauerkraut. There were a number of compotes and stews that were packaged in the same way, but sauerkraut was going to be my trademark. If my poetry was linked to only one product, it would give the press something more to think about (Sauerkraut Poet Strikes Again!).

With any luck, the press would contact a couple of psychiatrists who could tell the readers a bit about what frame of mind the mysterious poet found himself in. Why did he target sauerkraut and nothing else? Something to do with his childhood, presumably. Dominating mother. Drunkenness and beatings in the home. The pickled cabbage could possibly be a symbol of the soured atmosphere that had prevailed in the poet's childhood home. Who was the poet? In all probability a confused young man, with no friends. I chuckled as I sat there. Thinking about my friends. About Kjell Bjarne, Reidun and Alphonse Jørgensen. And the two young tomcats that gleefully skipped around me day and night. I also sent a thought or two to my mother. My kind, dead mother who could never do enough for me. I'd have to go and tend to her grave one of these days.

I hid the sauerkraut packet at the very back of my wardrobe and got ready to go. Elmer and Pepper were sitting side by side in the hall and looked up at me in surprise. They always did this when I was about to go out. They looked thunderstruck. Are you going out now? Why can't you just stay at home? Yes, it hurt to look at their innocent, questioning eyes. Sometimes I felt like an ogre when I left them like that. I decided to talk to Kjell Bjarne about it. Surely we could let them out, in a controlled environment?

On the way over to Hjelmsgate, I popped into a tobacconist's and bought ten Bellman Lights. Mild cigars, but with character, as the man behind the counter said. He recommended that I lit them with matches and did not inhale. It was almost as if he realized that I had not smoked for over twenty years.

However, I do still intend to count myself among the ranks of non-smokers. To relax every now and then with a cigar is not the same as abandoning yourself to nicotine hell. Everything in moderation, as they say. I lit one up on the way and noticed to my surprise that my mouth accepted the pleasant-smelling smoke without any protest whatsoever. It was as if all the years that lay between my days of dabbling with American menthol cigarettes and the present had never existed. It all felt so very natural and no-one even so much as smirked at me, either. They obviously just thought that here was a man with a cigar in his mouth. Fair play to him. It's nothing to do with us.

My entrance was a success. I think I dare to say that. Alphonse and Reidun were sitting at the small garden table and Kjell Bjarne was bent over the Buick. Naturally, the cigar caused quite a commotion among these people who knew me as a non-smoker, but I puffed away and pretended it was nothing extraordinary. The fact was that I enjoyed smoking a cigar every now and then. And I always had. There was nothing to make a fuss about, quite the contrary.

'You never smoked at Brøynes,' Kjell Bjarne said. 'Not even at Christmas.'

'That is because I like to show consideration,' I said. 'I smoke outside every now and then. But only good cigars, mind you. It's hardly the life of Riley, is it?'

Kjell Bjarne put down the monkey wrench. He looked pretty comical, to put it mildly, in Alphonse's overalls which were a couple of sizes too small. They were tight around the groin and the trouser legs stopped halfway up his calves. 'Alphonse says we can go to his cabin when I've fixed up the old banger!' he said.

'To his cabin?' I said. I didn't know quite what to think. It sounded a bit frightening to me, but at the same time tempting. Sitting by the fire every evening after long days out in the fresh air. Ludo and instant soup. Mouse droppings in the cupboards and water in the well.

'I've got a place down south by Nevlunghavn,' Alphonse said. 'I haven't been there for ages. I've rented the whole place out for the past few years. I thought that if the weather was good at Easter . . . Well, you and Kjell Bjarne obviously have to talk to that Frank chap first, but if it's OK with him . . . ?' He looked at me questioningly.

'This is nothing to do with Frank,' I said.

'No, no, but all the same . . .'

'I'll talk to him,' Kjell Bjarne said. 'Elling'll just start to argue. He's coming on Thursday and he's usually in a good mood after the pictures.'

'You will not get involved in this, at all,' I said sharply. 'It's time that man was put in his place and I will be the one who does it. I'm not the sort of person who grovels to council employees!'

Alphonse didn't say anything, but snapped his fingers hard two times.

'I'm sure he won't be difficult!' Reidun said. She giggled. 'And if he does make a fuss, Alphonse and I will go alone. Won't we, Alphonse?'

Kjell Bjarne started to rub his temples with his filthy fists, but Alphonse was quick to save the situation and said no, the motto here was 'all for one and one for all'.

I wound myself up. I most certainly did. And with good reason, too. I paced restlessly around the yard, with the extinguished cigar in my mouth, and imagined Frank's mocking face. A trip to a cabin? Out of the question! That was absolutely not why we were being given an allowance once a month. I convinced myself that he would say no, just for the fun of it. Out of pure sadism. Foaming at the mouth, I had a furious, imaginary conversation with him. I was going to go on this trip to the cabin, if it cost me both my home and my allowance! I had never been to a cabin in my life and it was about bloody time! I kicked the washing-line pole and punched the air every time his self-righteous face appeared in my imagination.

Suddenly Alphonse was there. 'That's enough, Elling!'

And it was enough. More than enough! I spat out the wet cigar and started to cry. I wanted to go to a cabin, just like everyone else! Was that asking too much?

'I think we've done enough for today, Kjell Bjarne,' said Alphonse. 'Let's go back up to my flat, all of us. It's starting to get cold.'

And it was true. Suddenly I realized that it was really cold. My whole body was shaking and once ensconced in Alphonse's flat, I had to rest under a blanket on the sofa. Reidun made some more tea and stroked my hair when Kjell Bjarne wasn't looking. I lay quite still, with closed eyes, and listened to my heart thumping in my chest.

# 11

Frank's nostrils quivered. I had noticed it before – his nostrils quivered when he was ruminating on something. His nostrils flared and small black hairs protruded from under his nose and blended into his unkempt moustache. On odd occasions I had had an almost irresistible desire to stick my finger up one of his hairy grottoes, but at this particular moment the idea disgusted me. I thought he was revolting. Almost obnoxious. A thin string of melted cheese hung from the corner of his mouth and down into his stubble. He was chewing at a piece of pizza and ruminating.

'Well, what's it going to be?' said Kjell Bjarne, helping himself to the biggest piece of pizza on the table.

I kicked him on the shin. This was my department. I had prepared a tough riposte that I wanted to launch at Frank if he didn't let us go on this trip with Reidun and Alphonse. If he refused to give us permission, and he probably would, at least I would have the pleasure of peppering him with the most unpleasant words to be found in the Norwegian language. I had lain awake half the night preparing myself. I had got so het up and was talking to myself so loudly that Kjell Bjarne had woken up. Right, I thought. You snot-nosed reptile!

'Of course you can go on the trip,' Frank said. 'I just need to have a little chat with this Alphonse . . . what was his name?'

'Alphonse Jørgensen,' Kjell Bjarne said.

You could have knocked me down with a feather, as they say, and after almost being knocked down by a feather, I was so relieved I was as light as a balloon. Before I knew what I was doing, I had stood up and was tap-dancing! Tippytitap, tippytitap. Round and round. Snapping my fingers at the same time, just as Alphonse always did. I raised my right arm over my head and snapped away. People were staring of course, but I didn't care. In my mind's eye I was already sitting in the front seat of Alphonse's huge American car, unapproachable and mysterious behind my sunglasses. We were roaring down the wild roads of Vestfold. I was overtaken by a sudden burst of euphoria, I was free and I could hear the sound of mental chains breaking.

Frank waved me back into my chair. 'Alphonse Jørgensen?'

'We just call him Alphonse,' Kjell Bjarne said. 'Or Alf. That's what he likes best.'

Frank looked at me. 'Not bad. The evening you rang to tell me about your argument you didn't mention that it was with Alphonse Jørgensen.' He laughed. 'You've got a nerve! Arguing about literature with Jørgensen.'

'He didn't like Kvilekvål's book,' I riposted. 'But I did. It's all water under the bridge now. I did as you said, didn't I? I rang him up and apologized.'

'Yeah, right. Take it easy. Jesus!'

'Did he do anything wrong?' Kjell Bjarne asked. 'Since you seem to know who he is.'

'No, for heaven's sake. It's just that he's very well known. Was, anyway.'

'Well known?' Kjell Bjarne repeated. 'Has he been on the telly?'

Frank shrugged his shoulders in indifference. He liked to boast that he almost never watched television. He still had one of the old black and white sets in his cellar room. 'Alphonse Jørgensen published two collections of poetry in the mid-Sixties,' he said. 'He was considered a promising young talent. I was studying the history of literature as my subsidiary subject at the time and everyone raved about him at university. Then it went quiet. Two collections of poetry and that was that.' He shrugged his shoulders again.

I was absolutely bowled over by the news. I was the personal friend of a poet! Not any old poet, but a poet who had been considered promising by the gang of carping critics at Oslo University. It was unbelievable! Why hadn't he said a word of this to us? Or at least to me? Telling Reidun and Kjell Bjarne would be a complete waste of time, like casting pearls before swine, but why had he not let me into this secret? I quickly came to the conclusion that there must be some tragedy lurking behind this somewhere. It was true that I kept mum about my own poetry, but that was a different matter! The whole of my campaign rested on my remaining anonymous; no-one was meant to know who was hiding behind the stark 'E' signature.

Alphonse Jørgensen had done what I eschewed. He had published collections of poetry under his own name, probably through one of the big publishing companies. Why had he suddenly given up? Could the truth be so awful that it was in some way connected with his wife's death? One thing was sure: I was definitely not going to ask him why he had put away his pen. For me he was Alphonse Jørgensen, a friend and benefactor. I intended to rise above the fact that he still enjoyed celebrity status amongst ageing academics like Frank. I said this to Frank, too. I forbade both him and Kjell Bjarne to mention these two collections of poetry in any way at all, with the justification that it might be a terribly sore point for Alphonse and we had no right to even broach the subject. The strange thing was that Frank nodded in agreement. I had never dreamt that I would experience such a thing in the course of one single life on earth.

'And what about Reidun?' he asked Kjell Bjarne.

Kjell Bjarne turned his back and sent me a questioning glance. No! He would have to manage this one on his own.

'Is she your girlfriend?'

'None of your business!'

'Take it easy, pal. I'm only asking.'

Kjell Bjarne looked away.

'I'm asking because I think you're doing really well. Barely a month ago you were in your flat struggling to make sense of the remote control. Now you're getting on a lot better, aren't you? Personal friends of Alphonse Jørgensen! Kjell Bjarne has a lady friend . . . and she's already pregnant into the bargain.' He winked at me and I winked back with warmth. We liked each other now. We had each other where we wanted. It was a good, heart-warming feeling. 'Why the hell didn't you tell anyone that you could fix cars, Kjell Bjarne?'

'Because no-one ever asked!'

Frank nodded. He was pleased with the answer. It was an answer he could use in any lecture in the field of health and welfare.

I took my Bellman Light cigars out of my pocket and blew blue smoke across the table into his face. I was unshaven and appropriately cool. He had given up trying to get me to take off my sunglasses. He had accepted that I had an essence all of my own, like everyone else.

I had been working up to this for a long time. I had steeled myself. For reasons of circumstance – an unforeseen breakdown – I had not been able to be present when the urn containing my mother's ashes was placed next to the urn containing my father's ashes. I was being accommodated at Brøynes Rehabilitation Centre against my will and when I returned to Oslo . . . the cemetery was covered with snow and ice, and I was also somewhat ashamed. I had spent a little over a year at Brøynes, and, deep down, I knew that Sister Gunn would have accompanied me to the grave in the cemetery if I had asked her. But the death of my mother and everything that reminded me of it was like a knot inside me. The pain was excruciatingly connected with the desperate days I had spent on my own in the old block of flats. To all intents and purposes, I had repressed everything.

Slowly, however, I was beginning to feel ready for it. One day, when Kjell Bjarne and I were already due to go for a walk in Frogner Park with Alphonse and Reidun, I took my decision! I would walk a little way with them, but at a certain point I would beg their indulgence and retire, that is, I would go to the cemetery behind the park. There was something I had to do. Someone was waiting for me. They would simply have to excuse me for half an hour.

It was a magnificent day. It wasn't quite Easter yet, but it was sunny and warm. The thought of what a pleasant trip we would have to Nevlunghavn, so long as the weather held, filled me with happiness. Alphonse was almost completely restored. He strutted around the park with his coat open and his hat pushed to the back of his head. Reidun had managed to find some lighter clothing and it was only really now that you could see how large she was. She waddled around like a globe on legs. Kjell Bjarne and I had bought a lead for each of our cats, but although we had tried to train them in the flat, by and large the system didn't work. We came to the conclusion that cats weren't made for leads. The simplest solution was to take off the leads and drag them behind us. Then the cats followed us faithfully. Two grown men walking along and dragging leads behind them looked silly, of course, but we rose above this.

I had bought a lovely bunch of daffodils in a flower shop. This was very apt since Mother's favourite colour had been yellow. I explained the situation to my friends when they noticed the flowers. I was going to visit a grave. I had neglected it, but now the time was ripe. They understood that, they said. That is, Reidun and Alphonse did. Kjell Bjarne said that he wished he also had a grave he could visit. 'Then I would know where to go every time I needed a piss.' He couldn't resist the temptation.

I put the lead in one coat pocket and Elmer in the other. He was so big now that he could sit in the pocket and peep out. He obviously liked that because as long as I kept moving he would stay quiet. We agreed to meet by the Monolith after half an hour.

At first I couldn't find the grave. It was years since I had visited my father's grave and in the meantime several hundred urns had been placed in the earth. There were flat stones everywhere in the grass and I became increasingly desperate. Ashamed, too. What kind of person does not know where their parents have been laid to rest? An ignorant good-for-nothing, in my view. I began to jog along the rows of stones, but it seemed a little disrespectful to me, and, anyway, Elmer was protesting. He didn't want to be shaken about; he preferred a calmer ride. I was hot and sweaty, and almost in tears by the time I was finally able to crouch down by a greyish-blue stone surface on which the names of my parents were engraved. I took Elmer out of my pocket and let him sniff around while I laid the flowers down.

Well, I thought, there you are and here am I. Your boy. I've brought flowers with me and a little cat. In the park three of my friends are walking and talking about God knows what. Alphonse's old car, perhaps. We're going to go on a little trip one of these days. Frank has given us permission. While I was crouching there and chatting away to the stone I thought I could hear my mother's happy voice. I knew exactly how she would have reacted if she had been alive and had seen with her own eyes how I was surrounding myself with animals and friends. It would have pleased her more than anything, as she herself had often tried to persuade me to join in with other people.

Scouts, wouldn't that be an idea? Thank you, but no thank you! Boys masturbating together and helping each other up from holes in the ice. Paedophile scout leaders and soaking wet sleeping bags. Meaningless sailors' knots. I was even sent on a Christian summer camp twice, but that didn't give me anything, either. I was the kind of person who felt lonelier in a group of people than on my own in my room.

It seemed to me that I could see behind everything, that I could see through the happy boys running around after one another. They weren't happy. They weren't even boys. They were like me, lonely souls trapped in bodies of flesh and blood, intestines and undigested food. They could play volleyball and talk about Jesus Christ on the cross as much as they liked – but they hadn't understood that they themselves would have to die. Every time they saw themselves in the mirror they actually believed in the image they saw – of that I was convinced.

I wasn't made like that. I could sit in the classroom and see the teacher decomposing and disintegrating. His words would often become meaningless sounds, completely detached from everything. Elling? My own name? Name? They could shout this ridiculous code of letters at me, but when I was in that frame of mind, and frequently I was, I just saw lips and tongues moving, and occasionally a moist uvula in the red darkness. I was in my own world.

I lay down. I ran my hand across the grass and talked a little to Mother. It seemed more natural to turn to Mother; after all, I had never met my father. I told her a bit about Kjell Bjarne. About all his special qualities, about his parent-phobia. He really had had a bad time before we got to know each other. However, I was able to tell her that I had got him back on the rails, yes, I had even organized a woman for him. Her name was Reidun Nordsletten. Soon to become a mother. She did have a round potato nose, but she also had a heart of gold. She washed dishes at the hospital so that the patients could eat from clean plates, drink juice from sparkling glasses. An industrious ant in a huge system.

And what was I doing? Oh, a bit of this and a bit of that. Mostly I took care of Kjell Bjarne. I kept an eye on his social benefit, and made sure he changed his socks and underwear once in a while. Otherwise, there was my poetry. My poems, or, to be more precise, my poem. The packets of sauerkraut that had to be smuggled back into the shops. As always, I had quite enough to keep me busy. It would probably be some time before I would be able to devote myself to love and to perpetuating our family name. If indeed love should ever smile at me. It was better not to know about these things. As a famous Norwegian poet once said, some have many and others have none.

I curled up on the grass and let my thoughts flow freely as I teased little Elmer with a piece of grass. I must have forgotten both time and place, for suddenly they were standing around me in a semi-circle. Kjell Bjarne, Alphonse and Reidun. They seemed worried and said they had been looking for me for almost an hour. Could that really be possible? I thought I ought to say something sensible, so I told them that Elmer and I had had a near-death experience and we had lost track of time and place. We had seen Mother standing in a radiant beam of light at the end of a long tunnel. We had also heard otherworldly classical music playing. It was marvellous. I was filled with an inner harmony that no words could describe. After this I would never again be frightened of meeting death.

'Bollocks!' Kjell Bjarne said.

'Don't be so unfeeling, Kjell Bjarne,' Reidun said. 'I've read about this in a magazine. Is it really true, Elling? Did you see your mother in a tunnel?'

'I most certainly did,' I said, getting up. One trouser leg was soaking wet near the top, and I brushed the grass and soil off me. 'I would recognize my own mother, wouldn't I.'

'Cool!' Reidun said. 'Some people are supposed to have seen Jesus Christ.'

Alphonse snapped his fingers twice. 'Let's go.'

That evening Kjell Bjarne got the car started. Suddenly we heard the heavy sound of an engine coming from Alphonse's back yard. Eight cylinders functioning with American precision. In my confusion I looked at Alphonse, who closed his eyes and smiled. Reidun came running in from the kitchen, a big question mark written all over her face.

We went to the window, all three of us. The shiny Buick stood in the yard with its engine running and blue exhaust belching out into the spring evening.

On the grass by the washing line, Kjell Bjarne was doing a handstand. He stood there for ages. He was as solid and constant as a rock.

# 12

For once, things turned out exactly as I thought they would. Maundy Thursday was sunny and warm and Kjell Bjarne, Reidun and I made our way to Alphonse's flat for ten o'clock, as agreed. Kjell Bjarne had a rucksack on his back and another on his front, and Reidun's two suitcases full of clothes and food in his hands. I carried the cat box with Pepper and Elmer. Alphonse was already busy putting his own luggage into the car. Two days earlier we had done a little test drive up to Maridal and everything had worked perfectly, except for a few problems with the radiator. I had no idea why you needed a radiator in a car, but I got the impression that it had to work, whatever the reason.

Kjell Bjarne insisted on wearing his overalls all

229

the time, just to be on the safe side, in case he needed to look under the bonnet on the way. Unnecessary, of course, but Alphonse and I backed him up, because we, as men, understood that this piece of clothing had something to do with Kjell Bjarne's new identity. Now he was the man who fixed things. Head of all things technical. He had his sleeves rolled halfway up his arms and had neglected to do up the top buttons, so that the black mat of hair on his chest came into its own. Reidun conceded to his outfit more or less immediately.

The only thing that did not live up to my dreams was that I was in the back seat with Reidun and the boys. I had envisaged myself in the front with Alphonse, with my right arm hanging lazily out the window, or resting against the roof panel. My old self would definitely have made a song and dance about this, but I had now developed a more generous ego and I took it all very well. Besides, there was definitely a grain of truth in Kjell Bjarne's argument that he, as the mechanic, had to be where it was all happening. And, strictly speaking, he had also earned himself this seat of honour, as it was his tireless efforts that had made this trip possible.

So I didn't sulk more than was absolutely necessary and took my seat in the back. And I can tell you, there was plenty of room there! Quite a ballroom in fact! Reidun and I could almost stretch out our legs and even with the cat box between us there was room for another three or four bottoms in there. Generous people, the Americans. Family-oriented. This car had been built for Father and Mother, some planned (or unplanned) children, Uncle Henry and Auntie Sally and nieces and nephews.

Alphonse started the engine and slipped gently into first gear, then we glided out through the gateway and into the street. On the far side of my sunglasses, the spring morning was bluey-green.

'Now we can leave it all behind!' said Alphonse. 'Now it's just us and the road!'

A couple of perfect lines, as far as I was concerned. Almost American. We all nodded and heartily agreed and Kjell Bjarne put on one of his Johnny Cash cassettes. We thundered out of Oslo to the sounds of 'Man in Black' and 'Folsom Prison'. It was all 'cooler than cool' as Kjell Bjarne said. Even before we had passed Sandvika, the E18 had become Route 66 and sequences of revolutionary poetry ran through my mind. We passed newly ploughed fields and I championed the farmers' cause. Then Drammen: the urban hell of the city where people lived and died in the shadow of factory chimneys and stinking bars. And then on in the direction of Vestfold, where poverty and misery had forced young boys to sail to Arctic waters in search of whales and good fortune. I thought about all the sailors during the war, being torpedoed in the Channel or sitting in nicotine-stained bars by the Liverpool docks feeling homesick. The prostitutes with a night's comfort to sell and their own tragedies throbbing between their moist thighs.

My poetry belonged to the people, ordinary men and women, small wretches who crawled around in chaos, people who had no prospects, but who had dreams and vision. The car journey provided me with endless inspiration. I grinned to myself at the thought of the notebook, made in China, that I had bought the day before. In the evening I would walk along the shore and jot down my notes, with the salty wind and the eternal complaint of the seagulls ringing in my ears. A Norwegian version of Lou Reed, in one of his sober phases.

Just outside Sande we were stopped by the police. Things couldn't have been better! I immediately felt very nervous, because in a way I was still somewhere in the Midwest and it usually means trouble when the police and the sheriff turn up. We were, of course, totally innocent, but everyone who has seen American films knows that being innocent is not always an advantage. Quite the opposite, in fact. The less guilty you are, the more the local psycho law enforcer torments you. He can't stand you to start with, because you didn't happen to have been born in the same sleepy, small town that he was. And in this case, there was a good chance of being done over as none of us had any connection with Sande. At least, not as far as I knew.

Yep! The man coming towards us was that sort of man, I could tell. Self-confident and swaggering in the slightly ridiculous uniform that the Norwegian Police Force had recently acquired. American baseball caps and broad reflector stripes around each trouser leg, so that it looked like they were wearing fishing boots, the whole lot of them. If I was not very much mistaken, he was the sort who had wet his trousers throughout his time in the Cubs and Scouts and therefore had chosen a profession where he could throw his hate around in all directions. If he could torment a poet with a couple of days in a padded cell, it would probably give him sexual satisfaction – and a lot of it. In this man's world, poems that didn't rhyme were crap and Picasso couldn't draw. I mentally prepared myself for being forced to stand with my legs apart and my hands on the car roof as he felt around my whole body with his rubber truncheon. I repeated my date of birth over and over in my head, in case he should ask. Civil status? Should I say . . . I couldn't really say cohabitant, could I?

'Hey ho,' Alphonse said. 'At least we weren't speeding.' He wound down the window.

There was some mention of registration papers and driver's licences. In a southern accent. Even though I was of course relieved that the man was not from Sande, I was also a bit disappointed. In a way it would have been quite stylish to be arrested here and now. Nerd poet arrested on E18! With a picture of me lying in the dust, my hands behind my head. If they found the poem in my left top pocket, there was a danger that I might be linked to the case of the sauerkraut packets. Two days earlier I had smuggled six packets back into two local supermarkets, so now it was just a case of waiting and hoping for the best. It was somewhat disappointing to find out that the policeman was obviously not the brutal type, but more of an enthusiast when it came to old American cars, because now I actually wanted to be caught. I felt a violent urge to confess, to put all my cards on the table and accept my punishment.

I would stand up for what I had done; it was all a stunt to show up modern consumer society, a friendly poke at the packaging industry and everything that passes as ready-made food. I sat there with a pounding heart, sweaty palms and the knowledge that the poem nestling in my pocket could secure my place in Norwegian literary history, if only this Southerner would order me out of the car and do a superficial body search. I wound the window down, stuck out my head and stared hard at him. Tried to look slightly drunk, so that he understood the potential seriousness of the situation. But no. The man just carried on talking enthusiastically with Alphonse about models and original car paint, and obviously couldn't even be bothered to check the brakes. Every now and then Kjell Bjarne joined in the conversation, so I felt completely left out. I didn't like this policeman. I realized that I had actually never liked grown men who talked enthusiastically with soft vowels, that there was something unmanly about the accents south of Kragerø, something soft, rather indistinct.

I thought that the guy probably had as much balls as a jellyfish. Lord only knows how he managed to end up in the police force at all. Maybe they had a special quota for 'softies' at the police academy, so they could tone down their aggressive image. Unnecessary, in my opinion, as long as the recruitment of female officers continued at the pace it was going. When I was a boy, there wasn't a policewoman to be seen anywhere. Now they were everywhere. And I have to confess that I did sometimes have very erotic fantasies about what it would be like to be handcuffed by a blonde bursting out of her uniform. But only in the days when police officers went round in sweet little uniform caps and light blue uniform shirts that tended to ride up in the struggle during an actual arrest. However, the one time that I had been arrested there had certainly been no room for eroticism. The two spotty youths from Toten or thereabouts hadn't even handcuffed me. It was simply a case of 'Come with us' and 'No more nonsense now!' And then straight to Brøynes.

Were they never going to finish? Obviously not. Out of the car clambered Alphonse and Kjell Bjarne and up went the bonnet. Kjell Bjarne gesticulated enthusiastically. The policeman nodded eagerly and was obviously hanging onto every word. Really, eight cylinders! Wow! This was not a rigorous inspection of anything, just a lot of boyish enthusiasm, to the point of negligence of duty. They were a micro-society, which I, as a back-seat passenger, was excluded from. I had often noticed this: the person sitting in the back seat was some-how not really there. The real conversation always happens in the front seats. As a back-seat passenger you are just carted around and thrown scraps from discussions about the roads, driving conditions, speed and oil pressure. As a back-seat passenger, you are a second-class traveller.

I thrust open the door and took my place in this masculine camaraderie. I pulled and wiggled a piece of something that was sticking out. The bobbit was loose, I exclaimed. Bobbit? Kjell Bjarne asked me to let go of the coil. I gave them a brief intro-duction to the slang from my part of town. It had never been anything other than bobbit where I grew up. Coil was for the snobs from the West End of Oslo. I instantly realized that I now lived in the west of Oslo myself, but no-one held it against me. They just asked me to let go. But I didn't want to. I insisted that we could not drive all the way to Nevlunghavn with a loose bobbit. I thanked the policeman for having pulled us over. There could have been a terrible accident. I had read in one of my general-science magazines about a man from Montana who had got a bobbit right in the face. Oil everywhere. One father-of-four less, and only because he had ignored the car mechanic's advice to tighten the bobbit as far as it would go.

Kjell Bjarne was starting to get angry now. I had bluffed my way into his domain and I think he realized that. He was about to take me by the ear and lead me back to the car. So I retreated a few steps and kicked the tyres to check the pressure. The policeman and Alphonse took a short walk over to the patrol car and then back. Kjell Bjarne and I were each given a pat on the shoulder by the law enforcer – there was no limit to his friendliness. It wouldn't have surprised me if he had given each of us our very own pen with 'Drammen Police' on the side. What had Alphonse told him? That Kjell Bjarne and I were men with a past? Had he mentioned Brøynes? Well, what did I care! I slammed the door with more force than necessary when I got into the back seat again and did not answer when spoken to until we had passed Sandefjord. On the outskirts of Larvik, the other three got out to have a hot dog. If that's what they want, I thought. And stayed in the car.

But I pulled myself together and repressed the urge to take a train back to Oslo. After my stay at Brøynes I had become a real expert at pulling myself together. I pulled myself together in shop queues, I pulled myself together when Kjell Bjarne dropped his smelly socks everywhere, and now I pulled myself together with my three friends. Whenever my stubborn side reared its head, I heard the echo of Gunn's voice, and tried to find something positive to focus on. Like now. When the others were standing by the kiosk, pretending that the sausages were delicious, I observed the first fly of spring as it paraded proudly past the car window. And blow me, if there wasn't a wagtail on the other side of the road, wagging its tail. I thought of the enormous distances it had travelled and all the dangers that this little life had faced in order to come here, right here, right now, to give me some pleasure. It had survived the Italian bird hunters. Likewise the sudden gusts of wind over Gibraltar. And now it was standing there, dipping its tail. A small grey, white and black globetrotter. Seeing the bird cheered me up and when the others came back, I surprised them with applause and an effusive welcome.

Alphonse Jørgensen's cabin was the cabin of dreams, straight from a holiday paradise. It had seen better days and it wasn't big either, but the location! It lay in a sheltered spot between two large rocks, and from the sitting-room window and the veranda you could look straight out to sea. The shore was only fifty metres away and the small paradise was encircled by bushes and windswept trees.

'It's so beautiful here!' Reidun said, as she rubbed her lower back and pushed out her belly.

'Not bad,' Alphonse said. 'As long as the tenants haven't used everything inside for firewood, we should have a good couple of days. We can borrow the neighbour's boat, if any of you want to go fishing. You should have good sea legs, Elling, if your grandparents came from Sandefjord.'

Kjell Bjarne chuckled to himself, as he lifted the luggage out of the car.

I looked at him sharply, but of course he avoided my eyes. What was he thinking? That I didn't have good sea legs, only because I'd lied to him about my time at sea? The truth was that I was very comfortable with boats. My grandfather had had a wooden fishing boat, which had kept us amused, summer after summer. Sometimes enormous waves pounded in down the fjord and crashed against the gunwale so that we got quite a shower. But the one who always felt safe and secure was me. Mother had a habit of screaming when things like that happened, but my grandfather and I stood firm in the face of the elements.

I assured Alphonse that we could no doubt catch enough fish for a meal or two, and added that it was probably best if Kjell Bjarne stayed in the kitchen. To my moderate irritation, Kjell Bjarne thought that was fine. He couldn't stand being on the water, he said. And as Kjell Bjarne couldn't stand being on the water, neither, obviously, could Reidun stand being on the water. Fair enough. And I thought to myself that they were beginning to behave more and more like an old married couple.

Alphonse clicked his fingers and pulled the cabin keys from his jacket pocket. We carried in the luggage in two goes.

'An open fire!' I was ecstatic!

'Yes, we'll put some pieces of wood on straight

away and get some warmth in here,' Alphonse replied.

'Where'm I going to sleep?' Kjell Bjarne asked. He was standing in the middle of the floor, with a suit-case in one hand and his sleeping bag in the other.

'The bedrooms are through there,' Alphonse said. 'Beside the kitchen. Choose whichever one you want, but it's maybe best that we men . . .'

'I want to sleep with Kjell Bjarne,' chipped in Reidun, then disappeared out again.

'As you wish,' Alphonse mumbled distractedly, as he scrunched up newspaper to put on the fire.

Kjell Bjarne stood like a statue in the middle of the floor. In fact, at this moment, I don't think his blood was even moving in his veins. I think he was brain-dead and his heart had stopped. We stared at each other. We stood there staring at each other without blinking, while Alphonse, unperturbed by this historical sequence of sentences, whistled away and lit the fire.

I don't remember precisely what I thought and felt at that moment. Everything was just chaos. Never in my wildest dreams – and at times they could certainly be wild – had I imagined the situation that now faced us. That Reidun Nordsletten would suggest, no, demand, to share a room and perhaps even a bed with Kjell Bjarne. Reidun's condition had in itself prevented me from thinking such depraved thoughts. She was due to give birth in only a matter of weeks! Surely she was not stupid enough to plan intercourse with Kjell Bjarne under such circumstances? Surely it was illegal, tantamount to child abuse? Was it actually physically advisable, let alone possible? Was I going to have to be present when Kjell Bjarne made his sexual debut, separated from him and Reidun by only a thin wooden wall? No, thank you! A thousand thanks, but I would rather spend the night on the outside toilet!

Kjell Bjarne shook himself out of his apathy and reeled off into the bedroom nearest the kitchen. I followed. I closed the door behind me and grabbed hold of him. 'You must realize that it's just not possible!' I hissed.

'Go into your room!' he said and shook himself free. 'You've got no business in here.'

'What you two are planning to do is sick!' I said. 'It's not natural.'

He smirked and I saw that his hands were shaking as he loosened the cords on his sleeping bag.

'You'll suffocate the baby!' I whispered. 'Do you want that? Do you want to become a killer for the sake of some perverse sex?'

'Bugger off and catch yourself a couple of flounders,' he said and unrolled his sleeping bag on one of the beds. 'Let people get some privacy.'

'You are not going to do it!' I wagged my finger hysterically.

He looked at his watch and yawned. 'I'm knackered already, I am. Think I'll hit the sack early tonight, Elling.'

I was about to threaten to tell Frank when Reidun came in with the rest of the luggage and I had to withdraw. The fire was crackling and Alphonse and I unpacked in the other room. Through the wall we could hear Reidun Nordsletten giggling.

Afterwards I went for a long walk along the shore, without managing to cobble together so much as a single usable line. The hard-hitting lines that had come to me on the drive down here had been wiped from my memory and the only thing that was fixed in my mind was a picture of Kjell Bjarne's and Reidun's naked bodies. And I felt guilty, as it was I who had more or less brought them together. I had cunningly steered Kjell Bjarne into Reidun's arms and now I had to face the consequences, the fatal consequences. I had not considered that Kjell Bjarne's pent-up sexual frustration might make him both blind and mad. Nor had I realized that Reidun Nordsletten was open to sexual deviancy.

When I returned, rather wet after a sudden downpour, dinner was ready on the table. Sausages and mashed potato, real holiday food. We talked about this and that and pretended that nothing was afoot, but, with the possible exception of Alphonse Jørgensen, we were all thinking about the same thing, all of us. About the night that would shortly be upon us and about what would happen then. I searched for signs of remorse on Reidun's face, but she was in fine fettle, slightly manic, in fact. She joked and laughed and told funny anecdotes from her cleaning job at the hospital. Alphonse snapped his fingers and roared with laughter when she told us about Freddy from Togo, who, after only four months in Norway, had become an expert in a certain Norwegian folk-dance step that involved kicking a hat from a beam. He had used a cake tin on the end of a broom handle to practise.

And obviously Kjell Bjarne laughed as well; he just behaved like a lapdog, sending me vigilant looks all the time. Personally I didn't see any reason to be amused by a folk-dancing black man who damaged the kitchen equipment at one of Norway's largest hospitals. I kept a rather stern face, let me put it that way. And each time Kjell Bjarne glanced over at me, I most certainly looked him straight in the eye. I did not budge an inch. If he wanted to participate in an indecent act, there was nothing I could do about it. I was quite simply powerless, as was so often the case. However, I did want him to know exactly where I stood on the matter. If the child was stillborn or had a club foot, there would not be much comfort to be had from my quarters. Quite the opposite, in fact.

It was a strange evening. The fire blazed and we played Monopoly and drank Coca-Cola. Kjell Bjarne bought and sold as if there was no tomorrow and went 'straight to jail' with a smile. He was losing spectacularly, without any threatening remarks whatsoever, something I had not experienced before.

I calmed down after a while. I came to the conclusion that Reidun would not be so stupid as to let
him have his way during the night. She had
certainly shown herself to be irresponsible from
time to time, and she smoked like a chimney despite
being pregnant, but she could not be completely
devoid of maternal instinct. After all, she had
chosen to have the child, even though there
had apparently been plenty of good advice from the
child welfare office. It was another matter altogether
whether she knew what she was doing, inviting
Kjell Bjarne into her room. To be sure, he was as
kind as kind could be, but he was a man, after all.
And a starved man, at that. And on top of that came
the pitiful fact that his sex drive was already
abnormal. For example, I was as good as un-
interested in sex, compared with Kjell Bjarne. And I
was, when it came down to it, quite interested in
sex.

Alphonse snapped his fingers and built a hotel in
Park Lane. Kjell Bjarne, recently released from
prison, threw a perfect five, went straight to the
dogs and was unquestionably out of the game.
Reidun, who was doing quite well by now, offered
to lend him money, but then I put my foot down and
got Alphonse on my side. Rules were rules, full
stop! Kjell Bjarne wandered out into the kitchen to
eat some of the leftovers, eagerly followed by
Pepper and Elmer.

By about ten o'clock, Kjell Bjarne had polished off

what remained of the sausages and mash and had progressed to bread and cheese. I knew that it was sheer nervousness that was driving him to eat now. He flitted around in the cabin, restlessly, while we three allowed ourselves to be hypnotized by the shining embers. Well, I thought to myself, with a secret smile. Now we'll see what you're made of, you horny old goat! Let's see how much of a man you are when it comes to the crunch. It's easy enough to show off when it's daylight, but when night falls it might prove to be a different story.

At half past ten, Reidun yawned so hard that she looked like her jaw might split. Shortly afterwards she got up and went out into the kitchen, 'to get ready', as she put it. She wanted to go to bed now.

'Sit yourself down,' I said to Kjell Bjarne, as I fished out a cigar. 'You'll wear out your socks.'

He did as I said and sat down on the chair where Reidun had been sitting and started to leaf aimlessly through a magazine from 1968. Crown Prince Harald had just got engaged to Sonja Haraldsen.

'You must be exhausted,' I said. 'You were already falling asleep when we got here.'

Alphonse's face was in the shadows, but I caught a twitch at the corner of his mouth.

'Woken up again,' said Kjell Bjarne, defiantly.

'You could take a couple of magazines in with you,' I said. 'In case you can't sleep.'

He didn't answer.

'Or did you bring the Easter edition of Men Only with you?'

Alphonse was chuckling now, but quietly.

Kjell Bjarne put down the magazine. Carefully, right on the edge of the table. Suddenly, his face was three years old. He looked helplessly at Alphonse and me. 'I don't want to hurt anyone!'

'Of course not,' said Alphonse. 'And nobody thinks you do.'

Kjell Bjarne looked down at his clenched fists, and it seemed as if he was debating whether to rub his temples or not, but then he relaxed. 'Elling does,' he whispered.

'What nonsense!' said Alphonse.

I blushed furiously and was glad of the reddish glow from the fire. 'Not on purpose,' I whispered forcefully. 'But you can't . . . They can't . . . Reidun's due soon!' I shot a glance at the kitchen door and heard water splashing on the other side. 'Kjell Bjarne weighs a hundred and thirty kilos!'

The cat was out of the bag now. We were at the crux of the matter. In a way I was relieved, because now I wouldn't have to deal with it alone.

'I think that you and I should mind our own business,' Alphonse said. 'There are plenty of ways for a man and a woman to enjoy themselves.'

Oh?

'How?' said Kjell Bjarne.

Alphonse brushed it off. He seemed to find the whole thing a bit embarrassing, which it was really.

A bit, at least. 'Relax, Kjell Bjarne,' he finished. 'Reidun is a wonderful woman. That's all you need to know. The rest will come naturally.'

I couldn't help but laugh! Yes, I howled with laughter. 'The rest will come naturally!' I choked. 'You expect me to believe that!' I fell to my knees and rested my forehead on the tabletop and then collapsed in a heap.

'Idiot!' Alphonse said, but he didn't sound that severe. Fortunately, Kjell Bjarne did not pick up on it.

'I'm going for a walk,' I said and got up. The laughter was still vibrating in my stomach muscles, but I simply could not bear to be there when Kjell Bjarne was initiated into the world of sex by a woman. It was just too intimate for me; too obvious to see him going into the bedroom and closing the door behind him. It would be enough to have to spend the whole night awake with Alphonse, on the other side of the thin, thin wall. I knew myself well enough to know what sort of insidious fantasies were now lying in wait. I rushed out. It had stopped raining and the night air was chilly and salty.

About halfway down to the shore I noticed that someone was following me. For a moment I was gripped by an icy fear, as I imagined a local delinquent, the sort that could not stand people from Oslo, there were plenty of them, I knew. But when I spun around suddenly, I saw only the huge outline of Kjell Bjarne behind me on the path. He was standing completely still, staring at me.

'What is it now?' I asked.

'Nothing.'

'Well, go to bed then.' I carried on down to the shore, where the waves embroidered a white border on the sand and stones. What a lovely thought, the waves embroidering a white border. A beautiful image that could be woven into a poem. If only I could be left in peace now, new lines would come by themselves. I could feel it.

But no! Kjell Bjarne stuck by me. Like a hundred-and-thirty-kilo horsefly. Eventually I got a bit irritated. I sat down on a weatherworn stone and told him what I thought: I could understand that he was nervous, but I could give him no reassurance. I reminded him of the horrible fact that Gunn had revealed, that is, that all my stories about women were pure and utter fantasy. Lies. I was as much a virgin as he was. Absolutely untouched. I had no advice to give him. All I had to offer was crossed fingers and my sincere wishes for his happiness. From the bottom of my heart I wished him and Reidun a synchronized orgasm. But how they were going to achieve it, that was their business.

He towered above me in the dark.

'When did you change your underpants last, Elling?'

Excuse me! When did I last change my underpants? What on earth did that have to do with it?

'Two, three days ago?'

'I changed them this morning!' I replied, indignantly. 'As I always do!'

'Can I borrow them?'

Naturally, I was speechless at first. I had never experienced anything like it in my life. But at the same time I wasn't so slow that I didn't quickly twig what the root of the problem was. That Kjell Bjarne was a slob I already knew.

'And you?' I asked, forcing a degree of innocence, certainly not my natural style, into the question. 'When did you last put on clean underpants?'

'Not sure.'

'Easy to lose track of the weeks,' I quipped.

'Be nice!'

'I am nice,' I retorted. 'On principle! But that's not the issue here.'

'What is then?'

'The fact that you're a pig,' I said. 'That's what the issue is!'

'I wasn't to know that Reidun . . . That she would . . .'

'No,' I said. 'I admit that such a development did seem unlikely. But couldn't you have made an effort all the same?'

'Go on, Elling. Just for a couple of days.'

'You mean that you don't even have a change or two in your bag?'

'I said I didn't know this was going to happen!' he said, unhappily. 'I thought I'd be sharing a room with you!'

'Absolutely,' I said. 'And so there was no reason not to smell like a pig. And do you want to borrow my socks as well?'

Yes, please, if he could.

I gave up. Just resigned myself. He was a slob, but he was my friend. I thought to myself, my blood has mixed with his, so what's to stop him borrowing my underpants, as long as I don't have to wear his.

'But there's no point in putting on a nearly clean pair of pants, if you don't wash yourself first!' I informed him.

'Here?'

I pointed to a flat stone that lay some distance out in the water.

And while Kjell Bjarne knelt down to wash his organ in the salty water, I got undressed, quick as a flash, in the dark behind a bush. Kjell Bjarne's underpants were so far past their sell-by date that we agreed that the only thing to do was to bury them in the sand. No sooner said than done. Afterwards, he shook my hand in gratitude, as ordered, and then ran back to Romance. I continued to walk for a couple of hundred metres, but no poems came to me at this time. Not having any underpants on was disturbing, as if the cool night air was playing with my balls. And I would leave it up to others to write that kind of poetry.

When I got back, everyone had gone to bed. I moved through the cabin, all ears, but not a sound was to be heard, only the water and the wind. Was it really possible that the two lovebirds had achieved what they wanted so quickly? It seemed improbable. How long, on average, did intercourse between a man and a woman last? I had read something about it once in one of the Sunday papers, but now I suddenly couldn't remember anything about the article. And besides, it didn't really matter, as the kind of intercourse that was probably involved here was guaranteed to be anything but average. If something had happened, or was going to happen during the night, it would have to be seen as exceptional. Unparalleled. The most likely explanation was that my somewhat pessimistic prediction regarding the idea that things would come naturally had proved to be true. In which case, Kjell Bjarne was now sleeping like a baby, while Reidun lay listening in the dark, unsated and sticky. What had she been doing with him? I dispelled the horrible images from my mind and started to play Monopoly with myself.

I had just built a hotel on Euston Road when something happened. Reidun Nordsletten started to moan. At first, naturally I thought that Kjell Bjarne had induced an early birth. I mean, that was the worst possible scenario. The child would be born out here in the wilds. But then I heard her giggle between all the moans, and of course everything became clear. It was a case of heavy petting. I tried to imagine Kjell Bjarne as an accomplished lover, but it was totally impossible. The picture vanished before my imagination had even managed to evoke it. Did he still have my clean underpants on, or were they lying in a crumpled heap at the bottom of the bed? Had she peeled them off him with her small, deft fingers, so she could stimulate his briny-smelling organ with greater ease? Well. She laughed and moaned. There was certainly no oral sex going on here. All the same, I never wanted to see those underpants again. I certainly did not want to own them! Something had happened to them, they had found themselves in a situation that I, their rightful owner, had never even been close to.

If Kjell Bjarne were to return those underpants, I would reject them outright. I would quite simply tell him to go to hell. It was perhaps a bit petty on my part, I don't know, but suddenly I was completely obsessed with the thought that I never wanted to see those underpants again. Take them! Keep them! The idea of putting on a pair of underpants which Reidun Nordsletten's quivering fingers had slipped inside, was repellent to me. I flung the dice down hard and moved the yellow lorry, as if in a trance. I bought Mayfair. I bought the Electric Company. Stole a hundred-kroner note from the bank and paid the fine I had got because my dog had attacked the milkman.

Tears welled up in my eyes and things did not get any better when I heard that Kjell Bjarne had now also joined in the chorus of loud noises. He was making a sort of barking sound. 'Yuup, yuup.' Over and over again. Had they sunk to such depths that they had lain there, stimulating each other to fever pitch then waiting for the climax until they knew I was there? One thing was certain: they were going at it hammer and tongs now. What sort of a noise was that to make, anyway? 'Yuup'? Even the kittens, asleep on the rug in front of the fire, pricked up their ears. The yuups were coming thick and fast now, louder and louder – and then, just as I was about to put my hands on my ears and run for the door, the stillness of the night was shattered, as Kjell Bjarne roared: 'FUUUUUUUUCKING HELL!'

And then it was quiet. Almost complete silence. Only the sound of the wind and Alphonse's regular snoring. Not so much as a giggle. How was it possible for Alphonse to carry on sleeping undisturbed while those two nearly brought the house down in the next room? I could only imagine that he had taken strong sleeping pills. There was no other explanation. The cats looked at me anxiously.

Anger and indignation slipped away. And were replaced by sorrow. A deep sorrow. In a daze I moved round and round the Monopoly board, my thoughts flitting in every direction. A chapter of my life was over. I realized that after this, after Kjell Bjarne's roar, our relationship would be different from before. More complicated. Every time the conversation turned to women, that wild roar would lie between us and ruin the atmosphere. He had been somewhere that I hadn't been, even if it had only been a hand job. All the same. He would know that I knew and vice versa. After this, he would in fact have more in common with Frank.

In the time that I had shared a bedroom with him, I had got to know him as a quiet, discreet masturbator, the sort who does not plague others with their sexuality. Now it was yuup, yuup and fuuuucking hell. At full volume. Just meeting his eyes in the morning would be a bit of a trial, if I managed it at all. I could write off breakfast straight away, it would be too embarrassing for me to see them in action with their boiled eggs and marmalade.

But, I thought, life goes on. We are born alone and we die alone. And some of us go through life alone as well. I lay down on the floor and buried my face in the boys' warm fur coats. I tried to think about my poem, perhaps at this very moment being plucked out of a sauerkraut packet by a hungry carouser, but nothing seemed to matter any more. I was so psychologically exhausted that I fell asleep there and then. It may sound improbable, but that is actually what happened. The following morning I was found alive by a bright-eyed and bushy-tailed Alphonse Jørgensen.

A difficult day followed. I would put it as strongly as that. I was under the weather and stiff after having slept on the floor. Fortunately, the newly-weds slept long into the day, so the problem of breakfast was solved. But it was very odd. And sooner or later it would be time for lunch. Alphonse and I went for a long walk, to the farthest point on the Mølen promontory, and when we got back I knew that I would have to pull myself together and face reality. Meet the New Kjell Bjarne. There was no way I could suggest going for another walk now. My legs were tired and I was starving. The smell of fried pork wafted towards us from the kitchen window.

He was spread across the sofa! With a great big grin on his face! I had never seen such arrogance! Out in the kitchen I could hear Reidun singing a popular song while she fried and cooked. OK, I thought. They're following a well-trodden path and sticking to the traditional gender roles. I pretended to clean out my coat pockets and ignored his pathetic expression. I carried on doing what I had to do and looked the other way.

If he so much as attempted to tell me a single detail of what had happened, either now or later, I would break off all contact with him. I would not want to see him again. The most vulgar thing I could think of was men who bragged to their friends about their sexual prowess and told their women's secrets to the world. Utterly despicable, it was! Disgusting! I have always been of the opinion that anyone who is fortunate enough to enter a woman is, well, visiting and should behave accordingly. At the very least, you do not go around afterwards bragging about what you've experienced. Particularly when, like Kjell Bjarne, you have not really experienced much before. In fact, it was completely incomprehensible, and rather pathetic, that he was sitting there on the sofa with that stupid grin on his face. He hadn't even entered her! At least, I couldn't imagine that he had. Surely not!

During lunch he tried to keep the tone friendly. Chatted away about all sorts of nonsense as if nothing had happened. He wanted to know what it looked like out at Mølen. If the pork was tasty, etc. As far as I was concerned, if he wanted to know what it looked like at Mølen, he could go there himself. And that was that. I certainly saw no reason to reply. And if anyone at the table was to ask if the food tasted all right, it should be Reidun, who had prepared it, and she wisely kept her mouth shut. The pork was in fact a bit salty and the gravy . . . So what. Even though you know the lumps are just flour, it isn't exactly appetizing. I sat there, staring at her right hand. I couldn't help myself. It looked so pale and innocent as it held the fork. It was hardly possible to imagine that only a few hours ago that same hand had slipped under the elastic of my underpants, in search of Kjell Bjarne's penis. Not exactly an appealing thought. Had he told her that it was my underpants that she was pulling and clawing at? I hoped so. That is, I wouldn't have objected, as this loan could hardly be called anything other than utterly selfless.

Later on in the afternoon, Alphonse and I went out fishing. I was grateful for any excuse to get away from the two lovebirds. Kjell Bjarne kept looking at his watch, as if to reassure himself that time really was moving in the right direction, towards bedtime.

It was a mild, beautiful afternoon, sunny and still. The little boat had a ten-horse something or other, but Alphonse Jørgensen wanted to row. Which was fine by me. I sat at the back of the boat and philosophized about life while Alphonse rowed us out. I could never quite fathom why I was part of this strange drama. Light and shadow. Strange noises. People who came and went. Sometimes I was convinced that it was all utterly meaningless, with no point or purpose. At other times, like now, I humbly bowed my head. I could not see the pattern in the cloth, but felt a greater power, understood that I was part of a greater whole, something that went beyond me.

Kjell Bjarne's coupling had really put me to the test. It certainly had. But I had overcome it. I had a new experience to add to all the others. There was not a single person in the entire history of man who had experienced exactly what I had experienced that night. It had been painful, it's true, but I had emerged a stronger person. I could only hope that this experience would benefit me in another life, because I could not see what good it would do me in this one.

'You should sleep in the room with me tonight,'

Alphonse said. 'It's too cold to sleep on the floor.'

I shook my head and explained that I would rather sleep in the car. To sleep under the same roof as Reidun and Kjell Bjarne was impossible.

He studied me, with a strange look in his eyes, but said nothing more. In fact, he did not say much at all, which was all right by me. I didn't find it awkward in any way. We enjoyed the beautiful weather and each other's company, but we did not catch any fish and that annoyed me. All these anglers who claim that catching fish is secondary, that it's the trip and being outdoors that counts, they are just liars! If you go fishing, you want to catch fish! If the fish didn't matter, you might as well stay on the beach barbecuing sausages. I knew that under the boat, perhaps even directly under the boat, there were thousands of cod, coalfish, pollock and haddock, but no, the mussels that Alphonse Jørgensen and I had to offer them were not good enough. Just not good enough. After a quarter of an hour I pulled in my line and said that I wanted to go back. Despite the good weather, there was no point in sitting here making a fool of myself.

That evening, when it was time to go to bed, Alphonse gave me a little blue pill. At first I didn't want to take it. I had always been a cautious child. I had seen what drugs could do to people's lives.

'Just this once,' Alphonse said. 'And maybe tomorrow night.'

And so it was. I slept like a log and awoke at about

one o'clock the next day, heavy-headed but happy. I had been blissfully unaware of Kjell Bjarne's barking and noisy orgasms. If the biblical Easter pageant had lasted any longer so that good Christians had to take three- or four-week holidays, I would undoubtedly have become dependent on the small blue pills. But in the car on the way home, as I lorded it up in the front seat with Alphonse Jørgensen, I felt I was in full and absolute control. Behind us, Kjell Bjarne was asleep with his head in Reidun's lap. Exhausted by lack of sleep and unexpected joy.

# 13

Reidun Nordsletten was due on 4th June, and Kjell
Bjarne and I suddenly found ourselves caught in the
sweaty throes of something as mundane and absurd
as preparing for childbirth. Yes, we really did. We
were getting ready for the big day. As well as we
could. On pure impulse we went out and bought
tiny socks and yellow rompers the day our social
benefit came in. I think it was the male protective
instinct kicking in. Most evenings we tended to
ignore the television, preferring to sit and practise
various breathing techniques with each other.
'Push,' I would shout. And Kjell Bjarne pushed.
This nonsense had no real practical significance in
what was about to happen, but I think we wanted to
show each other our totally committed solidarity

with the woman upstairs. We sat in our flat breathing and pushing.

The relationship between Kjell Bjarne and Reidun had already entered a more serious phase when we returned from Nevlunghavn. The holiday was over, if I can put it like that. There was nothing to giggle or yelp about any longer. The way I understood it was that the foundations had been laid, and as the birth approached it became less and less important for them to grope each other's nether parts. Kjell Bjarne might stay upstairs until very late in the evening but he always came down to our bedroom when he was ready for bed. Worked up, of course, but with his dignity intact, I'll say that for him. And, fortunately, he didn't breathe a word about how he and Reidun organized their sex life. In a way this was naturally rather disappointing, but mostly it was a great relief for me not to be drawn into the details of the relationship between a man and a woman. I certainly had my own ideas about how they resolved the matter from a purely technical point of view, but it was liberating not to have your smuttiest fantasies confirmed.

Kjell Bjarne behaved more and more like the shining knight he had dreamt about, the evening he came to Reidun Nordsletten's rescue with my help and assistance. Now and then I was immensely proud of him, something which I did not omit to mention every time I had Frank on the phone. If he kept on the course he was steering now I imagined that there would be assisted employment waiting for him at some point in the future. And he truly deserved it. For myself, I was not interested in the acknowledgement that a job would bring; I was answering another call, but I understood Kjell Bjarne when, at difficult moments, he fantasized about having a job to go to.

Anxious as we both were by nature, we could not help feeling daunted by what was about to happen to Reidun. There were many long nights without much sleep. We both tried as well as we could to comfort each other, but there was no ignoring the fact that a very large baby was on its way. To stop us worrying, Reidun suggested we put the telephone in our bedroom in the evening. She promised on her honour that she would ring us the moment she went into labour so that we could spring into action. Kjell Bjarne had nailed up a piece of cardboard over his bed, on which he had written the telephone number of the taxi company in red felt pen. We were ready.

It started on the first of June. Three days early, in other words. It was eleven o'clock at night when the telephone rang. Kjell Bjarne and I were exhausted after talking to Frank about our lives all evening and we were just about to go to bed. We had had an argument as well, so the atmosphere wasn't great. We had talked ourselves into believing that it would be a boy and we ended up having a meaningless argument about names when we arrived home; as if it was up to us whether the little fellow would be called Glenn-Kenneth, or Trygve, after my father. It was probably our nerves playing tricks on us, and when I blurted out that the boy should be called El Bjarne so that both his Spanish father and the two uncles were represented, Kjell Bjarne was on the verge of laying me out flat on the carpet.

Then the telephone rang, as I said. We looked at each other. Nobody rings us at this time of night. Frank rings at eight o'clock, at the latest. Alphonse never rings after ten. Assuming it wasn't a wrong number, there was only one call it could be. Kjell Bjarne, who only a few seconds before had been menacing and loud-mouthed, immediately began hopping about, rubbing his temples and screwing up his eyes. I had to answer the phone.

And bingo! A remarkably calm Reidun Nordsletten informed us that the pains were frequent now and it was time to make our way to the hospital. I beg your pardon? If the pains were frequent now, that meant that they were not so frequent earlier in the evening! Throughout our pizza evening Kjell Bjarne had rung Reidun at regular intervals to find out if there was any news. We had also given her the number of Peppe's Pizza in case of any developments. She hadn't mentioned a word about any labour pains. When I, sick with worry, asked her if she had lost her marbles, she just laughed! She said we had plenty of time and she hadn't wanted to ruin our evening together with Frank.

Frank! I screamed at her that there was nothing in this world that could ruin an evening with this man since the evening was already spoiled, by definition, the moment he appeared. Frank? Did she imagine that we had gone out of our own free will to eat pizza with this wretched local council spy who interfered in everything we said and did? We were forced! We had no choice if we wanted to keep our flat and the few privileges that went with it. Frank? A miserable lefty who told other people what pizza they could have, and was even paid to do this by Oslo City Council!

'Elling!' she interrupted. 'Ring for a taxi and ask Kjell Bjarne to come upstairs. I have to pack a few things.'

Then she put the phone down.

I didn't know what to believe. The situation was out of control. Without thinking about what I was doing, I whacked Kjell Bjarne to bring him back into the land of the living. It worked. He stared at me in disbelief, rubbing his cheek where I had hit him.

'Get yourself up to your girlfriend's,' I screeched. Yes, I screeched. My voice went into falsetto and became even shriller. I had absolutely no control over this part of my body any longer. I could see a breech birth well under way, one floor up. I raced round the flat with the telephone in my hand. Taxi! A taxi right now. 'Get going!' I repeated as he was still hesitating. He stood where he was for a few seconds, hyperventilating, then he ran to the door.

Taxi! Taxi, taxi, taxi! I ran into the bedroom and tore down the piece of cardboard with the number of the taxi company on.

And was put into a queue! I threw the telephone receiver hard at the wardrobe. You could contact people on the other side of the globe in two seconds with the Internet, but you couldn't get through to Oslo City Taxis. A sudden urge to run amok came over me – to smash the telephone, to knock over the wardrobe, to jump all over the beds.

Thankfully, for all parties concerned, God, that capricious figure of authority, sent me inspiration before I let loose. 'Alphonse!' my brain sang. I punched in his number at a furious speed and, mercilessly, let it ring again and again until I had his voice on the phone. I explained the situation as concisely as I could. The birth had started. Complications looming. A matter of minutes to go and there wasn't a taxi to be had. They had said point-blank 'no' at the Oslo City Taxis switchboard. So he could imagine the rest! I made no secret of the fact that our friendship was at this moment being put to its ultimate and sternest test.

'All three of you go down to the street,' Alphonse said. 'I'll be there with the car in five minutes.'

Five minutes? Did he need five minutes to drive his car five hundred metres? I read him the riot act and told him in no uncertain terms what I thought about people who leave you in the lurch at the crucial moment. Was he going to have his evening meal first? Finish watching some lousy film on TV Norway? I was jeering at him now. The humanistic ideals he had so often talked about in such glowing terms were just a bluff, a thin veneer to cover over the sad fact that he was a miserable turncoat, a man totally devoid of his own opinions and backbone. He could take his damn car and go to hell in it.

'Elling!' he shouted. 'Now you do what I tell you. Go and get Reidun and Kjell Bjarne and be down on the street, all three of you.'

Then he put the phone down.

Fine. There was nothing else I could do. There was no other option; everything was riding on this one card. It wasn't a good card, but it was all I had.

Reidun thought we were being hysterical. The only reason I didn't emphatically put her in her place was because I knew all about the un-predictable nature of a woman's psyche. I had read that their menstruation made them emotionally unstable and I automatically assumed that child-birth would not be particularly stabilizing, either. To me it looked as if puerperal fever had set in.

She refused to be carried by Kjell Bjarne. However, Kjell Bjarne had regained his composure now and imposed his will. Without saying a word, he picked her up and carried her down the stairs like a little child. No dilly-dallying, in other words. I took care of her bag with the change of underwear and toiletries.

Alphonse was already in position. The car was parked on double yellow lines and halfway up the pavement; the driver was leaning against the bonnet, waiting. I immediately went for him. Was I right that it didn't take five minutes to come and pick us up, or not? We could take that up another time, he said, opening the door for Reidun.

'Yes, you can bet on it!' I shrieked.

'Take it easy, all of you,' Reidun said. 'There's plenty of time.'

'That's what I thought,' Alphonse said.

Oh, really. So that's what he thought, was it! Plenty of time or not – that wasn't what this issue was about. The point was that when I ring and say that it's a matter of urgency, then it is a matter of urgency. He has to take my word for it. Or he can put my friendship on the scrapheap. I took my seat at the front and slammed the door. Several times.

We drove through the city at a snail's pace. I had never seen so much dawdling and dithering around. Every time I saw an opportunity to overtake or I suggested a short cut Alphonse told me to shut up. Just like that. After a while Kjell Bjarne also got involved. On Alphonse's side! In other words, it was three against one, soon four. But resistance makes you stronger. I gave them an earful for not taking the situation seriously. Reidun I was willing to excuse, after all she wasn't in her right mind, but I took note of every single critical remark made by the two men. And stored every word in my heart.

When eventually we arrived, words failed me. There was no-one there! Not a soul. I had been there when Reidun informed the hospital of her arrival immediately before we left the flat, and naturally enough I had expected a show of health-service staff at the door. But no. Not so much as a stretcher in sight. Was this the Norwegian welfare state or were we out somewhere on the Mongolian steppes? As far as I could see we were caught at the centre of a hospital scandal, the kind we are used to reading about in the tabloids. The left leg becomes gangrenous and the right leg is amputated. A patient suffering from stomach ulcers is sent home with his stomach full of mislaid surgical instruments. And now this. A woman about to give birth is left to her own devices or at the mercy of casual acquaintances. Had it not been for the fact that Kjell Bjarne and I had found Reidun Nordsletten as drunk as a chimp on the stairs that time, the Minister for Health and Social Services might have had one, perhaps even two, lives on his conscience.

Corridors. Swing doors. The antiseptic atmosphere of a hospital. After the huge row in the car and my disappointment over the lack of a welcome, I slipped into a semi-unreal state. Voices were buzzing around me, but I didn't register a single word, just the melody of the language. As I walked I started to hum the melody to myself. I was indifferent, somehow. In retrospect, I understand that this reaction was an expression of relief. After all, we had managed to get to the hospital, and even though the consultant was conspicuous by his absence, surely someone would be at hand when Reidun Nordsletten's waters broke.

To cut an unpleasant story as short as possible, when the administrative formalities and the vacuous questions were over and done with, this awful battleaxe of a woman asked us to leave. Alphonse, Kjell Bjarne and I were shown the door. I was immediately a hundred per cent back on the ball and demanded my rights. I refused to move one millimetre and I pointed out that Reidun did not have any family. We were her friends and we did not intend to abandon her, even if personally I didn't think I had the stomach to be present at the actual birth. The woman insisted that there wouldn't be much point sitting around in the corridor and tried to sell us the line about it being a long time 'before things actually got going'. What rubbish! When the pains start coming with ever shorter intervals, it's a sign that the birth is on its way. And that was precisely the situation with Reidun Nordsletten. I said this to the ignoramus in white. She couldn't fob us off with some cheap bluff. I knew my rights!

We were outside in no time. I was disappointed that it was Kjell Bjarne of all people who dragged me away when I had been basically defending his position. After all, he had taken the place of the Spanish father. He should have been taking active responsibility instead of standing around like a spare part and staying shtum. But that was typical Kjell Bjarne. He let himself be pushed about. And, of course, Alphonse was obediently waggling his tail to authority as well. How this man was capable of writing poems that had stirred the emotions of students in the Seventies was a mystery to me. It was an even greater mystery than why he had stopped writing poetry.

Well, fine. The battle was lost, but at least Reidun was at the hospital. With some reservations, I agreed to go back home in the car with the others. It would be a long night; we would have to conserve our energy. I saw, however, no reason to make any comment when Alphonse started to joke about my honest endeavours. I have a generous capacity for self-irony, but somewhere there is a limit, even for me. On the other hand, I was extremely relieved that he obviously wasn't angry with me. I would be distant with him for a while, but in my heart of hearts I liked the thought that our friendship could stand the odd storm. Kjell Bjarne sat at the back and kept his mouth shut.

Alphonse drove on to his flat. It was after twelve, when all was said and done, and he was an old man. Kjell Barne and I sat up without quite knowing what to say or do. The telephone lay on the table between us; some matron or other had passed us a piece of paper with the appropriate telephone number on. But when could we ring? And how often?

Something in her tone had told me that she didn't want to hear from us at all, that they saw us as two troublemakers who hadn't even impregnated the woman they delivered. Had it been daytime we could have consulted Frank, but he would be furious if we disturbed him at this time of night.

Our nerves slowly began to frazzle. I saw the most terrible scenes before me, such as Reidun Nordsletten bursting open. Splitting open with a cra-a-ack. I saw the child come out, strangled by its own umbilical cord, with a humpback and two club feet. What if it were Siamese twins? To be a Siamese twin had always seemed something of a nightmare to me. Not to be able to go to the toilet on your own! The risk that your own brother might drink you senseless! I didn't wish our little boy a fate such as that. Yes, I had begun to think of him as ours now. A new member of the exclusive tribe we had established during our trip to Nevlunghavn. The sparks could fly when the different personalities in the group clashed, but we all pulled together when it mattered. As indeed it did now. It really mattered.

'Let's go out,' Kjell Bjarne said suddenly.

'Out? Now?' I had never gone out on the town at this time of night in my life. It was half past twelve. On the other hand, we would have to stay awake until this was over. We had each been given a telephone card by Frank, so we would be able to ring the hospital from a telephone kiosk. There was no fear of random violence since Kjell Bjarne was with me. There are very few people who are so blind that they would attack a man who looked like an orangutan. Perhaps Kjell Bjarne's idea was not so bad. As the situation was now, our cosy home was simply an unbearable place to be. Thinking about all the things that could go wrong only nourished worse thoughts when we had nothing else to look at except each other and the stupid telephone on the table.

It was a wonderful warm summer's night. First of all, we strolled a little in Frogner Park and tried to strike up a conversation, alighting on one inconsequential topic after the other. Without much luck, I have to say. And soon we were back in the same devastating rut of child deformity and death. Reidun was abnormally large, Kjell Bjarne thought. And that was right. I could hardly imagine that a tiny Spaniard was on the way. On the other hand, if the baby had water on the brain, it would need plenty of room!

It just became worse and worse. We wound each other up. If we had not been outside in the open air, our mental state would have slumped back to zero, that is, where it was when we first moved to Oslo.

In the end I realized some action was called for and I hit upon an extremely unorthodox idea. I invited Kjell Bjarne to a glass of wine.

At first, naturally, he thought that I had gone mad. We were both as good as completely abstinent. We didn't drink and that was all there was to it. The strongest drink I had ever seen Kjell Bjarne have was half a bottle of low-alcohol beer. For my part, I had a little more experience; after all I had been on a package holiday to the Mediterranean with Mother and on that occasion I had sampled a glass or two of the local wine. It was a question of culture, rather than binge drinking and vomiting. Kjell Bjarne and I were both revolted by binge drinking and vomit, that's why we were so good for each other. It had struck me in Spain, however, that the little drop of wine I drank had a calming effect. Yes, it had simply cooled me down. I explained this to Kjell Bjarne.

'It's the exception that proves the rule,' I said.

'Oh yeah,' he said. He still wasn't very taken with my idea.

'We never drink alcohol,' I said. 'So we can allow ourselves a glass today.'

He didn't follow the logic of that. Basically, I didn't either, but I tried to explain to him that we were in a very special situation. Our nerves were very much on edge, quite understandably.

'And it helps to drink? Are you off your chump or what? When my mother drinks she becomes totally hysterical.'

'That's because she drinks every day,' I elucidated.

'OK then, but just one glass. And if it doesn't help I'll be hacked off.'

We found a little café not far from the Palace. As usual, it cost us quite some mental effort to go in, but we were two men and we had acquired the art of geeing each other up. Before we knew it, we were sitting at a marble table in the corner. Kjell Bjarne was staring around with large eyes while I was developing an introverted, world-weary look. I had noticed that many of the people in the audience at Nordraak Café had looked rather world-weary and, basically, I liked this look. Sometimes I practised precisely this expression while tinkering with my beard to give it the three-day-growth look. The difficulty was trying to appear slightly morose while sending out the signal that you had nevertheless accepted that you were part of what was going on around you. You had read everything, heard everything and seen everything – but so what. You might postpone committing suicide for a month, though you had some reservations. In the meantime you would kill time drinking a glass of wine, smoking a mild cigar, preferably in a café in the middle of the night. You didn't expect any miracles and you did not wish to be saved.

'Funny place,' Kjell Bjarne said.

Yes, indeed it was. I am almost positive the art on the walls was original and all the various potted plants were a hundred per cent genuine. The clientele were like me – intellectuals. Artists and writers, I assumed. I felt at home.

The waiter came mincing up. Yes, really! Clippety clop, clippety clop. Shaved head, black T-shirt and tight leather trousers.

'What's it to be, boys?' He smiled at Kjell Bjarne and me as he took out a small notepad from his mini apron.

I asked for two glasses of their finest red wine and explained that we were celebrating. I didn't want him to think that we pushed the boat out every day.

'A Bordeaux perhaps?'

Yes, absolutely! That was exactly the one we wanted! Two glasses of Bordeaux.

He scuttled back to the counter. Kjell Bjarne leaned over towards me. 'D'you think he's a poof?'

'Yes,' I said. 'I'm sure he is.' And so that Kjell Bjarne shouldn't get any stupid ideas I whispered to him that it was very common to find homosexual waiters working at the slightly better places. The best thing to do was to behave as normal. Only out and out bumpkins on a rare visit to town made a fuss about it. 'Don't forget that it's absolutely natural,' I concluded. The psychologist at Brøynes had told us that.

'Bloody isn't!' Kjell Bjarne said. 'Because then, then there wouldn't be any kids! We'd have snuffed it!'

'Perhaps that would be for the best,' I joked. 'Then there would be some peace and quiet in the world.' The last thing I wanted to do was to discuss this topic with him now, because I could see the waiter coming towards us with the wine. I pointed to the telephone by the stairs leading down to the toilets. 'Talking about children – ring the hospital!'

'Can't you do it?'

'No,' I said. 'It's excellent training. Anyway, you're the boyfriend, not me.' And I added, 'Or am I mistaken there?'

He stood up with a snort.

The wine was superb. Almost exquisite I would say. A bit sharp, but never mind, I knew that it was supposed to be like that. I took a large sip and pulled out a cigar. I kept my eye on Kjell Bjarne. He was gawping at the waiter while waiting to be put through. Afterwards, when he was connected, he turned his back on the café and held his hand over his left ear.

On his return he was shaking. 'They said it's started.'

'Started?' I said. 'It started several hours ago. That was why we went to the hospital!'

'Started properly,' he said, throwing the whole of his wine down in one gulp. He dried his mouth with the back of his hand and frowned. 'They said I should phone again in an hour.'

My nervousness had eased a little since coming to the café, but it soon flared up again. Didn't they say in the hospital that this could take quite some time? And now, just a couple of hours later, it was in full swing! She must have fallen on the bathroom floor. I couldn't imagine any other reason. The mere thought of it made me feel sick. However, I was glad they hadn't told Kjell Bjarne anything about it – he couldn't have handled that kind of information. I felt that instinctively when I saw how out of it he was.

'Like shit it helped!' he said menacingly, looking round for the waiter.

'Now just calm down!' I reproved. 'This is wine, not juice and water. And besides, alcohol doesn't work immediately.'

'I want another glass!'

'Only if you drink it very slowly,' I said. 'You don't want to get drunk, do you? If you get drunk, I'll call Frank, even if it's the middle of the night! Then it'll be quick march, back to Brøynes, and who knows who you'll be sharing a room with. You might not be as lucky as last time.'

'You're not in charge of me! And you've almost finished your glass, too!'

Yes, indeed! I must have been sipping away while Kjell Bjarne was phoning.

'I just mean that we should be careful,' I said. 'Neither of us is used to alcohol. You said yourself you only wanted one glass.'

'I wanted a proper glass,' he grumbled, playing with its stem. Basically he was right, they had given us two miserable little wine glasses, just egg cups really. They weren't full, either. I made an elegant waving gesture with two raised fingers and attracted the attention of the waiter. It cheered me up that I could make contact with the house management in such a playful way. I raised two fingers and he nodded and understood. Words were superfluous between us. He knew what the two guys in the corner were drinking, and now they were thirsty again. I decided to come here more often. I wasn't frightened of a homosexual or two, and the atmosphere of the place appealed to me. I was filled with a warm feeling of peace. I belonged here.

When I was well on my way down to the bottom of the second glass I began to understand what Alphonse had meant. I won't say that I regretted the wigging I gave him, but now that I had a little distance I could see that my commitment could have been interpreted by others as hysteria. It wasn't his fault that he didn't see the nuances. After all, he was an old boy. I took the matter up with Kjell Bjarne and he was in total agreement with me. He said he had been so nervous that he had simply let me take charge. He even shook my hand and thanked me.

'Forget it,' I said. Then I explained to him how wonderful it was that we humans were so different. I expatiated on the diversity of nature. He listened and nodded. He even added that no two snowflakes were identical. It was something I would never have expected of him, to be quite honest. He had grasped my meaning, even though what he said was beside the point, of course. Naturally, I had been thinking most about living organisms, and I clarified this. But he was emboldened now, and said that snowflakes were also part of nature – which I had to concede. Yet you could only really talk about different individuals in the animal and plant kingdoms, and that was why I was being a bit pedantic. Nothing he should take amiss. I just didn't want an argument. He laughed heartily at this. He didn't take it amiss at all, and he didn't like arguing either. He only argued when he was frightened, he maintained, and at the moment he felt almost secure. He was so grateful to me for suggesting a glass of wine. I was absolutely right.

He wanted to shake my hand again, but I said that it wasn't necessary for such close friends as we were to keep shaking hands all the time. It would be enough if we only did it when he thought I had really done something outstanding. I just had, he said, and shook my hand again. He had been like a cat on hot bricks all evening, but now he was almost completely relaxed.

We drank a toast to the new arrival and to the world's most wonderful woman. Our glasses were empty and before I knew what I was doing I had waved two fingers in the air again. My arm described a perfect arc in the air, and I revelled in the sight of the waiter taking my order and getting the bottle of wine and glasses ready. It was a wonderful feeling just to sit there giving orders instead of taking them from others. I had taken enough orders. Now it was my turn. My blood was racing.

When the wine arrived I couldn't prevent myself from winking at the waiter. Looking back on this now, I have to say that it was lucky I was wearing sunglasses, but at that precise moment it felt right. I had such a strong desire to demonstrate to him that I had no objections to his sexual orientation. I sincerely wanted him to feel as comfortable as I did because now I was absolutely at my ease.

Kjell Bjarne went for a pee. I used the opportunity to wave to my new homosexual friend. He totally misunderstood and brought two more glasses, but I wasn't bothered. I explained to him that if Kjell Bjarne seemed a little high or edgy it was because his girlfriend was having a baby at this very moment. Within half an hour he might well be a father. Yes, I used the word 'father', because it seemed so natural. Anyway, it was a lot easier to say that than to go into all the ins and outs of the relationship.

'Well, aren't you the lucky ones!' the waiter said, rolling his eyes. 'Tell me when you have some news and it'll be champers on the house all round!'

One thing was for sure: we were among friends here. I had spoken so loudly and clearly that the next table raised their glasses in a toast when Kjell Bjarne returned from the toilet. We raised our glasses in return; we were having the evening of our lives. It suddenly seemed to me that I had never felt so good in all my life. Champers on the house! I told Kjell Bjarne and he was so moved that he had to bring out his handkerchief.

'What's champers, Elling?'

'Haven't a clue,' I said. 'Makes no difference. The main thing is these people want to make a fuss of us.'

Ten minutes later he was back on the phone. He was more confident now, I could see that. He punched in the number with authority.

Then something strange happened. A hush descended over all the tables around us. Most faces were turned towards Kjell Bjarne, who for some reason was gesticulating with his left hand while holding the telephone with his right. The homosexual was standing with crossed arms and a burning cigarette hanging from the corner of his mouth. Deep in concentration.

Kjell Bjarne put the phone down slowly. And when he turned around he just stood there, smiling and crying at the same time. I had never seen anything like it and so I started smiling and crying too.

'Come on then, say something, man!' someone shouted.

Kjell Bjarne took a run at it and then roared: 'IT'S A BLOODY HUGE GIRL!'

A salvo of applause! People were yelling and screaming, and then, there was Kjell Bjarne, walking on his hands in the middle of the room. Pandemonium broke out. People were standing on chairs, clapping and egging Kjell Bjarne on as he lumbered around; he looked a bit like a bear I had once seen in the circus with Mother. Thinking about Mother in the middle of all this joy made me sad. I cried and cried. I would have loved her to see this.

Kjell Bjarne let himself back down onto his legs and staggered back to the table. His face was flushed and his tears had run into his sparse hairline. He looked funny. The waiter ran over with two large green bottles and a tray of tall glasses; the cork flew up into the ceiling. Soon we were in the middle of a storm of well-wishers, a hurricane of friendliness and bubbly drinks. People we had never seen before warmly congratulated us. We were soaked in sweat, we were hot and we drank the ice-cold champagne to cool us down. 'This is a good drink!' Kjell Bjarne kept yelling. We welcomed the child to the world with a toast. We drank to her mother and we drank to Kjell Bjarne. We drank a toast to Gro Harlem Brundtland and to the King. In that order.

After a while I began to feel a little dizzy. Not a lot, just enough to notice it. I registered it, so to speak. I also noticed that Kjell Bjarne was beginning to leave out important words in his sentences and that his eyes were bulging. Of course I knew what was happening, but it seemed so natural to go with the flow of wine, life and all the friendly people. Brothers and sisters of all ages. I told myself there was a big difference between being a little merry and drunk. Yet we had to go, and I informed Kjell Bjarne. After all, there was something waiting for us, or rather someone. Or perhaps he wanted to wait until tomorrow to see mother and child? Of course he didn't. He wanted to make a beeline for the door, but I held him back. I am not the kind of person who leaves others holding the bill.

I stood up to go to the bar where my friend was pouring beer. I'd never known anything like it. The room was turning! It made me laugh. Pictures were dancing on the walls. I tried to count out my money and got into a complete mess. In the end I put all my notes on the bar and asked him to take the money he needed. At the same time I thanked him for a nice evening and invited him to come to our flat the following evening. We were broad-minded people after all; we didn't harass people who stuck their fists up each other's arseholes. We accepted every-thing. Absolutely everything!

'I'll get a taxi for you, my friend. I think that would be well advised this evening.'

A brilliant idea. I agreed on the spot and ten minutes later we were actually being accompanied to the car. Kjell Bjarne couldn't stop laughing. I don't know why. Someone must have said some-thing funny to him as he left.

However, there wasn't much to laugh at when we arrived at the hospital. The taxi driver's erratic driving had left me feeling slightly nauseous and when, on top of that, he started wrangling about the price, I put him in his place. He came up with the cheap con trick about how I had confused the clock on the dashboard with the fare meter, but I didn't fall for it. He obviously noticed that we'd had a couple of drinks and thought it was worth a try. I told him that he could save that kind of trick for bumpkins and fishermen, but it wouldn't work on city folk like Kjell Bjarne and me. Did he fancy a punch-up right there and then? I nudged Kjell Bjarne in case things turned nasty, but he was talking to himself about Brøynes and women. When the driver came and hauled me out of the cab, I therefore decided to pay up anyway. And I gave him a generous tip so that he didn't actually realize his threat of ringing the police. I took all the notes and coins I had on me and threw them in his face. I didn't want to serve Mammon, it was too childish. I had my own life to lead.

What happened after that I don't remember, because the next minute Kjell Bjarne and I were standing outside the hospital hammering on the door. We wanted to see the child! Kjell Bjarne had brought half a bush with him since the flower shops were still closed. Rosehip, as it turned out, and he was bleeding like a stuck pig, but he kept his composure. It was the hospital, after all.

I have no idea how we made it home. I will probably never find out, either. A large piece of one night in my life was torn out of my consciousness. And Kjell Bjarne can't help me solve the mystery either, because he can't even remember leaving the café.

It was like waking up in a nightmare. I lay diagonally across Kjell Bjarne's bed, bathed in my own vomit. My eyes were glued together with the stinking contents of my own stomach. When I finally managed to open them so that I could take in the full misery, I saw Elmer sitting on a chair watching me in wonder. I was sicker than I had ever been before. My head was hammering, it was on fire, and my stomach started churning the minute I got onto my feet. I spewed up green bile into Kjell Bjarne's trainers, I couldn't help myself. But the worst was the fear. The awful fear. I was frightened of everything. Mostly I was frightened that, since I had woken up in his bed, I had killed Kjell Bjarne. When I found him asleep with his arms around the toilet bowl, all sorts of other fears emerged. Did we beat up the taxi driver? Where was our money? I could find only one 50 kroner note crumpled up into a knot in my sticky pocket. But worst of all, what did we get up to at the hospital? I didn't have an inkling. That is, I did; I had several inklings and they were all frightening.

I took my clothes off and forced myself into the shower. I spewed up and showered, spewed up and showered. Kjell Bjarne was beyond earthly contact. He had clearly been trying to undress when consciousness had departed. His shirt hung around his neck and the buttons were scattered around the floor. He was using his blood-encrusted right hand as a kind of pillow. In the sink there was a grey suit jacket that didn't belong to either of us. Did we go on somewhere else after leaving the hospital? Well, yes. Why not? If we had been capable of getting home under our own steam then we were probably also capable of all sorts of other things, too. I shuddered at the thought of what we might have done. How was it possible for the warmth and pleasure, and the intense sense of belonging we had felt over the glasses of wine to develop into such a smarting defeat as this? How deceptive alcohol was!

Now everything was ruined. I knew that. It was sad, but it was a fact. Oslo City Council had given us a chance, and we had abused it. If I hadn't felt as frail as I did, I would already have begun to pack. In my mind's eye I could see how sad Gunn would be when Kjell Bjarne and I returned to Brøynes, each with an alcohol problem. And she had put such trust in us. Most of all I felt like crying, but I simply didn't have the energy. Instead I changed into clean underclothes and rang Frank.

I told him everything. I told him that the evening's drinking had undone us and it would be impossible for us ever to show our faces in public again. We had no idea what we had been doing for a large part of the night; I, at least, had a total blank. I told him that Kjell Bjarne was lying unconscious in the toilet and that in all probability he had stolen a grey suit jacket. I had literally thrown away all our social benefit money into a taxi driver's face. As taxi drivers stick together like glue, there would be no chance of me ever feeling safe anywhere, except perhaps in Brøynes. What did he have to say?

Nothing. He laughed! He roared with laughter and

said that it served us right. I wanted to know when we would be taken back to Brøynes, but he wouldn't even hear of it. Brøynes was for screwballs, he said, and then he maintained that what we had done was basically very normal – at least at the beginning. And what exactly did he mean by that, might I ask?

'For Christ's sake, Elling. You were out celebrating the birth and then things got a little out of hand. Take an aspirin and go to bed. Are mother and child OK?'

'How should I know?' I answered. 'I can't even remember if we talked to anyone in the hospital. It's absolutely awful. I've never experienced anything like it. Imagine if I had tried to rape someone!'

'I don't think you need to worry on that score, Elling.'

Eh? What was that supposed to mean?

'Never mind. Clear up the vomit and try to shake a bit of life into Kjell Bjarne. And one more thing. Go out and buy a litre of milk to help you get over it.'

Milk? Was he mad? Just the sound of the word made me feel like throwing up.

'I'll drop by tonight,' he added. 'I'll check the sell-by date. I don't want you bloody hibernating in the flat just because you were naughty boys on a piss-up.'

'I'll never manage it,' I said, and it was true. The thought of all the people out there scared the pants off me. I would throw up waiting in the queue at the checkout. I would fill my pants.

'I hereby prescribe a large glass of milk,' Frank persisted relentlessly and put the phone down.

I could hear that Kjell Bjarne had woken up in the bathroom. It sounded as if his guts were coming out through his mouth.

# 14

Everything passes. Or rather, to be more precise, things change and are replaced by something new. I have learnt to take comfort in this, whenever life throws me a punch. I was standing in Alphonse's flat by the open window, watching Reidun set the table in the back yard. Coffee cups and yellow serviettes. Kjell Bjarne and Frank were sitting against the wall in the sun and Kjell Bjarne had the little girl on his lap. He only let go of her with extreme reluctance and Reidun nearly had to wrestle with him every time the child needed a feed. Out in the kitchen, Alphonse was pouring the coffee and tea into two big Thermos flasks.

'I brought today's Dagbladet with me for you,' I said as casually as possible, as if I had just remembered. Just so I don't take it home with me again, sort of thing. I had two perfect copies of the same newspaper at home already.

'That's kind of you,' he said, without paying attention. 'But you know I buy the paper every morning.'

'So you do,' I replied. But he could, of course, have forgotten to buy it for once. Who knows how many times I had already done it, but I unfolded the paper and looked at the front page. Down in the left-hand corner, in the shadow of the headlines which were all about Princess Diana's emotional life, was the good-news story of the day, black on a yellow background. 'SAUERKRAUT POET STRIKES!' See page 17. So I did. Again, I should add.

To tell the truth, I blushed with pride when I saw the picture of Kaare Svingen holding up the packet of sauerkraut at home in his kitchen in Hovseter. An elderly, kind-looking man, who despite the fact that he preferred poems that rhymed, said that he thought the whole episode had added a certain spice to everyday life. He had no intention of taking legal action against the manufacturer. The spokesman for Grimstad Preserved Foods, a certain Arne B. Johnssen, said that of course such things should not happen, but expressed his relief that at least the poem had not been found inside the actual plastic packaging. Then he would have been forced to instigate an internal investigation, as he put it. But best of all: the poem was printed in its entirety, in a fancy frame, no less.

I had made my debut and in Norway's best cultural paper at that! Now there were thousands of people sitting around the country, discussing who could possibly be behind this mysterious E. I was the talk of the town! I imagined the buzz in the canteens at various Norwegian publishing houses. Would it be possible to trace the anonymous poet and gain his confidence? The answer to both questions was the same and very simple: no. I preferred to bathe in the glory of my self-chosen anonymity and had no faith whatsoever in the link between culture and big business. I had benefit money and I intended to maintain my artistic integrity. Naturally, it would be flattering to be recognized on the street, or at Nordraak Café – but not if the price was my own self-respect. I would live and die as the man with no face, the anonymous voice from the silent night streets.

'Did you notice the thing about the sauerkraut poet?' I asked, and followed this with a small dry laugh. I was perhaps giving myself away a bit, but not too much.

'Yes, blimey,' Alphonse said. 'It wasn't that bad either, the poem.'

Then he stiffened. He was standing with his back to me, screwing the top onto one of the Thermos flasks, and I could see his neck muscles tighten. He turned slowly and looked directly at me, and I could feel myself blushing as I stood there. Rumbled. Naked.

'E . . .' he said, surprised.

I didn't answer. Somehow there was nothing to say right then.

'It just didn't occur to me,' he continued, 'I have to admit.'

'Why did you stop?' I asked. I had determined never to ask him that question; in fact, I had forbidden anyone else to ask, but now it just popped out of my mouth. For a moment I was frightened that he might get angry, or, even worse, that I had put him in a difficult situation, ripped open an old wound, something dangerous. Instead he just smiled, and gently shook his head.

'I'd said what I had to say,' he told me. 'I got bored with my own voice. I came to the conclusion that others could take over.'

And as he said the last words, the baby let out a furious howl down in the back yard. A thin sound that rent the air and seemed to fill the space in which Alphonse and I stood.

'Sounds quite dramatic,' I said. 'But really all she wants is milk.'

'Yes,' he said. 'It's as simple as that.'

THE END

ABOUT THE AUTHOR

One of the most critically and commercially
successful contemporary Norwegian authors,
Ingvar Ambjørnsen has written eighteen novels
and three collections of short stories, as well as
several children's and young adult titles. The
recipient of many literary awards, including the
prestigious Brage Prize (1995), he currently lives
in Hamburg with his German wife and translator,
Gabriele Haefs.